MISERY *loves* COMPANY

SCARLETT HOPPER

Scarlett Hopper

Misery Loves Company
Scarlett Hopper
Copyright © 2021 by Scarlett Hopper
Cover Design © 2021 by Amanda Simpson Pixel Mischief
Design

Formatted by Brenda Wright, Formatting Done Wright

Edited and Proofread by Rebecca Barney at Fairest Reviews

Misery Loves Company
By

Scarlett Hopper

Semi-Charmed Life by Third Eye Blind

Breathe by Michelle Branch

Keeping Your Head Up by Birdy

Stacy's Mom by Fountains of Wayne

Hands To Myself by Selena Gomez

Ms. Jackson by Outkast

drivers license by Olivia Rodrigo

If You Were Here by Cary Brothers

Seventeen by Sharon Van Etten

Anything Could Happen by Ellie Goulding

(You Drive Me) Crazy by Britney Spears

Everywhere by Michelle Branch

You Shook Me All Night Long by ACDC

When You're Gone by The Cranberries

Holiday by Little Mix

If It Makes You Happy by Sheryl Crow

Complicated by Avril Lavigne

Do What U Want by Lady Gaga &. Christina Aguilera

Love Me or Leave Me by Little Mix

Jumper by Third Eye Blind

Blondes by Peach PRC

Josh by Peach PRC

Painkillers by Rainbow Kitten Surprise

Shameful Company by Rainbow Kitten Surprise

Coming Down by Dum Dum Girls

Scarlett Hopper

Part 1

September 2018

Chase

Life is good.

No, scratch that. My life is *fucking epic.*

I look around the locker room, filled to the brim with my teammates, some starting their first season, and others, their final. We are all ready to win our first NHL game of the season, and it's hard to deny just how lucky I am. Lucky to be here, with this life, this career, and the people surrounding me. At 25, I'm living the dream of every hockey player out there.

"I'm taking everyone out for drinks on me after we win this game tonight!" I yell out to my teammates, my voice filled with confidence.

My gut tells me this is going to be our year. I'm starting center, my entire summer spent training for this moment. Correction, my entire life.

With a strong team at my side, I know we've got this. Some could say my arrogance is presumptuous, but I know we are ready. I know *I'm* ready.

"Big tab you're going to have, Mathews," Chapman, our captain, says from next to me. His freshly shaved face is void of its usual stubble, his pale skin sticking out against our orange uniforms.

"Ah, we all know he can afford it. We all saw this cocky son of a bitch on *GQ* with Saunders," Taylor throws out as he tosses a tee shirt onto his duffle. His curly brown hair, sitting right at his shoulders, shakes along with his laughter.

Dude needs a haircut.

I think back to the *GQ* cover I did with my best friend, Logan Saunders, last summer. Although we may be on different teams in the NHL, our friendship goes back years. It wasn't exactly his idea of a good time, but I can't lie, I didn't hate it. Shaking my head, I'm immune to their teasing. "You all are just jealous this face is bringing in the big bucks."

"Better hope no one tries to damage it tonight," Taylor replies.

I smooth my thumb down the side of my cheek. "Precious cargo here."

"Okay, enough fucking around," Chapman calls out. "It's our first game of the season, let's not fuck it up. We've trained like crazy, we've got the best of the best, there is no reason for us not to win this. We win this and we're one step closer to the cup!"

"Now let's win this so Mathews is stuck with the tab tonight," Coach jokes as we exit the locker room.

The sound of the crowd screaming makes my body buzz. It's a high. And I fucking revel in it. Revel in how the fans get just as into the game as we do, sometimes even more so.

I look out into the arena, breathing in a lungful of the frosty air. Never take a moment of this shit for granted. Not now, not ever. Sure, you can get caught up in the glam, the girls, and the money, but it can leave as soon as it arrives. But I sure as shit don't plan on being left behind.

"CHASE, WE LOVE YOU!"

I turn to see a man and a woman aggressively waving posters with my name and number on them. I laugh it off, knowing my focus needs to be on warming up and winning.

"Mathews, head in the game!" Coach yells at me. I flash him a smile.

I spin back around, ready for our team to crush the start of this season and secure the Stanley Cup, the championship trophy in the NHL.

The next fifteen minutes pass by in a haze of cheers and torn-up ice. Skates slice across the ice, the sound of the puck swooshing back and forth between players rings in my ears. The roar of the fans is drowned out, my mind only able to focus on the game. From the first drop of the puck, our team wastes no time in asserting its dominance. With three minutes left in the first period, I have the puck, looking out for Chapman who is ahead of me. My foot presses down on my skate while my other leg propels me forward.

I can practically taste the impending first period victory, but it's quickly replaced by the metallic tang of blood along with what feels like the impact of a truck against my left side.

My vision goes sideways as I watch the crowd spin, or is it me? My body is quick to slam into the ice, my head bouncing off it. But that isn't where my issue lies. It lies in the sharp shooting pain that explodes along my left knee.

As it plays out, it feels like a slow-motion car crash of my life, my mind knowing, like any athlete would, that everything is about to change.

The arena goes silent as I lie there, the behemoth who took me down quick to skate back to his team like a coward. Coach Lee screams a bunch of expletives, clearly distressed at my current state.

I want to get up. Want to tell him I'm okay, that I can shake it off. But the spinning in my head and the ache in my leg keep me down.

Lee's head appears above me, but when it splits in two, I know focus is a lost cause.

Within minutes, I'm lifted onto a gurney and wheeled out of the arena, leaving my teammates behind. My focus comes in and out, enough to notice the team doctor and Coach sharing huddled whispers. If the pain in my leg didn't tell me something was seriously wrong, this does.

I'm taken to the nearest hospital, alone, as the team has a game to win. A game I'm no longer a part of. When I'm more lucid, they ask me who I want to call, but I shake my head. No point in worrying my parents back in Seattle, when I'm all the way here in Boston.

I'll call when I know more. When everything is certain.

A man in a white lab coat comes in hours later, Coach Lee finally at my side post win. I'm silent. Trying to be stoic as I hear him tell me news I already know.

"I'm afraid I've got some bad news. It appears your ACL has been torn in the fall. Along with some superficial bruising you'll have over your right side, you've also suffered a concussion. Of course, these two things can be fixed with time, but the ACL won't be as easy. You'll need surgery at the very least and at best, months of physical therapy. I'm sorry, Chase."

I bite down on the side of my cheek, my eyes staring straight ahead as he continues to talk, yet I've heard enough already.

My career as a hockey player is over.

Mentions of rehab and surgeries fly around, but mentally, I'm already checked out. My head turns, mindlessly staring out the chipped hospital window.

As I lie here, all I can think about is the fact that my hockey career is over. Yet, life will continue on, as if it hasn't just categorically changed due to just one moment in time.

December 2018

Georgia

"Are you sure I can't bring anything?" I ask my best friend, Ash, as I browse the aisles of Baby Land. My left arm is full of onesies and baby booties, and some may say that the pile I've already left at the counter is a bit over the top.

"Georgia, I don't need anything else, you've gone above and beyond. If I'm being honest, I'm not even sure what half of this stuff that's arriving at the house right now is."

I smile, even though she can't see me. My hand stops on a pair of denim overalls with a matching baby blue hat, and I quickly add it to my pile.

"Georgia?"

"Sorry, just shopping, I got sidetracked."

"You better not be buying me anymore baby clothes. Henry hasn't even been born yet and he already has a bigger closet than my and his father's combined."

"Eh, that's not really too hard, Ash. You own like two pairs of combat boots, a tee shirt and skinny jeans. And don't get me started on Logan."

"Hey, I'll have you know my tops and jeans are very comfortable, well maybe not while extremely pregnant, but comfortable nonetheless."

I walk over to the register, my eyes passing over strollers, toys, outfits, and baby monitors. All things I made sure to put on her baby registry. My eyes roam over the Aston Martin Silver Cross Pram with a price tag of over 6 thousand.

"I'm sure they're great. But enough about that, did the cake arrive yet? I'm just picking up some last-minute essentials, then I'll head right over."

I place the clothes on the worn-out counter, probably touched by hundreds of excited or exhausted parents or their grubby little kids. The brunette sales clerk's eyes widen at my mini haul, but she quickly starts scanning.

"Yes, the cake arrived and do you want to tell me why it looks like it serves 100 people? I only invited 20."

"Yeah, but it's so cute! It's got a zoo on it to go with the theme. You're going to love it all, Ash, I promise."

"You don't have to tell me twice, G. I know if you've done it, it will be amazing."

"Only the best for you."

"So, are you bringing a date?" she asks.

I groan. "God no. I swear the universe has thrown the worst of the worst my way these past few months. I've officially decided I'm on a break from men. So, moving forward, it's just Georgia. I'll be your third wheel."

"Yeah, I can't blame you there. And you can be our third wheel anytime."

I hear a distant shuffle of clothes over the phone before what sounds like a stream of water.

"Bitch, are you peeing while on the phone with me?" I ask her, trying to hold back my laughter. The store clerk pauses at my words, before hastily continuing to ring me up.

"I really had to go. It seems like all I do is eat and waddle to the bathroom."

"I will let you get back to that then. I'll see you in twenty."

We hang up as I walk back to the register, passing a baby cot called a Snoo that costs well over $1000.

I am not having kids anytime soon.

"Is that everything?" Sue, from the looks of her name tag, beams at me as she rings me up.

"Oh, I've got everything I need, thanks. Probably too much." I grimace as I look at the small mountain.

"For yourself?"

I practically recoil at the question. At 25 and single, for the first time in a while, pregnancy is the last thing on my mind. Sure, one day, but definitely not now or anytime soon.

"A friend," I quickly add.

"Oh, well she is very lucky to have you."

"I'm the lucky one. Ash is the best, more like a sister."

We talk for a few more minutes; she tells me about some of the other gadgets they sell, things I'm hoping Ash doesn't want, as I've yet to get them. But then I remember Ash is also buying stuff, despite my need to spoil her rotten.

I leave with two massive shopping bags digging into my arms, no doubt about to leave some marks. Now the question is how I'm going to get everything wrapped before the baby shower, that starts in a few hours.

I waste no time throwing everything into the back of my Audi, the engine purring to life as I squeal out of the parking lot, headed to the outskirts of Seattle to Ash and her husband, Logan's home. Since he started in the NHL three years ago, privacy has been at the top of his priorities. Luckily, I have my own key. I don't think Ash could get rid of me now, even if she wanted to.

Ash and I grew up here in Seattle, having been best friends since childhood. We've been through everything together. Makeups and breakups, deaths and births, you name it. She is the very definition of a ride or die. Despite her having some other friends outside our friendship, at the end of the day, she is the only person in this world, besides my parents, I can truly count on. Growing up with someone allows this invisible link to be formed between two people, and the ones who make it out together, well, let's just say I think those friendships are meant to be.

And as life continuously moves on and changes, Ash's has transformed the most in the past year. Now she's married and pregnant. To say we've gone down different paths is an understatement, but thankfully, it hasn't diminished our connection.

The fact that she and Logan still live in Seattle is another bonus as I love having them close by. I'm basically an extension of their family, which is why I've infiltrated their lives and all things baby.

I tried to get everyone here today, but due to the holidays coming up, a lot of Ash's college friends couldn't make it. I know she's upset about it, so that's why I've stepped up to ensure that today is the best it can possibly be.

I am not even fazed by Logan's best friend and dickhead extraordinaire, Chase Mathews, coming along.

No one will ruin this day, not even Chase.

Over my dead body.

Chase

I take another sip of my beer, it's warm, therefore shit, kind of like my life right now. The dull throb in my leg is never-ending, along with the reminder of all I've lost. Despite surgery to repair my ACL, life isn't going to be the same. I can't play professional hockey anymore, but I'm not sure what else I'm supposed to do. Four months have gone by since my injury, yet it feels like I'm standing still, watching the world continue on without me.

I spot Ash and Logan across the room, his arms wrapped around her ever-growing middle. They're happy; they're starting a family. And despite my terrible mood of late, I'm glad I'm still a part of all of this, even if the blonde-haired devil in disguise is running around.

Refilling drinks like a goodie-goodie and throwing out the used paper plates when people have hardly finished eating, I'm sure she's doing more harm than good. Classic Georgia Monroe, always wanting to be the best friend to Ash and now Logan. I'd make more of an effort, but I can't exactly prance around the baby blue room at the moment.

Georgia Monroe has, unfortunately, been around for the past five years, being a lifelong friend of Ash's. But Logan and I have been best friends since we were kids, and I won't let some demon in Prada run me off from celebrating the upcoming birth of his son.

Despite the overwhelming scent of flowers and blue streamers dancing above my head, I put on a good face for Logan.

"Hey, brother," Logan says, stepping away from Ash and finding me people-watching across the room.

"Hey, man, nice party." I tip my beer up, gesturing around. About thirty people litter their living room, including Ash's brother and some friends from our college days at Breslin University. Perks of being Logan's closest friend, I know everyone he does.

"The guys from Breslin couldn't make it?" I'm referencing our old teammates, most of them still living on the east coast.

"Nah, with Christmas so close and this being so last minute, there wasn't any time. But Ash and I will do something for Henry when he's born, so everyone can be here. This was supposed to just be a small get-together, but I think Georgia got a little carried away." He laughs at the thought.

I don't know why, but he seems to like the little hellion, while all I can see are her ridiculously annoying tendencies.

I shift in the chair I'm on, grunting at the pain that shoots up my leg. Logan turns my way, his full attention now on me.

"You gonna go see your doctor again?"

"What else can he tell me? Nothing I don't already know. My career is down the drain, I'll never play again." I hate the anger that slides over every word. I've never been an angry person. I'm the fun-loving jokester who doesn't take life too seriously. Now look at me. A miserable prick who can't even keep a smile on his face at a baby shower.

"You need to keep going back, Chase. Even if you can't play again, this shit needs to be properly looked after, or you could have lifelong issues."

I run a hand through my hair, pulling at the overgrown ends. That, along with my stubble-covered face, are enough to tell Logan I'm not doing great. A buzz cut and a clean shave were always priorities for me. Now I'm lucky if I'm wearing a fresh tee shirt.

"I know it's hard, shit, I can't even imagine what it would be like to lose the game. But Chase, you're losing yourself too."

I bite the inside of my cheek, my eyes laser-focused on the now warm drink in my hand. Logan's been in the NHL as long as I have, three years, and I've never met someone who loves the game more than him. But the reality is, he's right; he can't imagine what I'm going through.

Not wanting to be the one to ruin a day of celebration, I put on a smile. "It will all work out. I'm gonna go see Dr. A next week and get it all sorted." I turn to him, patting him on the back. "Thanks for looking out for me, brother. I appreciate it more than you know."

His lips tilt upward. "Always, Chase. We're family."

"Another?" I ask, holding up my beer. He nods and we both get up, walking toward the bar. At least Georgia did one thing right.

Ah, speak of the devil. She prances over, her green dress swaying as she goes. "Logan, I thought, if you wanted to, we could do presents soon?"

"Yeah, sounds great, thanks G."

She beams at him before her eyes land on me. I get the usual eye roll accompanied by a raised upper lip.

"What, no hug?" I tease, smiling at her annoyance.

"Eww, I think I'd rather not die from whatever grimy disease you've caught from your current flavor of the month."

What she doesn't know is there has been no one in months, not since this all went down. I guess my cocky playboy persona went down the drain with my career.

"Hey, your mom isn't that bad," I retort, but she's unfazed.

"My mom's got higher standards than washed-up athletes." She gives me a sickly-sweet smile.

"Brat."

"Prick," she snaps back.

"Okay you two, let's find Ash, so we can do presents and get this day moving. From the look on her face, she's only got so much socializing left in her tank."

My head swings to her and Logan is right. Poor Ash is stuck in conversation with some distant family member of Logan's, who blondie over here invited. Ash looks like she's trying to stay involved, but there is only so much the girl can take.

"Excuse me while I go save her," he says, slipping by us.

Georgia wastes no time following him, putting on her best superficial smile while getting Ash out as Logan speaks to his family.

I, on the other hand, go for another beer. It's going to be a long day.

Georgia

I finish wrapping up the last of the cake, jamming it into the overstocked fridge. Ash warned me we didn't need cake for 50 people, but me being me, I got carried away. Your best friend only has their first baby once.

"Ash has just gone down, you go, Georgia, I can finish this up," Logan says as he enters the kitchen.

I scan the room. The marble countertops are still covered in trays of food.

"No way, go relax," I reply, far too comfortable in their house. Most people would hate it, but I think Logan is just so used to me popping up everywhere. Anyway, he has his annoying sidekick, Chase, basically living here, so I doubt I'm overstepping as much as him.

"Seriously G, no way am I letting you clean up after everything you did for today. I've got it."

I know Logan, so I know when he's serious. Relenting, I put down the cling wrap and raise my hands in the air. "Okay, Saunders, just this once. I've got a big day at the office tomorrow, so I'll let you have it."

His pearly whites are on display as he smiles at me; it's easy to see why GQ wanted him on their cover this year. I remember how much Logan hated it, but Ash thought it was cool as shit. Girl got bragging rights for years from one cover photo.

"Thanks again, G. Today meant a lot to us, especially Ash."

"She's my girl, I'd do anything for her."

I grab the last of my things before walking through the massive TV room. Chase's form is sprawled out on the couch.

We eye one another as I pass. "Bye, Asshole!" I sing sweetly.

"Bye, Brat," he responds.

I roll my eyes, opening the front door and slipping into the night.

As I unlock the door and climb into my Audi, I can't help but hope I never have to see Chase again. But fate has a twisted way of laughing in our faces at the absolute worst times, and little did I know, I was about to witness it.

April 2019

Georgia

"It's a shame, she's a real prize."

I nod to the burly-bearded man in his stained overalls, trying not to grimace as I watch my 2017 Audi Q3 be hooked up to the jittery tow truck. The final slice of my old life about to be driven away. I knew I shouldn't have sold my red Prius last year, but Dad insisted I use the company car.

And that all turned out so well.

"It's okay, it's just a car." I lift a shoulder, not wanting to explain to a complete stranger that the loss of the car means nothing. It's more so the meaning behind it; the fact that it being gone means it's time to start anew.

"The dealership should be in touch once I drop it off, but aside from that, just sign here and we're done."

I hastily take the pen from him, scribbling my name against the white paper.

There. It's done.

I don't bother watching as he drives away, my Gucci heels ringing out against the pavement as I make my way to the Starbucks across the street. God, I'd kill for a caramel macchiato right now, but people who are trying to save money drink coffee at home. Right? I mean, I feel like that's what they tell you. Though I'm not really sure who *they* are.

Rocking back and forth, I wait for Ash to pick me up, her grey Mercedes not yet in sight. I pause in front of the store, instead focusing my attention on the black leather strap rubbing against my toe and my aching soles. Perhaps this outfit was a stupid choice, but I needed to feel some semblance of control and normalcy. I'm still deciding if it's working. I feel ridiculous for wearing these shoes today. I mean, I'm dressed for the office, not for whatever today is anyway.

Cars pass by me, slotting into the Starbucks drive through, as I continue to wait. My mind can't help but linger back on the moment everything changed for me.

"You're broke?" I taste the words against my tongue, unsure how to fully process what I'm hearing. Peering into my father's blue eyes, ones that mirror my own, my mind attempts to grasp any semblance of comprehension.

My father nods, his aged face solemn. "I made a bad investment," he pauses, "more like I invested everything in a project that failed. Therefore, I failed."

"I know it's a lot to take in, Darling, but don't you worry. Your father and I are taking care of it," my mother quickly interjects. Her hand comes to cover my own. The cold feel of her expensive rings burns against my skin.

Will she have to sell those, is that their level of broke?

"It will be a time of adjustment and change for everyone, that is for certain, but we will get through this, I'm confident." My father smiles at me, the lines under his eyes more pronounced than in his previous years. Perhaps I was too self-focused to notice the change, the stress so clearly gnawing away at him.

I rake my fingers through my hair, my blonde curls slightly tangled, causing my hand to get caught in the mess.

"Is there any way I can help? I mean, I have savings. I could give you what I have and we can cut my salary at the company too." I pause. "I can work for free for a few months. I'll move home, help you and Mom out more, I mean that has to help, right?"

Even as I offer, the thought of moving home hurts, somehow feeling like a regression. But for my parents, I will offer anything. Everything.

I've been working for my dad's real estate company for the past four years, since I graduated college here in Seattle. I interned there all four years, worked long unpaid hours just to prove myself, not only to him but to everyone there, including myself.

I work in his marketing department with Jill, my senior advisor. I couldn't have been given a better boss than Jill. She doesn't give a shit who my dad is; if I fuck up, it's not taken lightly. I'm treated like everyone else in this company.

I may only be 25, but I know my shit and work every day to earn my place. Sure, my life will change if I move back home, but if taking a personal financial hit will help them, then you bet your ass I'll do it.

My father closes his eyes, a defeated sigh leaving his lips. It seems that as my mind has drifted, my parents' silence has only grown louder. My gut clenches, as my hands wring together.

"Georgia, there isn't going to be a company. In order to even begin to get out of this mess, I have to sell. Jack is buying me out."

So this is why they sat me down.

"And that means?"

"As much as it kills me to say it, you will be out of a job, we both will." He stops for a moment, swallowing a few times.

"What?" My voice comes out an anguished whisper. But not for myself, for my father. This company is his life; it's all he's worked for.

"But Jack's your friend, I'm sure he could give you a position in the company."

I hastily look to my mom, whose eyes have yet to find my own. "Right, Mom? Jack won't just leave you two high and dry, he will help. That's what family does. When one falls, the others help pick them back up."

"Jack isn't family, Georgia. I know he has been in your life for a long time, but at the end of the day, money is greener than blood."

That's when it hits me. I'm shocked at how naive I am not to have realized. "He wants control." It isn't a question; rather, a fact, one my parents both confirm with their dejected expressions.

"It appears Jack wants to do a little bit of an overhaul at Monroe West Agencies. What did he say, darling, 'out with the old and in with the new?'" My father's eyes crease at the memory.

"He said that?" I ask.

"Oh, he said a lot more than that, Georgia, but we will spare you the details," my mother adds. She rounds the table, coming to perch herself on the edge of the couch next to my father. Taking a sip from her waterglass, her nude lipstick leaves behind the faint remnants of a stain. "But what he

said really doesn't matter anymore. What's done is done, and now we work on moving forward."

My head moves up and down, knowing she's right. As much as I'd love to find Jack West and give him a big ole piece of my mind, what good would it do? He didn't get my father into this mess; he's just profiting from the fallout.

"Okay," I say, smoothing my hands down my pants. "What's our next move? Dad, how can I help?"

My parents spare a glance at one another. "That's the thing, Georgia," my father begins. "We don't want you to help us with this. I did this, and I refuse to bring you down with me. We love you for wanting to help us, but this isn't your fight. You're twenty-five, your entire life is ahead of you, you can start fresh."

"No, I want to help," I cut in. "I don't need to start fresh. I can help."

"Darling, I know you can. But I want to do this on my own. I must do this alone. The best thing you can do right now is try to rebuild what I broke for you. Find a new job, something you love. I'm just sorry I had to put you in this mess to begin with. I can deal with my own mistakes, but knowing they've hurt you and so many others at my company, that -" His voice cracks, leaving him unable to finish his sentence.

Despite the lump in my throat, I reach both my hands out, resting them respectively on my parents' legs. Because I understand this is far worse for them than me. If I'm out of a job, that means Dad certainly is too.

"You're worried about me?" I ask, before pulling a hand away and swiping it through my hair again. What can I say, nervous habit.

"I'm going to be just fine, Dad. You don't have to worry about me, just focus on what's best for you and Mom. I'll be fine."

A familiar car horn pulls me out of my depressing memory; it's Ash pulling up in front of me.

The window rolls down, my best friend's familiar silver hair burning bright against the sunlight. "Need a ride?" She grins at me, unlocking the door as I pull it open.

"You have no idea." I laugh, letting my back sink into the soft black leather. I turn my head around, noticing the car seat is empty.

"Henry with Logan?" I ask of her newborn son and husband.

"Yeah, thankfully. Logan has the day off of training, so he and Chase took Henry for the day. I'm so fucking exhausted all the time, it's a huge weight off my shoulders."

I nod, not bothering to ask about Logan's best friend. The guy has always driven me crazy. He's like an itch you can't scratch or ignore: always there and ever annoying.

"Thanks for picking me up, Ash. I know motherhood isn't easy and the last thing you need is to pick up your loser friend."

She reaches over, smacking my arm, the car momentarily swerving into the other lane. A man in a green Honda has no issue beeping at us, Ash waving her hand at him in apology.

"Don't say that shit, Georgia. You're not a loser. So you lost your job, that shit happens all the time, it doesn't make you a loser. You're smart, qualified, and a catch, you will find another one."

"It's not just the job, Ash. I know people lose their jobs all the time, I get that part. It's just how everything has gone down, and all at once. I worked my ass off at that company, staying late frequently, with no pay for the first few years. I was desperate to prove the job wasn't just handed to me on a silver platter. And now it's all gone. And that isn't even the worst of it. All these other people are going to lose their jobs, too. People with partners and children. What the fuck are they going to do? I mean, I'm losing my apartment because there is no way I can pay that kind of rent, but I don't have a child. Can you imagine what it's like for all those other people?"

Her head snaps to look at me, before refocusing on the road. "G, you never mentioned the apartment. When is this happening?"

I shrug. "I got off the phone with the agent yesterday. My lease is up next week and I just played it off like I wasn't interested in a renewal. What's even more embarrassing is he knows me and I'm sure has heard about Dad selling his part of the agency. The problem with both of us working in real estate."

Although she tries to conceal it, I see pity in her eyes. I hate being pitied, just like I know Ash does too. At least she's trying to hide it from me. That counts for something.

"Where are you going to stay?"

Ah, the dreaded question.

"I was going to ask Callie if I could crash at her place for the week until I found somewhere cheaper."

At the mention of my old college roommate, Ash's face scrunches up.

"Uh Callie? Fuck no, you're staying at my place. Logan and I won't even be home for the next two months. You can have a break and get yourself together. You don't need to be sleeping on her couch when you can have your own space."

"I don't need to impose on your life any more than I already do. I should stay with my parents, but with everything going on, the last thing I want to do is stress them out more. I've told them everything is fine, but clearly, that's bullshit."

"And that is why you're going to stay at my house. We don't need to go back and forth about it, it's settled."

"You just want me all to yourself."

She laughs. "No shit, Sherlock. You're my best friend. It's my duty to look after you when you're in need!"

"Well, your king-size bed does sound better than Callie's couch."

"Duh!"

I grin, thankful I have Ash to keep me sane.

"So, I don't have anywhere to be for the rest of the day. How do cocktails and fried food sound?"

"Perfect," I tell her, thanking whoever was looking out for me the day I was lucky enough to meet Ash. "It sounds perfect."

Chase

"You know, I bet if you sat up right now, there would be a Chase-size hole in my couch." Ash grins up at me, her hair piled atop her head while her eyes shine, glinting with mischief.

I groan, rubbing the sleep out of my eyes before hauling myself up, my left leg feeling a slight twinge from the movement.

"You're probably not wrong, Ash. But if I get up, then that means I'll have to walk around the house and that will probably end up with me driving you and Logan mad, and don't get me started on Henry. I doubt he'd want me taking all his attention away."

Her lips tilt up at the side, probably thankful some of my humor has come back. I've always been the joker, the class clown. The friend who took nothing too seriously, until that day last year. The day when everything turned to absolute shit and my career was snatched from my fingers with one wrong move.

"Hey," Ash nudges my shoulder, "You know we love you here. How else would Henry get all this one-on-one time with his favorite godfather?"

I can't help but smile at the mention of their two-month-old son. "I'm his only godfather."

"Eh, potato, potato."

"What about one of your special lady friends? I'm sure they could cheer you up!"

I grimace at having to have this conversation with Ash. "Uh, let's not talk about those things together."

"Why not? You talk about them with Logan. I can be one of the guys. I'm sure you've got a special someone in your phone you could go see." Her eyes are wide as she leans forward. Far too hopeful and giddy for me to get laid. Is this how far I've fallen?

"Not interested, but thanks, Ash."

"Oh god, if you don't want to see a lady friend, this is bad."

"Can we stop calling them 'lady friends?'"

She winks at me, before Logan enters the room, dressed in all black, clearly ready for a workout. When you play in the NHL, you never have downtime. Unless you seriously fuck up your leg, then you can get all the downtime you need. But the catch is, it will cost you your career.

"I'm heading to the gym, wanna come?"

It is the daily question he's been asking me for the past month as I've leeched off of them. Instead of staying in my condo, which happens to be under construction, the two of them insisted I move to their place, just outside of Seattle. Family sticks together. That's what they told me when I got here. It's what they tell me every day. And despite it all, I can't seem to pull myself out of my own head.

"Nah, not today, Man, maybe tomorrow."

Logan nods, but I see the pain flash across his face. This is supposed to be a happy time for them, and I can't help but feel like a dark cloud invading their bubble. I see Ash slip out of the room from the corner of my eye before Logan takes a seat at the end of the L-shaped sofa.

"Chase," he begins, but I put a hand up, effectively silencing him.

"I don't need to hear it, Man. I already know what you're gonna say."

"See, I don't think you do."

I lean back, letting myself sink into the plush sofa, my leg still elevated. I don't know why, but having this conversation with Logan, in this position, makes me feel weak. Like somehow, even sitting down, we're on different levels.

"I appreciate everything you've done for me, Man. I won't ever be able to thank you enough, but I'm just not ready. I rarely leave this couch, the last thing I'm gonna be able to do is skate on ice."

"I know that, Chase. I'm not your dad, I don't need to lecture you on hockey. I know how much you loved the game, how much it kills you not to play. I'm not gonna sit here and pretend I understand what you're going through. In fact, what I came in here to tell you might make the situation worse, so apologies in advance."

At this point, I'm not sure what could be worse.

"Well, don't keep me waiting, asshole." I laugh, but the hesitation on his face keeps it from being genuine.

"So, you know how Ash is coming with me for my upcoming games, right?"

I nod, already knowing they need me to take care of the house.

"So, it turns out Georgia has fallen on some hard times and needs somewhere to crash." He pauses before delivering the blow. "Ash offered our house."

At just the mention of the demonic blonde, I already feel like sprinting back to my car and living in my partially-demolished condo. I mean, it has to be better than being stuck in a home with 'Little Miss Nightmare' for a few weeks.

"Oh god, Logan. You're really trying to kill me here."

Logan laughs and if my leg wasn't so fucked up, I'd reach across and elbow him in his side.

"It won't be for that long, only until she gets on her feet."

"You're telling me Georgia's rich little family can't get her a hotel or shit, maybe even buy her a spare house?"

Logan grimaces, his hands coming together as he leans forward. "That's the thing, Man, they can't. I don't know the full details yet, but from what Ash told me, they've lost everything."

I try to ignore the flash of sympathy that hits my gut for Georgia.

I doubt this will keep her down for long, I quickly tell myself.

"I figured, since maybe you'd understand what she's been going through, you could keep an eye on her for us? Ash is really worried and doesn't want to leave, but Man, I can't be without her and Henry for two months. I've been without her before, and I just can't do it again."

And so, despite how much the girl drives me mad, with her side comments and constant flying off the handle, I know I will agree. Logan's been there for me my entire life. He is my family; I won't keep him from his.

"Of course, Logan. You know Georgia and I are all talk; it will be fine just us two."

He moves his head up and down, perhaps attempting to convince himself that my words are true. Because lord knows I don't believe them.

"Thanks, Man, I really appreciate it. And who knows, maybe the two of you will end up finally finding a middle ground and get along."

"Maybe," I say with a smile.

But not fucking likely.

Georgia

"Oh god, Ash. Tell me you're fucking joking. Chase of all people. He's a gross man-child who fucks everything he sees and hasn't had to deal with anything real in his entire life. I mean, the guy walked naked on graduation! He took a fucking bet and walked naked for god sakes. Who in their right mind would do that?"

Ash's lips pin together, but I see her desire to laugh.

"It was a little funny, G."

Maybe if it were anyone else, sure. But Chase has rubbed me the wrong way since I first met him, hell, since I heard about him my junior year of high school. He's a show-off and completely reckless.

"Enough about that, G. You're basing judgments of him off of interactions from three years ago, over seven years, if you go back to high school. He's changed."

I narrow my eyes at her.

She grins. "Okay, maybe not so much, but who cares! The house is so big you won't even have to see him if you don't want to. He doesn't even leave his room most days, so you're gonna be fine!"

"Doesn't leave his room?" I scoff. "I find that hard to believe. I'm sure he has a harem of women coming in and out daily."

"A harem of women? When did you become such a prude, Georgia?"

My face reddens. We both know I'm not a prude in the slightest. I practically majored in boys in college. Yet with Chase, I think I could find something wrong with everything he does.

"I'm serious, Ash. How do I know he hasn't screwed some poor girl on my bed?"

"Georgia," she says, her features no longer playful, "Chase tore his ACL last summer. He's been bedridden for most of it, and I can guarantee he hasn't brought home a single girl in the time he's been staying with us. But really, even if he had, I know you, that shit doesn't get under your skin."

Ugh. That is the issue with having a lifelong best friend. They know you better than you know yourself.

"Chase is a good guy; Logan loves him and so do I. I don't know what happened between you two all those years ago to make you guys always be at each other's throats, but you're both Henry's godparents and it would mean the world to me if you could get along. Chase already agreed to it, so that just leaves you."

Oh god, the guilt card. Plus, the insinuation that Chase is being more mature than I am. Fuck that.

"You're right, Ash. I'm sorry I overreacted. It's been a stressful few weeks and I'm just not myself right now. Of course I can handle it. I'm just lucky I've got somewhere to stay."

"Okay, now you're laying it on a little thick. You don't have to be that grateful. I'm sure he will drive you crazy."

A laugh escapes me because I don't bullshit her, she sees through all that.

"Hey," she says, pulling me into her side. "I'm always on your team, you know that right?"

I nod, my eyes suddenly feeling the familiar sting I've become so accustomed to lately.

"I know," I whisper, my breath hot against her grey wool sweater.

"And you never know, maybe you two can become friends and bury the hatchet." Her words are hopeful, and I don't dare crush them with the harsh truth.

It will be a cold day in hell when that happens.

I load the last of my things into my suitcase, my eyes regrettably scanning my bedroom one final time. This was my first apartment, the first place I got on my own, first place I actually *earned*. And now, after four years here, it will soon be nothing but a distant memory.

Without the income from my job, I can't risk dropping my savings on rent for a one-bedroom apartment in the heart of Seattle. Sure, Pike Place was only a ten-minute walk and my local Starbucks was right around the corner, but those things don't matter in the long run. My next step needs to be focused on getting a job and rebuilding my life, a life not supported by the relationship I have with my parents.

I reach for my black Gucci heels, the gold Gs that sit across the straps dimly shining in the light. They cost over $700 and I've worn them twice. Usually, I wouldn't think twice about buying things like that, but a designer wardrobe isn't exactly in the budget of the unemployed.

My phone rings on top of my white nightstand, the reading glasses on the side moving ever so slightly to the edge with the vibrations.

"Hello?" I answer swiftly, a white camisole hanging off my left hand.

"Hey, Honey, it's Dad. Just wanted to call and see how everything is going."

I pause, throwing the flimsy article of clothing on top of my bag. "Hey, Dad. Yeah, I'm not bad, just packing the last of the boxes before I head over to Ash's place."

"That's exciting, you'll have some girl time."

I laugh at his attempt to be relatable. "Yeah, it will be nice," I lie, before quickly changing the subject, "How are you and Mom doing?"

He pauses, his silence telling me all I need to know.

"We're managing, Georgia. It will take some time, but we will get back on our feet. We all will."

I move my head up and down, despite him not being able to see me. "Don't be too hard on yourself, Dad. Everyone makes mistakes."

"I just regret that my mess has spilled over into your life."

"Hey, I'm going to be just fine. You know I always land on my feet. Who knows, this is probably the perfect time for me to have some much-needed time off." The fib easily slips out, my goal never being to hurt my father.

"I'm sure staying at Ash's will feel like home, lord knows you're at their place enough."

I laugh into the phone. "Very true, Dad. Since you and Mom didn't give me any siblings, we should be thankful I found Ash!" I'm teasing and he knows it.

"I don't know if your mother and I could have gone through the teenage years twice, once with you was enough."

"Hey! I wasn't that bad." I bite my lip, knowing damn well that I *was* that bad.

"Tell that to your mother. I swear, the amount of times she'd catch you sneaking out at night, I'm surprised we made it to adulthood." His deep familiar laughter comforts me. I feel like I rarely hear it these days.

We speak for a few more minutes, laughing about the past, before I have to hang up. Less than ten minutes later, I get a text from Ash telling me she's five minutes out.

My actions are swift and mechanical as I zip the last of my suitcases, thankful I already sold most of my furniture.

I don't look back as I close the door on this part of my life, no point in dwelling on what you can no longer change.

Chase

"I know she drives you crazy, but dude, the house is big enough that you won't even have to see one another that much."

I nod. "It's cool, Logan. You don't need to worry about us, we're adults."

Any truth behind that sentence goes out the window mere minutes later when Ash and Georgia arrive. Ash has a sleeping Henry in her arm, and Georgia has their bags in hers. If it were anyone else, I'd help, but I'm sure she can manage.

It's a shame really. For all her annoying traits, the girl is a stunner. Her golden blonde hair sits just past her shoulders, resting against her olive skin. With bright blue eyes and full rosy lips, it's hard to deny she's striking. From afar she looks slightly delicate, that is until she opens her mouth.

"Hey, G, good to see you," Logan says, taking her luggage from her. He leans in for a quick hug that she easily reciprocates. Her smile is genuine when she talks to Ash and Logan, but it quickly falls upon seeing me.

"Ah Chase," she says with a fake sugary tone. "I heard you would be here. Good to see you." Her nose is turned up as she looks at me. I wink at her and I swear I see her shudder.

"Georgia, a pleasure to see you as always." My sarcasm is thick, to match her own.

Ash just laughs, handing Henry to Logan, who has just returned from putting Georgia's bags in what I'm assuming is her room.

"Good to see you two still getting along," Logan says. A giggle escapes Ash's lips, but she quickly covers it by coughing.

"What do people say, misery loves company? Maybe your mutual disdain for the world will bring you together." His voice is unusually chipper.

"Uh, if anyone is misery in this situation, it's him. I'm great company," Georgia retorts.

"Uh, no way, everyone wants to hang out with Chase Mathews."

She rolls her eyes. "I'm gonna go take a bath."

"Don't fall asleep in there!" I call out after her as she walks around the corner.

She flips me off before disappearing into her room.

I grin, maybe this won't be so bad, after all.

"Can you two try not to burn down my house while we're away?" Logan hands me a beer as we watch Georgia and Ash play with Henry in the living room.

"I will do my best, but I can't speak for Georgia."

"I never understood the instant animosity between you two. I mean, you're more alike than you know."

"I guess we just rub one another the wrong way. Not everyone is supposed to be friends in life."

His head moves up and down in understanding. "I get it, but could you try? Just for the next 24 hours before Ash and I leave. I know she puts on a brave face, but she's worried about Georgia."

I lean against the frame of the metal railing. It's cold from the frosty night air. Seattle never has been one to shy away from the cold.

"Of course."

I don't hesitate answering Logan. After all he and Ash have done for me, it's the least I can do. Playing nice for 24 hours won't kill me. But weeks stuck in this house with Georgia? That just might.

"Have you given any thought to what you're going to do next?"

I hold back a grimace. At 25, what the hell do I become now that my career has gone down the shitter?

I lift a shoulder, my gaze focusing on Henry.

"I don't know, Man. I gave my life to hockey and now that it's all over, I'm not really sure what I'm supposed to be doing."

Logan nods like he understands, but the truth is, he can't understand. He's living out his dream right now. He's got the girl, the baby, the house, and the career. He literally has it all, and I'm happy for him. I really am. But because he's never experienced his dream being ripped from him, he can't exactly relate to what I'm going through.

"But hey, when have I ever let a little hurdle get me down? I'll be back on my feet in no time."

It's a clear game of avoidance I'm playing, but he doesn't call me out. He just smiles, even though it doesn't reach his eyes, and I'm sure if I looked in a mirror, mine wouldn't either.

Georgia

I rock Henry in my arms, his skin soft against my hands. Thick blond eyelashes touch the tips of his cheeks, his body in a deep slumber.

"He really is perfect, Ash." I can't help the awe in my tone as I gaze upon him. The universe couldn't have created a more perfect baby boy if it tried.

Ash looks at us both, her mouth turned upward. "We're very lucky."

"He's lucky too, you know? He's got two incredible parents who think the world of him."

Her eyes close briefly and I wonder if she's thinking about her dad. After all, baby Henry is named after him.

"How's your mom doing?"

Her eyes open at the mention of her only surviving parent. Ash and her brother, Asa, only have their mom now. The death of Henry Ashford was hard on her entire family, particularly her mother. Although he's been gone for over three years, I don't think you ever stop grieving.

"She's good. Asa spends a lot of time with her. which is nice. Plus, her bakery is thriving. It all keeps her busy and I like to think, happy too." She lets out a long breath. "Losing someone so close to you, I don't think you ever really get over it. The pain somehow always lingers inside, but I guess you just find different ways to cope. My dad was my mom's soulmate and as much as I'd like for her to find love again, I just don't think she will or even wants to."

I nod, despite not being able to fully understand. I've had boyfriends for as long as I can remember, and sure, I think I've been in love. But what Ash is describing, what her mom had with her dad, what she has with Logan, I don't know what that feels like. And to be honest, I'm scared I never will.

"As long as she's happy, I guess that's all that really matters."

"That's true," she confirms, her eyes still lost as if clutching to familiar memories. I give her a moment, letting her relish in the comfort that only family can bring.

Eventually, she comes back to me. "What about you, G? What's happening at home?"

I lift a shoulder. "I don't know. Mom is looking for work again, but she's been out of the workforce for thirty years, so I don't really know what she is going to do. And Dad says he has it all under control, but who knows at this point. They're sort of keeping me in the dark about everything, but I'm not a kid anymore, I want to help them."

"You may be an adult, but you'll always be their baby, Georgia. They want to protect you."

I inhale the scent of baby powder and fresh laundry coming off a sleeping Henry. It's like an instant dose of serotonin. "I know," I whisper. "And I can't fault them for that."

"God, I could just stay here all day, holding him," I tell her, no longer wanting to think of the mess that is my home life.

"He's pretty great, isn't he?"

"That is an understatement. He's the greatest. Speaking of babies, how are Nick and Winona doing with Penny?"

Although Ash and I both went to college here in Seattle, she is a super genius who graduated before me. So, while I was stuck here finishing out my senior year, she moved to Cambridge, Massachusetts. That's where she met Logan and a bunch of other Breslin University students. Nick Wilder and Winona Clarke are a couple who Ash has been close with for the past few years. Last year, they welcomed their first child, Penny. From what I hear, she is already on her way to breaking hearts.

"They're great! Penny is coming up on her first birthday soon, I can't even believe it."

"I can't even believe people our age are allowed to have babies."

She laughs. "You're telling me! When they handed Henry over to me in the hospital, I felt like I needed some type of manual to know what to do. Logan, of course, was a natural while I had no clue what I was doing."

"Well, you clearly did something right."

I run my thumb up and down the baby's pillowy soft skin, momentarily jealous of how far Ash and Logan have come. Of the life they've built together.

"So, how's the new book coming along?"

I swear she grimaces. "I've pushed back my deadline yet again. I think they're going to kill me, but I don't really know what else to do. I'm hoping this time away with the boys will clear my head and this ridiculous mountain of writer's block I'm battling."

"God, I can't even imagine. Sitting at a laptop was bad enough when I had to write a 4,000-word essay in college. You do this shit willingly. But instead of 4,000 words, you're writing a 70-thousand-word novel."

A light laugh bubbles out of her. "When it's what you love, it's just different. There's this drive, this need to do it."

"I wish I felt that way about something."

Her hand reaches out, and she lays it on my knee. "You didn't feel that way at the real estate business?"

I lift a shoulder, my eyes suddenly very interested in my lipstick-stained glass.

"I don't know, Ash. At this point, I really don't know what I love and what I hate. It all just feels so jumbled."

"You'll figure it out. Use being here as a time-out, a reset."

I nod but doubt my mind will let me rest. It's always been hunting for the next best thing.

"You're free here, Georgia. For once, you've got no responsibilities. Take that and embrace it. Do whatever you want. Go on some dates, go on no dates if that's still where you're at."

"I think I will go with no dates. For the last ten years, all I've done is put myself out there and they always end up the same. Selfish assholes. I'm done, consider me taking the year off."

"I can respect that. Who knows, when you stop searching, the right person just might come along."

"I doubt it," I say dubiously.

As if sensing the end of our conversation, Henry begins to stir, a small wail, similar to that of a baby bird, coming out of his tiny mouth.

"I got him," Ash says, already on her feet. "Help yourself to anything, I'm just going to put him down."

I nod, not really sure what I would have done with him anyway. Although I love Henry, I'm not exactly the best with babies. As far as I'm concerned, all they do is poop, eat, and cry.

Ash ends up being gone longer than either of us expected, Henry's angry cries coming from the bedroom. I see Logan go in at one point, but my focus is fixated on my phone.

My fingers easily scroll through my Instagram feed like it's routine. Scanning countless posts without really seeing any of them. It's mainly filled with our friends or cooking videos I like. Everyone out there is living their best life with someone to love by their side.

It's sitting in this living room alone that I realize it's not just my job I'm sad about losing; it's the fact that when it's all said and done, at the end of the day, I only have myself. And man, that seems really fucking bleak.

Georgia

Logan, Ash, and baby Henry leave the next day. It's bittersweet as I want to be with them, yet I know this is good for their family, spending this time together. I spend the day in Ash's office, sending out resume after resume, leaving no stone left unturned. If I'm going to have forced time off, you bet your ass I'm coming out of it with a job.

By five p.m., I'm feeling a lot less optimistic. I slam my laptop down after seeing my first job rejection. At the rate I'm going, I'll be hocking everything I own in order to make rent when I leave this place. Feeling truly and utterly defeated, I walk into the living room, thanking my lucky stars Chase isn't out here.

I sink onto the couch that smells suspiciously like him, but that's not a shock. This has basically become his second home. I light up when I see *Legally Blonde* is on. Good, something I can chill out to, without thinking too much.

Five minutes into the movie, I hear a grunt from the doorway. A very shirtless Chase stands with his mouth slightly ajar, bowl of popcorn in hand. His overgrown dark blond hair sticks up all over the place while stubble lines his jaw.

I force myself to look away from him. Sure, he's attractive, most athletes are. Okay, that isn't completely true, but it's what I'm willing to tell myself for acknowledging his hotness. Hot people can still suck. There, that's it.

"Uh, you're in my seat," he snaps.

I dismiss him with a wave. "Didn't realize you paid for the couch." My eyes go back to the movie.

I feel the other end dip, while he exhales a puff of breath. In the next second, he changes the channel.

"Uh excuse me! I was watching that." I lean over to grab the remote from him, but he's too fast for me, tucking it under his ass.

"Seriously?" I fume, my fingers digging into the pillow I have in a death grip.

"If you want it, come get it."

I turn my nose up. "Ew, I think I'll pass. Even sitting near you is enough to risk catching something."

He just shrugs, shoving a wad of popcorn into his mouth. "Get your own seat next time."

"Well, if you didn't basically eat, sleep and breathe on this sofa then I wouldn't have to take it from you!"

"Someone's in a bad mood." He smirks, clearly loving the fact he's getting a rise out of me.

Fine. He wants to be an ass. Two can play that game.

"I don't think I've ever met someone as uptight as you."

My head snaps toward him. "To most people, I'm a delight, you just happen to bring out the inner psychopath in me."

He rolls his eyes. "Sureeee."

"Whatever, I'm going to shower, enjoy the show." My words are sticky sweet, like honey dripping off every word. I see his eyebrows draw together, but it's too late for him. I flick his bowl of popcorn as I walk by, the small yellow pieces flying all over him.

"Oops, did I do that?"

His eyes no longer sparkle in triumph; instead, pure annoyance has seeped into them. But I'm not finished yet. I'm not even close to being done.

I practically skip out of the room, taking a detour to the circuit breaker before my shower. In a matter of three switches, the power in the house goes out. It's not an issue for me, seeing as it is light outside, but I'm sure it will piss Chase off now that he can't watch his precious TV.

I'm smiling all the way to the bathroom, an extra pep in my step as I go. It isn't until I'm submerged in warm water, soap in my hair that I feel his retaliation.

I let out a scream as ice cold water shocks me out of my jubilation. It's such a surprise, I nearly slip on the tiles, my hands luckily catching the wall before I go.

I waste no time quickly rinsing my hair, knowing the asshole has turned off the hot water.

If Chase wants a war, then he's gonna get one. I've never been a good loser, and I'm not starting now.

It's on.

Chase

This woman is going to be the death of me. Less than 24 hours together and we're already biting each other's heads off. She somehow manages to push every single button I have, all at the same time. But today I will get my payback for yesterday's little incident.

I'm practically beaming as I fill her hairdryer with flour. I can just see it now. The pure horror that will cross her face. But that's the point, isn't it?

Georgia and I are similar in the sense that neither of us can lose with grace. To put it simply, we *need* to win. Too bad only one of us will come out on top of this.

I hear her talking on the phone in Ash's office as I slip out of her bedroom. I hold back a groan as I slyly try to make it down the hall undetected. My leg softly aches as I return to my spot on the couch, the ever-constant reminder of what I've lost.

It's pathetic really; I'm 25 and my biggest joy of the day is seeing the reaction of the prima donna getting pranked. But I can't seem to find it in myself to care. Getting a reaction out of Georgia has been the highlight of my days recently. And after the few months I've had, I'll take anything I can get.

I'm less than halfway through an episode of *SVU* when she emerges from Ash's office. Her blonde curls are piled on top of her head, different from her usual put-together appearance.

"What?" she snaps, clearly catching me starting.

I lift a shoulder, relaxing back into the feathered pillows. "You look disheveled."

Her eyes widen and her head jolts back. "Well, fuck you very much, Chase. I've been applying for jobs all day, unlike some people. Sorry if I want a career rather than spending my days melting into the sofa."

I force my body not to recoil at her words, instead giving her my best disinterested look.

"I've got enough money to last me the rest of my life, Georgia. I don't need a career." Although my words may be true, they're not genuine. The last thing I want to do is sit on this couch forever. I want to become something again, *someone*. But she's the last person I'm telling that to.

"Well, we can't all be so lucky," she mutters, turning on her heels and stomping to her bedroom. Well, if someone as small as her can stomp.

My gut clenches momentarily, my mind racing back to when Logan told me her family had lost everything.

Nope. Do not feel bad, Chase Mathews.

All is fair in hate and war.

Ignoring the momentary emotion I have no business feeling, I try to relax again, knowing I will probably only have to wait until the end of this episode to hear Georgia's meltdown. I get comfortable, grabbing the bowl of popcorn off the coffee table, careful not to make a mess on Ash's books. Logan's clearly proud of his wife and her success. Her debut novel is placed all over the house for everyone to see.

I'm nearing the end of the episode, watching Olivia Benson kick ass as usual, when I hear a high-pitched yell, followed by the screaming of my name and a slew of expletives.

I bite my lip as my chest begins to shake with laughter, but nothing could have prepared me for what greets my eyes.

A pasty white Georgia runs out of the bedroom, towel wrapped around her as she greets me. Her wet hair looks to have been coated in a paste as the flour has begun to mix with the water.

"Chase, you stupid motherfucker!" she screams. Her body lunges forward like she's going to jump me before she pulls back at the last second, clutching her towel. Seemingly realizing she can't attack me and hold up her towel at the same time, her face deepens to an even darker shade of red.

"Do you know how long this will take to get out!" She keeps ranting, calling me every name in the book, but I can't contain myself.

I howl with laughter, knowing this is a win for me.

"Oh, you think you're so funny? You're going down, hockey boy. Remember this moment, because it's the day you signed your death certificate."

"I'll make sure to pick out a nice casket," I tell her, not thinking any of her pranks can outdo this one.

"You'll regret the day you were born, Chase Mathews!" she hollers before exiting, leaving small wet footprints across the floor in her wake.

Who knew that was all I needed to feel better?

Georgia

I scrape the last of the flour out of my hair, grimacing at how much of my actual hair has come out in the process. I could kill Chase for this, but instead, I will just get even. Ruin not just his day but his fucking week.

My phone buzzes, Ash's name appearing on the screen.

"Hey Sexy," I answer.

"Hey Bitch," Ash replies.

"How's travelling life treating ya?"

"Not too bad. I've got an adorable baby and a sexy ass husband to keep me company, so I can't complain."

I grin into the phone despite the fact that she can't see me.

"Not too shabby," I reply. "Got a spare husband for your bestie?"

"The only single guy I would offer is the one you live with."

My lip turns up at the thought. The specs of now matted paste in my hair remind me that he is never going to be an option.

"Eh, I think I'll pass."

Ash's light laughter drifts through the phone at my words. "Speaking of Chase, how are you two getting along?"

Ash is my best friend in the universe. And usually, lying to her would be a no-no. But I also know she's worried about our current living situation, and I'm not going to be the one to add to her stress.

"Surprisingly fine." I let the lie slip out seamlessly. "You know, we just keep to ourselves. I'm busy attempting to get my life back and he's busy, uh, sitting on the sofa?"

"You're terrible." She chuckles. "You know, I usually wouldn't believe you two could keep it civil, but Chase told Logan the same thing when he called this morning. So, I'm choosing to believe you're not going to be dead when I get back next month."

"We'll be fine, Ash. I'm a big girl, if I can't handle Chase then I've got bigger issues."

"Okay," she replies, but she doesn't sound convinced.

"Anyway, enough about him, tell me about you. How's Henry doing? I already miss that little guy so much."

"Oh, Georgia, you should see him! Growing bigger every day. I swear he's gonna be as tall as Logan."

Ash continues on, filling me in on the past week as I simultaneously plot my revenge on Chase. After our call ends, I tiptoe out of the bedroom, finding a snoring Chase asleep on the couch. The guy really should go outside, even for just an hour. I don't think he's left the house since the day he came to stay.

His snoring alerts me to the fact that this is my chance for payback. Grabbing the plastic wrap, cream cheese and a bucket, I sprint to his bathroom, quickly wrapping the toilet in plastic wrap and replacing the entire contents of his deodorant with cream cheese. The latter takes a few minutes longer than I hoped, as I have to perfect the shape of deodorant.

One YouTube video too many lets me into a world of ways to ruin his day before he can ruin mine.

I'm quick to put everything back exactly where I found it, though I doubt he would notice either way. I sprint back to the kitchen, making sure he's still passed out on the way. Sure enough, he's still snoring away, yet the bastard looks good as he does it.

Ugh whatever, that's beside the point.

Back in the kitchen, I open the freezer and begin dispensing ice into the bucket before filling it with cold water.

Sure, three pranks may be taking it too far, but after having to spend over an hour getting the flour out of my hair, he doesn't deserve to get off so easily.

I shove my feet into my Nikes, not bothering to fully do up the laces. The bucket is heavy in my hands as I go up the stairs, careful not to spill it over the sides. I want to destroy Chase, not Ash's house.

Finally, at the top, I place it next to the balcony door, only a small amount sloshing out the sides.

Now to get Chase to the front door.

I run downstairs, finding myself standing directly in front of him.

"Chase, you've got a package at the front door!" I scream right into his face. We just miss smacking our heads together as he wakes up.

"Jesus, woman. Ever heard of an inside voice?"

"Nope!" I say with a pop before skipping out of the room. As I walk past the mirror on the mantle, I can see he's starting to rise from the couch, still groggy from his deep sleep. I use that as my opportunity to reach the balcony before he opens the front door.

And just in time, because the front door swings open below as I'm in position. He looks around a few times before running a hand over his face.

"There's nothing here," he mumbles to himself before looking one last time.

"Up here!" I yell.

His head looks up just as the bucket tips forward, small speckles of ice-cold water piercing my skin as it pours down on him.

Now it's his turn to cuss me out.

"Fuck!" he yells, but my ears only hear the sounds of my incessant laughter.

"I don't do well losing," I call out to him before retreating back inside. I know he won't risk getting water all over Ash and Logan's carpet, so I take my time going downstairs.

My ass is comfortably melting into the soft as he walks back in. He's taken off all his clothes except his briefs, clearly trying to contain the dripping mess.

"Oh Chase, you really shouldn't be walking around with so little clothes on in this weather. You really will catch a cold."

His scowl deepens as he eyes me in his seat. "Enjoy this victory, it won't last long."

"Oh, I will!" I call out to his retreating form.

Ah, victory is sweet. Especially at his expense.

Georgia

I wake up the next morning feeling more cautious than usual. I'm expecting big time retaliation for my latest stunt. Every move I make, every time I hear a noise, I'm on the defensive. My mind is on high alert, always ready for another prank that could be heading my way.

What started off as fun, a way to get my mind off of everything, now has me paranoid that Chase is going to get back at me. But at least I know it's getting to him too; his movements have been slightly jumpier than usual.

I refuse to be the one who folds first, though. And that's the issue. We're both too damn stubborn. But that's where our similarities end.

I peel myself out of bed, simultaneously thanking and cursing the blackout blinds Ash installed. I feel like I've been asleep for years.

My hands run through my hair on instinct, meeting tangled bits of resistance. Note to self: deep condition later.

I make it through the first part of my morning without spotting Chase. It's only when I'm going for the keys to Ash's Mercedes that he exits his bedroom, freshly showered and dressed for once.

He pauses for a moment, his eyes drifting to the keys. I spot them in the dish on the wooden credenza at the same time.

"Don't even think about it," I warn, quick to snatch them up. He lunges but isn't fast enough, his leg clearly holding him back. I feel slightly bad for him before brushing it off.

"Give me the keys, Monroe."

"No, I told you I needed the car!" I snap.

"Well, I forgot," he replies casually, lifting a shoulder. "I need to go see my doctor. I'm sure that takes priority over whatever it is you're doing."

"Sorry but where is your stupid sports car? You know I sold my car. Ash said I could use it."

"My sports car is parked at my condo while I'm staying here."

"Well take Logan's car."

His mouth goes into a straight line. "It's at the mechanic."

"Take an uber."

"No."

"Why not?" I shoot back.

"You take an uber," he retorts.

"No, I was here first, and I've got too much stuff to take an uber."

"I don't take Ubers, that's weird."

I roll my eyes. "It's not weird, Chase. It's totally normal. Have fun in your uber!" I say, deciding to put an end to this childish conversation. I don't have all day to go back and forth with him on this.

With a jingle of the keys, I rush out the door, my bag slapping against my side. Quick to enter the garage, I spot the Mercedes and slip inside, thankful to be rid of Chase.

Yet my joy is not long lived. As I'm waiting for the garage door to open, the passenger side door is pulled open.

"No," I say before Chase speaks.

"You won't give me the keys, then you can take me to the doctor." He happily sits himself in the seat, adjusting the side until he's reclined.

"I'm not taking you to the doctor. I have plans I can't miss, and I won't be finished for three hours. So get out."

"Good thing my appointment isn't until 3pm. I was just planning to get out of the house for a few hours beforehand. Now look how well it's all turned out. You're my own personal chauffer."

I grind my teeth, my hand digging into the leather covering the steering wheel.

Just ignore him.

I repeat that to myself the entire time I drive. This is supposed to be my happy time, the last thing I need is him ruining the little bit of peace I get from today.

We spend the forty-minute car ride arguing over what radio station to play until we settle on silence, both of us too stubborn to let the other one win.

When I pull into Whispering Palm Assisted Living, I find a parking spot right out front. It saddens me to see the lack of cars here, but it's always been this way. When you get old, people just forget about you. That shit is sad.

"You can wait here," I tell Chase. Unbuckling my seat belt, I grab my purse from the back then exit the car.

I begin walking toward the entrance when I hear another door slam. I pause in my tracks before turning.

"Yes?"

"I'm not waiting in the car. My phone's about to die, what am I supposed to do?"

"How am I supposed to know?" I look down at my phone, seeing I'm already five minutes late.

"Well, I'm stuck here because of you, so you might as well entertain me." He smirks.

"I'm not a dancing monkey, Chase. This is serious, I don't want you embarrassing me in here."

"We're in public, I'll be civil."

"Whatever," I mutter to myself before spinning on my heels and entering the building. The familiar scent of sanitizer fills my nose as I walk to the front desk.

Linda, the receptionist, does a double take when she sees me. Her white hair is piled on her head in a French twist while black cat eye glasses sit on the tip of her nose.

"Miss Georgia! I didn't know you were coming in today."

"I missed last week, so I owe it to Elaine. She'd hunt me down if I missed another week." I grab the familiar sign-in board, scribbling mine and Chase's names down.

"Who's your friend?" Linda asks, her eyes locked on Chase. I don't bother sparing him a glance.

"No one. He's just tagging along for the day." I hand her the sign-in sheet so we can get our visitor passes.

"That no one looks particularly familiar," she replies before scanning the clipboard. Her painted red lips turn up at the sides. "You know, some of the gentlemen in here are big ice hockey fans, won't turn that dang TV no matter how hard I try. After a while, the staff here starts to recognize some of the players."

Her eyes meet my own in a knowing stare.

"Hockey isn't all it's cracked up to be," I reply, taking the visitor badges from her. A quick laugh bursts out of her as she looks between Chase and me.

"And here I was thinking you'd gone and gotten yourself a boyfriend. Miss Elaine is going to have a field day with him."

Despite not wanting Chase here, I can't help but laugh. Elaine is a real ballbuster when she wants to be. I doubt Chase's usual charm will work on her.

"I'll see you in an hour." I wink, before turning and tossing the pass at Chase. He catches it with his free hand.

"Now I know everything with us is always a war, but I need you not to try anything in here," I tell him before we enter the main sitting room.

"I'm an adult, Monroe. I'm not going to pants you in front of the elderly. What are we doing here anyway? Did you get forced into community service because you committed a crime?"

"You're hilarious," I deadpan. "If you must know, I am friends with one of the women who lives here."

"You have friends?" His eyes go wide in shock horror, and I have to resist punching him.

"I mean it, don't be a dick."

"I'll be on my best behavior." He grins and it only makes the worry in my chest intensify.

Chase is public figure, so I'd have to assume he knows how to semi-behave in public. I mean, people seem to love him, lord knows why, so there must be something deep, deep, deep down that is redeemable. One has to hope anyway.

Not really having a choice of him coming with me, I push open the white-laminate door to the sitting room. Instantly, I spot a handful of familiar faces throughout the room. Some watching TV, others playing boardgames, but I know that isn't where Elaine will be. I spot her in her usual spot: in the corner reading a book in her worn green chair.

I beeline across the room, smiling at some residence before stopping in front of her. I take in her short, straight grey hair, stopping right above her shoulders. She's wearing her staple cream cardigan with grey pants and a white shirt underneath. A strand of white pearls is around her neck, Elaine always having to have some fashionable flair.

"I thought I might find you here."

Her head snaps to the side at my voice, her lips twisting upward when she sees me.

"You know, I shouldn't be happy to see you, you missed last week. But since I'm old and lord knows how many days I have left, I'll take any company I can get."

I roll my eyes. "You're 77 and in perfect health, I don't think you're going anywhere anytime soon."

"You never know what could happen!" she says before stretching her arms out to give me a hug. I don't hesitate, diving in, careful not to squeeze too tight. She may be in great health, but she's still skinny as ever, I fear if I hold her too tightly, she might snap.

"Did you bring any of those donuts?" she asks me, putting down her book on the worn wooden side table.

"I didn't have time to get to Pike Place today, I'm sorry. I had an unwanted visitor crash my plans." I tilt my head back to Chase.

Elaine looks behind me. "Who are you?" Short and straight to the point.

Chase's mouth drops open. I laugh.

"I'm Chase Mathews, Ma'am." He leans forward, shooting his hand out for her to shake. She looks at it as if it might be infected.

"Where did you find this one?" she asks me.

"It's a long story," I reply.

Chase stands there awkwardly before pulling his hand back to his body. I almost feel bad for the guy. Almost.

"Well, don't just stand there, sit down."

He's quick to react, taking the seat next to me. In all my years, I don't think I've ever seen him nervous.

"You look familiar."

"I used to play in the NHL," he tells her. I don't miss how his body straightens at the words. *Used to.*

"I don't watch hockey." She leans back in her chair. "But lots of the residence here do, maybe I've seen you on TV."

"Maybe," Chase replies. He smiles at her. Surprisingly, it doesn't seem forced.

"I saw Herb when I walked in," I say, changing the subject. Elaine's cheeks slightly redden at the mention of her on-again, off-again boyfriend. Apparently, there is a lot of drama in assisted living.

"Oh well, you know that man, can't seem to make up his mind. I think being single is the way to go."

I grin at her. "I would have to agree on that one."

"I still can't believe a lucky guy hasn't locked you down, Georgia. What happened to all those dates you used to go on?"

"God, don't remind me. I spent a long time dating losers, I don't have it in me anymore. I'm on a dating ban until further notice."

Her eyes look to Chase, who I forgot was sitting next to me.

"Hmmm," she says before returning her attention to me. "I would love a cup of tea; would you mind getting me one?"

"Of course," I reply, "Do you want some cookies too?"

Her whole demeanor brightens. "Oh yes, please."

"I'll be right back."

I'm quick to walk to the kitchen, not wanting to leave Elaine alone with Chase for too long. Or maybe I should, he's the one who should be afraid of her, not the other way around.

Chase

I stare at the old woman in the chair across from me, her eyes narrow as she takes me in. I'm starting to rethink why I thought this would be fun. I never in a million years thought Georgia Monroe's idea of a good time would be hanging out with grandparents. I doubt Georgia would know this, but I've been here before. Two years ago, my grandmother ended up here for a year before my parents moved her to an assisted-living apartment complex near our home.

"So, what are your intentions with my Georgia?"

"Sorry?" I say, leaning forward.

"You heard me."

"Uh, no intentions there, Ma'am. We're just roommates for the month, nothing more."

Her wrinkled hands come to scratch the side of her face. "I don't buy, but I'll accept it for now."

"Umm okay," I reply, feeling like I'm under interrogation. She stays silent, probably mentally dissecting every move I make.

"So, are you Georgia's grandmother?" I ask, trying to make polite conversation.

"Oh no, my grandchildren are little shits. Visit me once a year, if I'm lucky, or should I say unlucky. I don't need them to come by. Georgia's like a surrogate granddaughter, you could say."

"How did you two meet?"

Her deep green eyes soften at the topic of Georgia, it's clear she has a deep love for her.

"About four years ago, Georgia and I met at the center where my beloved husband Bradly lived. You see, he had had a stroke the month prior and was in a coma, never did wake up. Georgia's friend's father was also a patient there and I'd see those two girls come and go throughout my month there. I think Georgia started to notice me too, because one day, she started sitting next to me, making conversation while she waited for her friend. As the weeks went by, we developed a friendship and then finally when my Bradly moved on, Georgia was there, comforting me. After that, she never did leave."

"Ash," I say, my voice thick at the memory of her father. "She would have been there with her friend, Ash."

"Yes, that's who it was. Nice girl, terrible situation. She was lucky to have Georgia though. That girl was with her through everything."

I think back to the time when Ash's father died. Although we weren't close then, our friendship strengthened in the months after his passing. I never did see Georgia for more than an annoyance, but after being forced to be around her, I can't help but see a small glimmer of the person Ash has described to me all these years.

We're silent for a few moments; Elaine clearly lost in some thought. "What did you say your last name was?"

"Mathews," I reply.

"You wouldn't happen to be have been related to Joyce Mathews?"

My lips turn up at the sides from the mention of my grandmother. "She is my grandmother."

"I knew it! You looked too familiar for me not to know you. I was good friends with Joyce when she lived here. The two of us got along like a house on fire. I was very sad to see her go."

"She is a special woman," I confirm.

"Is she still in good health?"

I suspect this question is code for is she dead. God it's bleak that when you get to this age, you have to ask those questions so frequently.

"Yeah, she's happy and healthy. My dad wanted her closer to him so she's at an apartment now."

"Lucky lady. My kids have all but forgotten about me."

"Not Georgia," I find myself saying.

Elaine smiles. "Not my Georgia."

Speak of the devil, Georgia comes back juggling three cups in hand. "Miss me?" she asks Elaine, a smile on her face. "Sorry I took so long; I ran into Herb and he wouldn't stop talking my ear off."

"Well, I've actually been getting to know young Chase here. It appears I might have been too quick to judge."

"Really?" Georgia says, an eyebrow raised.

I take the cup, mentally noting I didn't ask for the tea, yet she got it for me anyway.

"I'm friends with his grandmother," she adds in.

"You have a grandmother here?" she asks.

"Used to, she moved," I reply.

"Oh."

"Joyce and I were good friends. She was one of the only people I could stand here."

"I'm sure she'd be open to visiting," I say before thinking. Elaine's aged face lights up at the prospect.

"Oh, I'd love that. You two would do that for me?"

"Of course," Georgia adds in, not letting Elaine catch on that us hanging out together again is unlikely.

"That reminds me of the time I first met Joyce," Elaine begins.

Georgia and I smile as Elaine goes on about stories with my grandmother. I'm taken aback by how friendly the two of them were. It's hard not to compare the fact that Georgia and I can't usually go five minutes without bickering but the closest elderly figures in our lives got along so well.

As the hour continues on, it hits me that this is probably the first adult conversation Georgia and I have had, and I haven't wanted to throw myself out the window during it. I chalk it up to being surrounded by other people, both of us being adults on our best behavior.

There's truly no other explanation. That has to be it.

After spending two hours with Elaine, Georgia regretfully says goodbye. Despite only just meeting her, I seem to have developed a soft spot for the older woman.

Our car ride to my doctor's appointment is had in silence, a stark difference to our usual back and forth.

Georgia waits in the car while I go inside.

My doctor looks me over, clearly pleased with my surgery, but I know the scolding is coming.

"Chase, if you don't keep up with your physical therapy, what's the point of having had the surgery?"

I look toward the grey carpet. "I know."

"But do you? You won't be back in the game, we know that, but there are so many other opportunities out there. These exercises can be done at home, you don't even have to leave the house. Don't make this all for nothing."

This is the issue with being close with your doctor. They're honest, brutally so.

"I just haven't been in the best headspace. But moving forward, I'll start back up, I swear."

His grey eyebrows close in on one another. "Chase, do you need to talk to somebody? I have a handful of resources at my disposal I can give to you. All you need to do is ask."

"Nah, I'm okay, Doc. I appreciate all you've done for me. I'm going to get my shit together."

His lips purse, probably because he wants to say more, but instead, he just nods.

I can't get out of there fast enough, who would have thought I'd be so desperate to get back into a car with Georgia Monroe.

I spot the familiar car, still parked right out front. If she really wanted to stick it to me, she could have driven off. That's what I'd do. Or is it?

I slam the door harder than usual when I get into the passenger seat. Frustrated at myself, more than anything, for slacking off these past few months.

"What's got you in such a bad mood?" Georgia mutters to herself.

"Nothing," I reply quickly. It's short and clipped.

She's quiet for a few moments, the only sound in the car is the blinker turning on and off as she pulls back onto the road. "Is something wrong?"

My eyes shoot to her, curious as to why she gives a shit.

"Nope. Just need to keep up my PT."

"Don't you have to actually do it to keep up with it?"

"It isn't that black and white."

"Well, if I was injured, I'd want to do everything to get better."

"Well, you're not, Monroe. I am." I snap at her, instantly feeling bad.

"Sorry," I mutter, wondering how I even ended up in this conversation. Spending the day with her was a mistake. It's humanized too much between us.

"It's fine," she replies, reaching out to turn on the music, "I overstepped."

Neither of us says anything while we drive home, yet my mind won't stop moving. I'm replaying the events of today and wondering how in a matter of hours, one's perspective on someone can change. Sure, I still don't like Georgia, but it's harder to be mad at her when I've seen this new side to her.

I'm just hoping she does something to piss me off in the next few hours, so we can right the clock and go back to hating one another. Lord knows our shallow banter is better than dealing with anything deep or meaningful.

Georgia

The sound of the TV alerts me to the fact Chase is already up. I need coffee before my mind is alert enough to deal with him. Not bothering to shower until later, I throw on the first pair of jeans I can find, tossing a tank top over my head and calling it a day.

I hear what sounds like a sports game playing as I exit my bedroom, noticing Chase's rigid demeanor instantly. He's hunched forward, arms leaning against his thighs, back tight. Eating up every word coming his way.

I'm about to make myself known when I hear his name come out of the announcer's mouth on the TV. Chase flinches, his body turning to stone, and I already know what is about to happen.

Sure enough, a bigger player smashes into Chase on the ice, resulting in him smacking into the ice at an odd angle. The arena goes silent as coaches and players alike rush to him, but both of us already know the outcome of this game.

I may not like Chase, but I feel for him. Having everything you've ever wanted in front of you, then gone in an instant, hurts…a lot.

I must get lost in thought, because the next moment the chatter of the television is gone and his eyes are on me. It's hard to ignore the feeling that I've been caught doing something wrong. Like somehow, I've interrupted a private moment. And god if I don't feel bad.

"Don't look at me like that, G. If you pity me, all of this isn't fun anymore, it's just sad. And how can I get the satisfaction of winning this war if you're looking all doe-eyed at me?"

My mouth opens, but words don't come out. I don't know this side of Chase. What do I say to him? What do I do with him?

"I'm gonna go think of more ways to ruin your day. See ya!" he chirps, practically skipping to the kitchen. I may not know him well, but I know him enough to see this is him giving me an out. To put the vulnerability that momentarily escaped just now back into the box. To keep things between us about rivalry and nothing more. We're not deep with one another. We don't share the ugly stuff we keep hidden from the world. Those things, those moments, well, they are for friends and we are not that.

"Not if I ruin yours first!" I call back to his retreating form.

I don't have to see his face to know he's smiling.

Chase

I scrub my hands down my face, my mind continuously attempting to rewind the moment in the living room with Georgia. Hell, the moments from the past few days. It's strange. Seeing one another on a different level like that, it's added a layer of humanity that we don't cross with one another.

These past ten days have been a battle of wills and wits, seeing who can piss the other off first and who will get the last laugh. She could have easily taken advantage of that moment in the living room and used it to her benefit. But that would be cruel and if I really think about it, it's never about that with us.

It's about annoying the other person or at least minorly inconveniencing them for a brief period of time; it's never about actually causing mental or emotional harm. If I really analyze it, it's about taking our mind off the shit that we've both been through.

Oh fuck, when did I develop a soft spot for Georgia?

This can't be good. The girl is a superficial barbie doll and here I am thinking about how much fun I've had having her around recently.

This is not good. Not good at all.

I spend the rest of the day making some calls, attempting to get my shit together. Despite what everyone else thinks, I always have a contingency plan, I just didn't want to say anything unless or until it goes through.

I exit the office to smells of cooked onion and tomatoes, my stomach automatically grumbling in response.

I've been surviving on takeout since Ash and Logan left. Logan being the better cook out of the two. Ash has some weird sugar addiction and her diet basically consists of Oreos and chocolate.

I find Georgia stirring a large pot, steam billowing in her face. Her head turns around as I pull out a beer and a bag of Lays. Making myself comfortable on the stool, I lean against the counter and begin to scroll through my phone.

We say nothing to one another as she cooks and I stuff my face, easily finishing off the bag. Despite no longer being in the NHL, I want to keep up my physique, so moving forward, I will probably have to lay off the chips. My muscle mass has already gone down since the injury, but I know with some intense training over the next few months, I can get back to where I was. I might not be a player anymore, but I refuse to believe this chapter of my life is over. There has to be an alternative.

I'm momentarily stunned when Georgia pushes a plate of food in front of me. A plate of vodka pasta, if I'm not mistaken.

I raise an eyebrow at her.

She lifts a shoulder and goes back to her bowl, covering it in silky parmesan cheese.

"Thanks," I reply, but even my words come out awkward.

"I just had extra," she responds, eyes on her food.

We eat in silence, neither of us saying anything else. The food is fucking incredible and I want to tell her that, but again, that isn't us. Chase and Georgia do not get along. We don't share food. We don't even share pleasantries.

So why does it feel like things are slowly changing between us?

Georgia

I quickly exit the kitchen after I scarf down my dinner, still unsure what's transpiring between the two of us. I don't know what came over me to offer him dinner, but I just couldn't watch him eat that shit anymore. I mean how many bags of Lays can one guy eat?

Apparently, if you ask Chase, a lot.

My footsteps are quick as I rush to the shower, no longer cautious for potential Chase-related sabotages coming my way.

It's weird.

Chase and I have never been nice to one another. It's always quick-witted retorts and comebacks. Digs at one another since the moment we met. A healthy dose of dislike from the beginning. I vividly remember our first interaction.

Ash was moving into her new house in Cambridge, Massachusetts, and then we found out Logan was her new roommate. And what's the one thing that always follows Logan? Pesky little Chase. Well, he isn't exactly little, but that's beside the point.

One look at him and I knew his kind: a cocky womanizer - one who clearly expected me to fall at his feet. But little did he know, that wasn't how I operated. I wanted to be chased, to be doted on. Yes, 22-year-old Georgia was a little bit of a princess, but who doesn't want that? I was just doing the female version of what he did!

Oh my god.

I stop in front of my vanity, gazing at myself in the mirror. The shocking mental revelation hitting me like a ton of bricks.

Am I the female version of Chase?

There is no fucking way. I refuse to even entertain the idea that we are similar.

He's cocky, demanding, too self-assured, and, not to mention, downright painful.

And I'm confident, stubborn, and Jesus fucking Christ.

No wonder neither of us have been willing to back down all these years in our back-and-forth rivalry.

Chase Mathews might be the male equivalent of me. And that thought alone is enough to send anyone to the nuthouse.

Georgia

A few more days pass in silence between the two of us. We go about our business, me applying for every job I can find. What Chase does, I'm still not really sure, but I'm not about to ask. Neither of us have tried to fuck with the other; it's almost like some unspoken rule has come down that it's over.

And the worst part of it all? The part I would never admit to another living soul. The part I have a hard time admitting to myself.

I kind of miss it.

Miss the back and forth, the excitement of always having to be on my toes. Of wondering what will happen next, what will I plan next.

With all that gone, the bleak reality that I'm twenty-five, unemployed, and living in my friend's house begins to set in.

My frustration reaches an all-time high when an already bad day becomes worse by burning my mini muffins.

Yes, I'm about to cry over mini muffins.

You know that feeling when the universe seems to be against you? When every little thing you're doing seems to go wrong and it all ends in the smallest of things tipping you over the edge?

Well, that's how I got here, cursing at a batch of blackened mini muffins. My face is hot and sweaty. causing the hair around my face to stick to my brow.

"Uh, is everything okay in here?" I turn to the doorway, my chest heaving as I take in Chase. He's clearly just gotten out of the shower, drops of water dripping past his hairline.

"No, nothing is fucking okay," I snap, tossing the muffins in the trash before exiting the kitchen. My accelerated heart rate is telling me I might be about to snap and if I am, the mortification of doing it in front of Chase would cause me to crack.

Vulnerability is great, but it's specifically reserved for the quiet of my own room or with close friends.

Chase is neither of those things.

His green eyes widen slightly, his hands out in front of him as he follows me into the living room.

"Georgia," he calls out, with a softness I've never heard before in his voice.

"I'm fine," I respond, attempting to hold back tears. This whole thing is utterly ridiculous and extremely embarrassing. My life really isn't that bad; I'm extremely lucky in most ways. Today just feels like it's all falling down on me. I feel stuck in a hole that I don't know how I'm going to get out of and that terrifies me.

"Georgia, wait," he says, calling my name again.

My footsteps come to an abrupt halt, my toes digging into the cream carpet. I focus my attention and energy on how it feels against my feet. Hoping the distraction will give me a moment to pull myself together.

And, sure enough, in true Georgia fashion, I manage to push it all back down before turning to face him. But if the pitiful look on his face tells me anything, I didn't do a good enough job.

"What?" I snap. "Isn't this the perfect time for a dig or a joke?" I try to egg him on, much preferring our back and forth to this.

He says nothing, just continues to stare at me.

"What? The almighty Chase Mathews has nothing to say?"

Again. Nothing. His silence only pushes me further.

"Look at us, Chase!" I yell, throwing my hands up in the air, "we were supposed to be something by now. Instead, we're three years out of college and both jobless and crashing on our successful friends' couches." I pause, trying not to let myself get overwhelmed at my impending downfall. "I really thought I'd have done something meaningful with my life. I mean you were always a dick, but it was clear you had drive."

He bites his lip, before a forced smile graces his lips.

"We were something, Georgia. You were a spoiled little princess, and I was a cocky prick, but we still were something. Both of us are products of crap situations. My injury, your dad, neither of us could have seen it coming, but it did. The reality is, life throws shit at the walls and hopes it sticks. Sometimes it doesn't and people narrowly avoid being hit. Other times, like ours, it catches us."

"Lovely, Chase, comparing our lives to shit." I walk to the edge of the sofa, sitting down.

He lifts a shoulder. "Am I wrong? Tell me it doesn't feel like the world has taken a massive dump on your head."

I burst out laughing, partially due to the comedic nature of his words, but also due to the truth behind them. Who knew his perceptiveness would be the thing to bring me back down to earth at this moment?

"Yeah, I guess you're right." I look down, my fingers picking at the hole in the thigh of my jeans. If I go at it long enough, I won't be able to wear this pair again.

"Feel better?" His question takes me by surprise, but then it dawns on me, I *do* feel better.

I nod. "thanks."

"Eh, more for my own sanity than yours. I don't do well with tears."

I roll my eyes. "There were no tears."

"Sure." He grins, and I know it's all to make me feel better. It's bizarre and feels like a slightly out of body experience. The two of us are having a civil conversation.

"I think the real comedy in this entire situation is that out of everyone, the two people most likely to rip one another's heads off are now stuck living together for the next month. It's like the universe really wanted to kick us while we're down."

I'm trying to make a joke, but Chase's reaction seems more thoughtful than jovial.

"So, let's change it."

I look up at him. "What?"

"Let's change the one thing we can control about our current situation, and that's our hate for one another."

"You can't exactly turn that off." I reply, knowing it isn't exactly hate I feel for him, probably more like a severe annoyance.

"Why do we fight all time?"

"Uh, cause you're annoying?"

He rolls his eyes. "And you're a brat, but all that aside, we have more reasons to get along than anyone. We're from the same town, have the same friends, both of us are godparents to Henry. If we both put down our weapons, it shouldn't be that hard to find some common ground."

"I mean, you are pretty annoying, Chase. I think I'd be the one doing all the sacrificing by being your friend." My words are light, a sneaky smile lining my face that I can tell he sees.

A soft green decorative pillow is launched at my head. "Oh, cause you're such a walk in the park!"

I stick my tongue out at him, my actions already more juvenile since being around him again. But instead of rejecting it, I try embracing it.

"Why do we hate one another? I mean Logan has asked me enough over the years, and I assume Ash has too?" he asks me.

"I don't know. I guess back in high school, I always heard about you and our schools were rivals. It just felt natural for us to be adversaries too. Plus, that first day I actually met you, I saw how you looked at me, like I was a conquest. So, I decided to be done with you before I even had a chance to start with you. You?"

"Fair enough. I guess that moment I took your reaction to my action as defensive. It seemed like you thought you were better than me and I didn't like that. Maybe it was a case of us getting off on the wrong foot?"

"Okay, Chase, let's call a truce for this month. If we don't kill one another, then hell, maybe we are meant to be friends."

"Then truce." He leans across the couch, his left arm digging into the sofa to hold up the rest of his weight while his right comes out in front of me. Even though I try to look away, I can't help but let my eyes momentarily linger on his physique. It's brief, but I could swear from the grin on his face that he saw it.

"Truce," I confirm, shaking my hand with his. This could be a terrible idea, but at this point, what's the harm in trying?

Famous.

Last.

Words.

Chase

It's been a few days since our truce. Not much has changed in our daily routines. Georgia is constantly looking for a job while I continue my attempt to become a part of the couch. It would be a lie to say her presence hasn't helped increase some level of my mood for the better.

Instead of constantly letting myself sulk, I've got her near me to annoy, and that's got to count for something. But now instead of it being genuine frustration toward one another, there is an element of fun in our teasing.

I've left my safe haven of fun to make a smoothie when I hear her growl. It's probably the fifth of the day, signaling another job rejection.

I grab an extra glass out of the cupboard, splitting my drink in two. Not exactly sure how to handwash this, I shove the blender in the dishwasher and turn it on.

Walking down the hall to Ash's office, I knock before entering. "Here," I say, placing it down next to her. She's hunched over at the desk, hair a mess, piled on top of her head. Yet there is something about a flustered Georgia that is entertaining. Compelling even.

She turns, eyeing the drink suspiciously. In the past, I could have potentially put something nasty in it, but since our truce, it's just a plain old smoothie.

"Thanks," she says, taking a small sip. Once realizing it hasn't been tampered with, she gulps it down.

"Wow, that's actually really good." A faint trace of pink lines her upper lip. My fingers twitch to rub it off, but instead, I keep my hands at my side.

"Uh, you've got a little-" My head tilts upward, indicating the remnants of the drink on her mouth.

Her face flushes slightly as she quickly wipes it, before standing up and walking back to the living room. I follow her.

Moving to the couch, she throws herself down on one end. I take the other. Although my leg has healed, it won't ever fully be like it was. There is a dull ache to it that never lets me forget what happened. How one moment took away what was to be my professional hockey career.

"So, how's the job hunt going?"

"Non-existent." She shakes her head. "It's just so frustrating. I feel like I've spent every hour of the past two weeks attempting to get somewhere and I'm still standing in the same place." She grabs a quilted pillow from next to her, hugging it to her chest. "I want a vacation, but I need money for that," she mumbles to herself.

"So, let's ignore it."

She turns to me, eyebrows raised. "Ignore it?"

"Why not? We're both supposed to be at the peak of our lives, but instead, we've both lost things that mattered to us. So instead of spending the next month crying about it, let's ignore it."

"Chase, you do realize when the month is up, I need to have another job lined up or I'll be sleeping on Ash's couch until I'm thirty." Her face seems to sour at the thought.

"Logan and Ash won't be home for another month. All I'm saying is take a break. I've seen you work like crazy the past two weeks. You will hear back eventually and if those ones don't work out, then you go back to the drawing board."

"That's so irresponsible." Her voice trails at the end, lacking its usual strength.

"Irresponsible? Maybe, but think how fun it will be. How long has it been since you spent consecutive weeks doing nothing?"

Lifting a shoulder, her blue eyes tilt downward. "I don't know, since college?"

"Exactly," I respond, her words proving my point.

A few moments pass, the running dishwasher, the only sound in the room. I think she might say no. And then not only will I feel stupid for asking her, but it will also be clear she thinks I'm even more of a joke than before.

"Why do you even want to ignore it with me anyway? You can't stand me."

I lift a shoulder. "You're more tolerable than I thought. Plus, if we're both here, we might as well make the best of it, instead of being miserable."

As dumb as it sounds, I started seeing the humanity in Georgia recently. I don't know if it was meeting Elaine or her making me dinner, but I've come to realize, I might have judged her prematurely. Perhaps she isn't the spoiled, self-centered princess I thought she was.

"Okay," she finally says, breaking me out of my thoughts. I rear back slightly.

"Okay?"

Her head bobs up and down. "Okay. Let's ignore it."

A full smile covers my face. For some odd reason, the thought of spending a month doing fuck all with Georgia, sounds like the best thing in the world.

"Okay," I confirm, wondering if when the month ends if we'll have formed a wonderful friendship or be ready to kill each other.

Georgia

Later that night, I'm lying across the sofa at one end while Chase is dissolving into the other side.

After our agreement to spend the next few weeks having fun, I quickly finished up the last of my emails before joining him for a Marvel marathon. I'm not really into superheroes, but I have to admit, they've been entertaining.

Thirty minutes into Captain America, Chase pulled out the tequila. I've never been one to say no to a drink, so I took it with glee, my body now happily in a state of fuzziness.

"Look at us," I say, "who would have thought we would be getting along for more than 10 minutes?"

He turns to me, his pearly whites on display.

"I do remember a time when we didn't hate one another," he says. My mind instantly goes back to that one night we declared a ceasefire. Sure, it was nice for a few hours, until he had to go and ruin it.

"Yeah, and look how long that lasted. A few hours, if I remember correctly."

"You know, Georgia," his voice halts before he expels a deep breath. "You know what, never mind."

"No, say it," I egg him on, even though I probably don't want to hear it anyway.

His deep green eyes lock onto mine, as if they're trying to speak to me without saying a word. Too bad I've never been good at mind reading.

"Why didn't you come find me?" he asks, finally ripping the band-aid off the old wound I so desperately tried to hide. It's not like we were in love or anything; I knew with Chase that it would only always be a fling. But it would be a lie to say the brief moment we shared our senior year of college didn't embarrass me.

"I did," I finally reply, feeling my cheeks heat. I hate thinking about it. Thinking about that one moment of stupidity on my part.

Chase's eyebrows draw together before he shakes his head. "I waited for over an hour, I think I would have known if you showed up."

"I did," I admit. "I came to your room and you were with someone else. So I left." I lift a shoulder, trying to brush it off, but Chase latches onto my arm, turning me to face him.

"No," he corrects, "I waited for an hour before I fucked off. I got wasted with Wolf, before passing out in Logan's room."

"You don't have to lie to me, Chase. I saw it with my own two eyes. Some buxom blonde was in your room."

I pull away from him, grabbing the cashmere blanket discarded in the corner of the sofa. I quickly begin folding it, making sure to keep my eyes down. "It wasn't anything serious to begin with, Chase. It was just supposed to be a night of fun and it didn't happen. It's no big deal."

"Being called a liar is a big deal to me, Georgia. I'm dead serious when I say I left after I thought you blew me off. I didn't hook up with anyone else that night."

Despite holding a teensy tiny grudge against Chase for the past few years, now hearing his side of things, I have to admit. I believe him.

"Okay," I reply.

"Okay?" he says, his voice skeptical.

He shakes his head. "So all these years, you thought I asked you to that room just to blow you off?"

"It's not something I really thought about too much, if I'm being honest. We had both had a lot to drink that night, inhibitions were low. I guess I just assumed you got tired of waiting and a better offer came along. The two of us had been bickering the entire year at that point, Chase. It's not like one night together would have changed anything. Hindsight tells me the universe made the right decision by making sure it didn't happen."

"Why do you say that?" he asks, body leaning forward.

"Messy. It would have been messy. My instincts now tell me that we probably would have killed one another after. It wouldn't have been like now. If the two of us hadn't been forced to live together, I doubt we would ever have had a civil conversation."

He looks down, scratching his stubble with his right hand. "You're probably right. I never really thought about it like that. I guess 22-year-old Chase never really did think with his head."

I stifle a laugh.

"It's in the past now. It wasn't a big deal then, but we can admit it probably didn't make our animosity toward one another any better. But I don't know, I guess it's nice to know the truth." I pause. "Now can we move on?"

"Yeah, we can," he says before lying back on the couch.

"Good," I reply, chewing on my bottom lip before turning my attention back to the movie. Yet despite trying to focus on a hot Chris Evans, my mind can't help but drift backwards in time.

May 2016

The music is blasting as I wade through the overcrowded living room. Ash has been living here in Cambridge, Massachusetts, for a while now, and tonight is the night it all ends. And since I graduated a few weeks ago, I thought now was the perfect time to visit her. Everyone here has just graduated and it's time we all grow up.

But that isn't what tonight is about. Tonight is about getting wasted and potentially finding a hot guy to kiss. I gaze around the room, biting my lower lip as I peruse the guys around me. Despite not going to this college, I see some familiar faces due to knowing Ash, others, though, not so much.

"Looking for your next victim?"

I don't need to turn to know Logan's annoying best friend is next to me. Chase Mathews is the spawn of Satan in my eyes. So fucking annoying and always seeming to appear whenever you don't want him.

"Shouldn't I be using that line on you?" I ask.

"Eh, the ladies love me, Monroe, it's more of a curse to me than them."

"Ew."

He grins, with that stupid cocky smile that makes women melt in front of him. That and the fact that he's on his way to the NHL, no wonder the guy's ego is bigger than Disneyland.

"You and me, I don't think we're that different."

"Oh yeah, and how's that?" I turn to face him, the buzz in my body warming my blood. He's closer than expected, our bodies practically aligned. I can't help but breathe in his scent, despite the whiff of tequila that I'm sure is surrounding everyone in the room, he still smells like fresh detergent.

"We like a challenge, and we love the chase, the thrill of it all." He tilts his head down, our breaths now mingling. I've never been this close to him in my life, I'm surprised I've yet to bite his head off.

"What are you trying to say here, Chase?" I whisper.

"One night, Georgia. One night of nothingness, one night of fun."

"We hate each other," I remind him.

He grins. "And wouldn't that make it all the more fun?"

My skin prickles, tiny goosebumps breaking out across my arms. I'm supposed to hate Chase, he infuriates me at the best of times. Yet, for some reason, I find myself replying.

"One night?" I ask.

"If you're interested, meet me in Logan's room in five minutes. If not, we never have to speak of this again."

Before I can get a word out, he's gone.

Leaving me standing there wondering what the fuck just happened. And why I liked it.

An explosion on the screen pulls me back to reality, my head quickly turning to the side to make sure Chase didn't see my trip down memory lane, as I'm sure it's written all over my face.

I never told Ash about that night; I never told anyone. It took me nearly thirty minutes to work up the courage to go to Logan's room. And as soon as I did, there were already two people in there. I guess my mind just assumed it was Chase. Gave me another reason to dislike him.

"I'm beat," he says.

I turn to him, nodding. "I think I've got a bit more energy to burn, I'm gonna keep watching."

He nods before standing, lifting his arms over his head as he lets out a yawn. I try to look away from the way his arms flex, I really do. But it's no use. I am only human. How he looks this good after being out of his usual training for months, I do not know. Nor will I ever ask or admit to this line of thought. I would never hear the end of it from Ash, that's for sure.

Some thoughts are better kept to ourselves.

"Georgia?"

I snap back at the sound of his voice, the tilt of his lips giving away that I've been caught staring.

"See you tomorrow," I tell him, opting to ignore the situation.

A soft chuckle escapes him before he nods. "See you tomorrow, Monroe."

I ignore the nickname, refocusing my attention on a guy who I can openly ogle like the rest of the world does.

Hello Captain America.

Georgia

The next morning, I wake up with a new sense of purpose.

To have fun.

Pigs must be flying because I've taken Chase's advice, determined to make the most of this situation. That's how I've ended up in the living room dancing like a lunatic with Third Eye Blind blasting at ten am.

Mid-dance I spot Chase coming down the hall. His steps groggy and slow.

"Uh, what are you doing?" Chase says, but I can barely hear his voice over the music, my body doing all sorts of flailing as I dance.

"I'm dancing," I say, as if it's the most obvious thing in the world.

He rubs at his eyes, clearly fresh out of a deep sleep. I should probably apologize for waking him, but wasn't it his idea to have fun this month? And that's exactly what I'm doing.

"I thought it was a strange dream I was having when I went to a Third Eye Blind concert."

I laugh before yelling over the music, "Hey, that would be a cool concert to go to!"

"You're nuts," he says, but his voice is light, the corner of his mouth turned up.

I dismiss him with a wave. "And you're a dick, but right now, I'm having fun and can't be dragged down by you!"

"I didn't paint you as a Third Eye Blind kinda gal."

I stop jumping, turning to face him. "I'm not, but I like this song and your constant talking is ruining it for me. So, either join me or be gone."

I give my back to him as I continue on, my feet digging into the soft carpet as I shake my non-existent ass, still belting out every word.

I'm surprised when Chase appears in front of me, singing along to the chorus. But what makes me really laugh are his moves. He looks like a baby giraffe on roller skates.

I really thought that with all that swagger he carries that he would have half-decent moves. But god, he's terrible. And it's great. But, most of all, it's fun.

We act like a couple of young idiots until the song ends, my labored breathing making it painfully obvious I need to get back to the gym.

"So, this is you having fun?" Chase asks as we walk to the kitchen. I chug down half a bottle of water as he makes his way over to the coffee machine. The room instantly fills with that beautiful bitter aroma and I know I need a cup.

"It is," I reply.

He nods. "I like it." He bites down on his lip, before looking around the room. "I've got an idea."

His long legs carry him out of the room with haste, my footsteps quick to follow.

"Where are we going?"

"You'll see."

He stops in front of Ash and Logan's hallway cupboard before pulling the doors open. I can't help but feel like a kid again when I see what he has pulled out, bursts of butterflies filling my stomach with anticipation.

"Holy shit, I haven't played this in years!" I tell him as he pulls out Rock Band.

Chase grins, clearly pleased with himself. To be honest, I'm pleased with him too. It's been way too long since I've played it.

"Okay Monroe, before we begin, I have a serious question for you."

"Hit me."

"Guitar or drums?"

I scoff. "Please, I'm a guitar and singer at the same time, all the way. I'm practically a real-life rock star at this shit."

He laughs and I can't help but smile at him. After we both put down our metaphorical weapons, it becomes clear to me why Chase and Logan are friends. Underneath all that bravado, Chase is a fun guy. Annoying as hell, but fun.

"Well, let's do this then, Mathews. I'm ready to kick your ass."

"You were close," he tells me, taking a sip of his cold beer. I lift a shoulder.

"But not close enough," I reply.

"No, not close enough." He laughs. "I guess I should have told you Logan and I still play religiously."

"So you had an advantage!" I lean forward, pushing my hand into his shoulder. A curl falls loose from my bun and Chase's eyes linger on it for a moment too long.

Oh shit. That feeling tells me I'm in the danger zone.

"I may have had a slight advantage, but I still beat your ass."

"Eh, I'll get you next time," I reply, keeping my voice cool.

"I'm sure you will."

"I will have you know, I kicked most guys asses at Rock Band in high school."

"I'm sure you had some tough competition."

"I did. I once played on expert level against Brad Wilcox for hours until I won with a perfect score."

"Brad Wilcox?" Chase asks like he recognizes the name of one of my high
school boyfriends.

Even though Chase and I went to different high schools, we both grew up in Seattle, so it's not suspiring that we have mutual friends.

"You know him?" I ask.

"Oh no, Monroe, don't tell me you dated him."

My mouth opens slightly before a guilty smile lights up my face.

"Wilcox, oh god, Georgia, for all that is good and holy, tell me you're joking!" Chase throws himself back on the couch, his stomach moving up and down as he laughs at me.

I lean over, smacking his side. "Hey, it's bad enough that I had to date him, don't make fun of me!" I mentally ignore how Brad cheated on me for the entirety of our relationship. I shove a handful of skittles into my mouth for a distraction.

"I just can't believe out of all the guys in Seattle, in our grade especially, you went out with him! God, the stories I could tell you about that guy. He was a douche!'

I cringe. "I don't want to hear them! Nothing can be worse than dating him. I'm pretty sure he dated half the girls in my grade while *exclusively* dating me."

"He's a dick," Chase remarks.

"It's been years, people can change."

"Last I heard, he was still up to the same behavior."

I squirm at the thought of him. "But you're one to talk, Ash told me you dated Crystal Jenkins."

Laughter ceases at the mention of her name. "Don't bring Crystal Jenkins into this. I'm still scarred from that experience."

Now it's my turn to laugh. "Aww, was poor wittle Chase scared of the big bad girl?"

"She made a photo album of what our children would look like after two dates! It was some 'How to Lose A Guy in 10 Days' type of bullshit."

I hold onto my stomach. "Oh god, I would have paid to see that." He tosses a marshmallow at me, but I grab it, stuffing it into my mouth.

"We've clearly both dated our share of crazy, but I'm sure many would say the same about us."

Now it's my turn to throw the candy. "Speak for yourself, I'm a dream. Anyone would be lucky to have me."

Chase smirks, just nodding his head.

We're silent for a few moments, both of us probably lost in memories of the past.

"Do you ever worry that all those years were our prime, and now we're just, I don't know, stuck?"

"Like high school and college?" I ask.

He nods, his eyes now looking anywhere but at me. I'm assuming this is vulnerable Chase, a side of him I've yet to see.

"I used to. I mean, I was this crazy fun girl back then, honestly, probably the female version of you. Life was all fun and games and then one day, I looked in the mirror and knew I had to grow up. Being reckless and impulsive was no longer cute."

"Yeah, tell me about it." He takes a long sip of beer before leaning back, his gaze now locked on mine.

"But I think if my time here this month has taught me anything, it's that growing up doesn't mean losing your inner child or stopping yourself from having fun, it's just finding different ways to express it."

"So, does that mean no more project X house parties?"

I burst out laughing, thinking back to high school when I went to a party where a guy drove a motorbike into the pool. Flashforward three years when I found out it was Chase.

"I will admit, that was a fun party."

He grins. "It was the best."

"You were still a dick," I toss in to make sure he doesn't think I'm going soft on him.

"Eh, can't argue with that."

There's another lull in our conversation before Chase opens his mouth again.

"Logan told me about your dad. Said he ran into hard times?"

I rear back, slightly taken aback by his bluntness. It's out of the blue, but perhaps it's a conversation that's been coming. I've yet to really talk about what happened with anyone but Ash.

"Uh, yeah, he did." I nod my head, my attention focused on my now warm beer. The label peels off slightly due to the condensation, my fingers itching to pick at it.

"Shit sucks."

His nonchalance makes me laugh, despite the situation being far from comical.

"Shit does suck," I agree. "But that's life. Shit happens, you've just gotta keep going."

I risk looking up at him, his eyes fixed in front of him, yet not focused on a single thing.

"It's not like I still rely on him to fund my life, but I worked for him and when he fell, I went down with him."

"You don't have to explain yourself, Monroe. I can see you're a hard worker, I doubt you'd willingly take something being handed to you."

I don't tell him he's hit the nail on the head. That one of my biggest insecurities in this life is that people will just assume I've been given everything. I worked my ass off to make sure I deserved to be at my father's agency. But despite my desire to get away from nepotism rumors, they're always there.

"Is your dad going to be okay?"

The concern in his voice catches me off guard, along with the fact he asked in the first place.

"I think so, I mean, he only needs to worry about my mom and him. I'm their only kid and I'm an adult, so I think he will be able to figure something out. I hope so, anyway. I don't have it in me to think otherwise. Like for me, I'm only just starting out in life, I have the ability to have this shit happen to me and still bounce back, but when you're older, the world constantly overlooks you. Like somehow looking for a job over fifty is a bad thing."

"People are assholes."

"Tell me about it." I expel a breath. "So what about your mom and dad?"

His gaze meets mine. "What about them?"

"I don't know, tell me about them."

He smiles, his eyes darting to the drink in his hand. "Dad works for an investment bank. Mom hasn't worked in a few years, but she used to be a teacher. They're good people, I wouldn't be where I am today without them."

"They've always supported you?" I lean forward, finding myself curious as to the people who raised Chase Mathews.

"Not just that. I'm adopted, Georgia. If my parents hadn't made that choice, then who knows where I would be today."

"I didn't know."

"Not something I really talk about. They might not have given birth to me, but they're my parents."

"Of course," I add in. "They're your mom and dad."

"Exactly."

His eyes meet my own. "You can ask more questions if you want, it doesn't hurt to talk about."

"Sorry, I don't mean to be weird, I just don't want to overstep."

Chase laughs. "You and me, we aren't the type to walk on eggshells with one another. I don't want you to change or to be sensitive to my feelings. The reason we can talk with one another like this is because we're blunt with each other, so don't get soft on me now, Monroe."

My mouth turns up at the side. "Okay, well, if you really don't mind me asking. Do you know what happened to your birth parents?"

I scan his face, making sure he isn't all talk and that I haven't overstepped.

"I do actually. As soon as I turned eighteen, I had the option to contact my birth mother, not really sure about the sperm donor. I decided against it, but I do know where she lives if I ever wanted to."

"Wow," I mutter. "I don't know if I'd have the control not to reach out, then again, I don't know if I'd have the balls to either."

"It's not for everyone. Some kids are content going their entire lives without searching for their birth parents, others don't have the option to, and then there are people who find them."

"So you've been sitting with their info for over seven years?"

He scratches his cheek. "Yeah, I guess so. My life feels like it's been on fast-forward mode for the past seven years, ever since I graduated high school. I haven't exactly had too much time on my hands to think about it." He pauses.

"Until now?"

"Until now," he confirms.

If the look on his face tells me anything, it's that the past few months of solitude has given Chase more than enough time to think about his birth parents.

"You could call her?"

He blinks a few times, before refocusing his attention on me. "I could. But you never know how that shit will go. If I decided to contact her, I'd want to visit in person."

"And where would that be?"

"She's an hour outside of Vegas."

"We could go."

The words are out of my mouth before I have a moment to rethink them.

What am I doing?

His eyebrows scrunch together as he looks me over. I feel embarrassed under his gaze, but I still don't retract my previous statement.

"Who would have thought the prom queen Georgia Monroe would be asking Chase Mathews if he wanted her to accompany him to Vegas to meet his birth mother. I think if the others saw us now, they'd be sure we'd had some type of head injury."

"I can't argue with you there." I take a sip of my drink, even though it's warm and tastes like piss.

"This feels too heavy," he says. He laughs, but we both know it's forced. "Aren't we supposed to be having fun, not swapping depressing family stories?"

"Come on then," I say, standing. I brush imaginary lint off my pants. "I'll get the popcorn and we can return to me kicking your ass in Rock Band."

"Hey, Monroe," Chase calls.

I pause, looking over my shoulder.

"Thanks."

I wink. "Don't sweat it. And don't tell Ash or I'll deny it till I die."

He chuckles. "I'd expect nothing less."

Chase

Our days together go by without a hitch. Georgia and I spend our time eating, dancing, visiting Elaine, and watching every Marvel film ever made. I finally restart my physical therapy too, deciding to no longer let myself rot. No comments are made about jobs or the future, both of us simply living in the now.

But despite all our good times, I don't forget her offer. To say it caught me off guard is an understatement. It shocked the hell out of me. Georgia and I are notorious for trying to kill, not to help, one another. So her offer to accompany me to see my birth mother has lingered in the back of my mind.

A part of me wants to go, the never vanishing curiosity living in the recesses of my mind. But the fear that sits there is just as prominent. A million 'what ifs' always make me chicken out in the end.

What if she doesn't want to see me?

What if I hurt my parents by seeking my birth mother out?

The list of questions is fucking endless.

Despite being a tough, cocky athlete, there's still a little boy who lives inside me. Fear of the unknown worse than anything else. It could be so easy to go see my birth mother, to just make that choice. But what if I don't like the outcome?

I want to jump on the offer from Georgia, like somehow going with someone who doesn't know me that well will make it less real. I don't know. I could never take Logan or my parents; I think the stress alone would kill me.

So despite previously wanting to kill one another, no less than three weeks ago, I can't help but remember her offer. And I can't help but also entertain it.

"Chase, come on!" Georgia calls out to me from the living room, my mind slowly slipping away from those burdening thoughts.

"Coming!" I call back to her as the intro to "Stacey's Mom" begins.

I'm not even slightly surprised to find her decked out in a feather boa and sparkly hat as she jumps around to the music.

She tosses a blow-up guitar my way before continuing to sway her hips. My eyes linger on them a little longer than they should before I quickly look away.

Georgia screams the chorus into the empty living room, her carefree giggles causing a grin to breakout across my face.

"Come on, Chase, this one is all you!"

I take the Rock Band mic from her, singing into it as she acts as my backup.

"Has got it going on!" We scream together like a couple of teenagers.

It takes me a few moments to notice that she's pulled up the photobooth app on her laptop, recording all of our antics.

"We're reliving our youth, Mathews," she calls. "Tell me you never made a music video!"

I grin, knowing full well that fourteen-year-old Logan and I did just that, a time or two, as a gag.

Never being one to take myself too seriously, I pull the feather boa off her neck, singing into the camera. My lungs may seriously be shot to shit after this, but what are you gonna do about it?

At the chorus, Georgia gets on my back, my arms going under her smooth legs to keep her from catapulting to the ground.

"Don't drop me!" She squeals as I spin her around, my grip firm.

"You're like 100 pounds soaking wet, I'll be fine."

Her arms link around my neck, our faces suddenly much closer than we've ever been before. I ignore the potential intimacy that is created from our proximity.

A few songs and a shit-ton of atrocious dance moves later, we're both beat, Georgia sprawled out across the massive sofa, her hair a disheveled mess while sweat coats her brow.

I run my shirt across my face, my own panting alerting me to the fact I need to work out.

"Admit that was fun," she says, her breathing labored.

"You've got me, that was fun."

A victorious smile paints her lips. She loves being right almost as much as I do. Again, a reminder of just how similar we are despite our ability to ignore that fact up to this point.

"But serious question, Monroe. Where the hell did you get all these props? Because I know Ash and Logan aren't into freaky costume foreplay."

She bursts out laughing, the image of our two friends getting it on with feather boas and blow-up guitars too much.

"As much as I'd love to say these are from Ash and Logan's kinky closet, I ordered them last night on Amazon."

I nod. "Ah Amazon, the land of everything."

She winks at me. "You got it."

"Beer?" she asks.

I nod. "I got it." Standing, I lift my arms above my head, my body feeling slightly stiff as it's been out of use for so long.

"A beer and a free show, what did I do to get so lucky?" she teases.

I throw a pillow at her as I walk to the kitchen, her laughter carrying along with me.

"Hey Magic Mike," she calls, "can I have a solo show?"

Apparently she's now a comedian. I walk back into the living room, two cold ones in hand.

"I'll show you mine if you show me yours, it's only fair." I smirk.

"Oh my god, tell me that look doesn't work on women!"

I lift a shoulder before diving back down next to her. Not close enough to create intimacy, but a friendly level of distance.

A friendly level of distance?

When did I start overthinking things as small as how close I'm sitting next to someone?

"I mean, it does most of the time."

"You're not serious."

"What's that supposed to mean?

She raises one of her perfectly groomed eyebrows at me.

"You're telling me that when you give women that little Chase Mathews' smirk, it works?"

"Almost every time."

"Okay, then it's settled, we're going out tonight. I need to see this work in person."

I laugh. "You're serious?"

"Of course I'm serious, I need to see you in action."

"I'm pretty sure we went to a lot of the same parties in high school; I was definitely using the charm then."

Now it's her turn to laugh. "Yeah, but you drove me crazy then and now you're tolerable, so I'm curious. Maybe I can learn a thing or two."

"Tolerable?" I tease.

"Hey, that's a big step from dislike, you should take what you can get."

"Fair enough. Also, I doubt you need help getting a date. As far as I can remember, you were almost always dating someone when you'd come visit Ash."

She wiggles her eyebrows. "Keeping tabs on my dating life, were you?"

"Ash talked about you enough, it was hard to ignore."

"Sure, sure."

"Well, if we're going to head out tonight, I need to start getting ready."

Pulling out my phone, I check the time. "Uh, Georgia, it's only 2pm."

"So?"

"You need four hours to get ready?"

By the look she is giving me, that was an asinine question. Spinning on her heels, she heads out of the room, but not before calling out to me one last time.

"Don't hate the player!"

Chase

"Okay Magic Mike, let's see what you've got."

I turn to Georgia. "You're about to eat some humble pie, Monroe."

She rolls her perfectly lined eyes. "I'll be the judge of that."

"Okay, so let's make things interesting. First person to get someone's number tonight wins."

You'd think I'd given her a new pair of shoes at the mention of a competition. There's the little hellcat I knew in college.

"I do love a wager, but what does the winner get?"

I pretend to think it over, despite knowing I've had the idea in the back of my head since this afternoon.

"Loser has to clean the house every day until Ash and Logan get home."

"Every day?"

I nod.

Her mouth tilts upwards. It's devious and entirely too enticing.

"I can't wait to watch you do my dishes." She slides her manicured hand into my own.

"We'll see about that."

On that note, she looks around the club before sauntering off, giving me a little wave on the way. I know I should look away, but my eyes are drawn to her getting up, understanding why it took her hours to get ready.

Her hair flows down her back, and she's wearing tight black jeans and a black top like a second skin. I'm sure she can get any guy's number instantly, so I've got to get my ass into gear.

I spot a brunette by the bar, taking one more glance at Georgia before I make my move.

Georgia

I take a sip of my vodka soda, pretending to give a shit about what the dude in front of me is saying. I keep smiling, but my eyes are sneakily trying to roam the bar and lock onto Chase.

I can't lie; I'm a terrible loser, especially when Chase Mathews is involved. Plus, I hate cleaning, so I'm ready to do whatever it takes to win.

"Tell me more about the practice?" I tell Tom, or maybe it was Tim, the veterinarian.

His eyes light up as he continues on, clearly not noticing he doesn't have my full interest.

I finally spot Chase across the room, speaking to some brunette. Her hand is already resting on his arm, so I know I've got to up my game.

I deliberately make a show of finishing my drink before batting my eyes.

"Oh, another?" He motions to my glass and I nod.

"That would be great." I walk with him to the bar, his hand on the small of my back.

As luck would have it, Chase is there too, ordering another round.

"Oh my god," the guy says from next to me. "Is that Chase Mathews?"

I tense, having momentarily forgotten he's a household hockey name.

"Uh, I don't know," I lie, placing my hand on the guy's arm to regain his attention. Even with dating, Chase manages to steal the spotlight. He's a star and the world wants to know him. I've got to give him credit.

"A vodka soda please," I tell the bartender, before looking next to me to see the vet is already talking Chase's ear off. On the flip side, the girl that was previously hanging off his arm is now gone.

"You know what, make it a shot of tequila," I tell the bartender. He grins at me, his handsome face covered by a beard. He looks like a sexy lumberjack.

"Rough night?" he asks, leaning forward.

I take the shot from him, downing it.

"You could say that," I reply, continuously checking what Chase is up to.

"Is he your ex or something?"

The question catches me off guard.

"No way, he's uh," I pause, unsure how to categorize what we are. "He's my roommate." It's not entirely true, but it's the easiest explanation.

"Gotcha." His face tells me he doesn't fully believe me but what do I care? I don't know this dude from Adam.

"Yep." I tap my newly painted fingers against the bar, thinking of how to beat Chase at his own game.

"You know, if you need any help in making him jealous." He doesn't finish his sentence, but the insinuation is there.

This could be an easy win.

"Can I have your number?"

His eyes widen. "You sure can."

He wastes no time scribbling it down on a piece of paper before slipping it my way. We're just in time, as Chase has managed to escape the vet and is coming my way.

"How did it go?"

I beam before holding up the paper.

"I guess you won then."

"Really?" I ask.

"Yep, I got stuck talking to some dude named Tim, apparently he's my biggest fan."

"Yeah, I noticed that. I would have helped save you, but I was too busy winning our bet."

"I guess I'm doing the cleaning." Clearly not too upset about it, he smiles down at me.

"I guess so. Wanna get out of here? As fun as this should be, I'm kind of desperate to get back to our movie marathon. My heels are killing me."

"Agreed," he says, and I follow him to the exit.

"You know, I totally forgot people recognize you until that vet came up to you. I know I have game, but I'm shocked you didn't get a number before me. I mean you are *the* Chase Mathews," I tease.

He shakes his head, laughing. "I'm sure I'm just off my game because it's been a few months. Let me get back on my feet and I'm sure I'll get you next time."

"We'll see about that."

After hailing a cab, we make our way home to finish *Avengers: Infinity War.* Twenty minutes into the film, Chase is passed out on the couch while I try to tidy up the living room.

Although he will be the maid for the rest of our time here, I can do one more load of laundry for us.

Picking up his jacket, I make sure the pockets are empty before throwing it in the wash. I expect to find a gum wrapper or his car keys, not the phone number of the girl he was talking to before the vet.

My gut hallows at the realization.

Chase let me win.

But the question is, why?

Georgia

I don't tell Chase that I know he let me win. I'm not really sure why, but the whole thing makes me feel uneasy. Our banter doesn't include being overly nice to one another. It's a fun rivalry and him letting me win makes me feel like we've somehow crossed into uncharted territory.

My phone rings as I'm mulling over last night, Ash's name appearing on the screen.

"Hey you," I say as I answer FaceTime. It's been a few days since I've seen her face and I instantly feel at peace.

"Just wanted to check in. Make sure you and Chase haven't killed one another yet!"

I hold back a smile.

"You'd be impressed, we're actually having fun together."

"Logan!" Ash yells out. "I think Georgia has lost her mind, she just said, her and Chase are having fun together!"

"Miracles do happen!"

The phone begins moving and, sure enough, the golden Adonis that is Ash's husband comes into the frame.

"Fun?" Logan repeats.

"Yes, you two, we are having fun. It's not the craziest thing in the world."

"But you two hate each other," I hear Ash say.

"Well, we've come to a truce."

"Oh god, are you sleeping together?" she says.

"Ash," Logan replies, clearly thinking it's none of their business.

"No!" I snap. "We're just trying to make the best out of a bad situation."

"Misery loves company," Logan calls through the phone, like somehow, he predicted we would put aside our differences. But, in reality, it's more than that. I dare say we've formed a friendship.

"Enough about me, what are you guys doing? Actually, scratch that, what is my amazing nephew doing?"

These two easily change the topic when Henry is mentioned, lifting the phone over his bassinet as he sleeps.

"Ugh, I don't even miss you two, I just want to kiss and squeeze his face."

"Did I hear you say Henry?" Chase pops his head into my room, my door now open more than closed.

"Shh," I snap at him, "he's sleeping."

Chase doesn't waste a second throwing himself on the bed next to me, getting far too close for comfort. I see Ash nudge Logan through the phone and try to scoot away from Chase, but if I go any farther, I'll be off the bed.

"Hey Chase," Ash says.

"Hey Ash, still looking like the hottest MILF I know." I jab my elbow into his side.

"What?" he has the audacity to say.

"Seriously?" I reply, eyebrows raised.

"Oh, don't give me that, Ash loves my compliments."

Shaking my head, I turn my attention back to our friends. Friends who are eyeing the two of us a little too closely. I know Ash, so I can tell the wheels are already spinning in her head.

"How's training going?" Chase asks Logan.

"Yeah, it's been better. Things change when you 're up half the night with a newborn. I somehow don't have all the energy I used to," he jokes.

My head tilts slightly, risking a glance at Chase's expression. I can't help but wonder if it hurts him to talk about the one thing he can no longer participate in. I've yet to gather the balls to ask him about it. Lord knows if I was in his position, I wouldn't want to talk about it.

"Yeah, I heard Simmons was a hardcore coach," Chase replies.

"Georgia mentioned you're back doing PT?"

Chase nods. "Yeah, figured I probably shouldn't let my leg go to waste."

They go back and forth for a few minutes before the front door rings and Chase moves to get off the bed. He quickly says his goodbyes before walking to the door.

"Who is that?" I ask.

"I got us pizza."

"With pineapple?"

"Of course, it's like you don't even know me!" he calls as he exits the room.

I grin, pleased he got my favorite.

"He knows your pizza topping?" Logan asks, joining in on Ash's questioning ways.

"So what?" I say a little too quickly, sounding defensive.

"Nothing." Logan holds up his hands in surrender.

"Well, as much as I'd love to stay for this inquisition, I need to go, but talk soon?"

They laugh, but we agree to FaceTime with an awake Henry later in the week.

I leap off my bed, leaving my phone and their questions behind, my mind only on one thing.

Pizza.

"I'm so full I could burst," I tell Chase, patting my stomach like an old man. He grins at me, clearly pleased.

"I could still eat dessert," he remarks.

I bite my lip and think about if I have room. Who am I kidding? There is always room for dessert.

"Okay," I concede, "I could do some Ben and Jerry's."

He claps his hands together. "Now you're talking!"

"But let me digest first!" I quickly add.

We keep watching The Avengers before I decide to just grow some balls and ask him about hockey. It's been on my mind, if I'm being honest, since I caught him watching the game all those weeks ago. Our friendship isn't based on deep conversations with one another, but the more time we spend together, the more I realize I want to know what is under the layers.

I want the answer to the question, who is Chase Mathews?

"Can I ask you something?"

He turns to me. His expression soft, unguarded. Something we've never been with one another until now. If I would have asked Chase a question any time before a month ago, it would have been met with an eye roll or an exasperated sigh.

But now, it's met with an openness I didn't realize we had. A vulnerability.

"Yeah?"

"Do you miss it? Hockey?"

I'm trying to tread carefully, rubbing salt in his wounds is not my objective. I know our situations can't even begin to be compared. What I'm dealing with right now, I know it's a temporary hurt. I will get another job and apartment. But with Chase, this is something he will carry with him for the rest of his life. The possibility of what was to come before it was all taken away.

Perhaps it's a stupid question, but it's a question to open the door. Test out the waters if he wants to speak on it or shut it down completely, either option I will accept.

He's silent a few moments, his gaze not focused on a single thing, rather lost in a riptide of memories.

"Yeah, I do," he admits. "I miss it, but the feeling is different than I thought it would be. I miss playing, sure, but more than that, I miss the sense of belonging I had with the team. It was a brotherhood, *is* a brotherhood." He pauses and I stay silent, knowing he has more to say.

"When I hurt my leg, I really thought it was all over. I wallowed in misery and self-pity for months. You saw the Chase-shaped hole in this couch," he jokes, but it lacks its usual mirth.

"I think I was more devastated to lose the one thing I'd worked so hard to attain my whole life. In a single moment, it was just gone. Completely out of reach forever. But over the past month, I think I've come to realize that it's something I will be able to get over. Not being able to play doesn't mean I can't still be a part of the team. I've been thinking seriously about coaching, and the more I think about it, the better it sounds."

I lean forward as he speaks, my ears eating up every word he feeds me.

"To be totally honest, I never really liked being told what to do, what to wear, or how to act. But the pull of community and belonging kept me there. Plus, I love the game, but maybe now it's just time for me to love it in different ways."

He rubs his hands over his face then tugs at his hair. It's slightly overgrown, with dark blond tendrils. Different to the buzzcut he had when I first met him all those years ago.

"Sorry, I'm sure you didn't want an answer like that when you asked me that question."

I can tell he's going to try to brush it off or turn it into a joke, so I'm quick to stop him. Reaching out, I put my hand on his leg. Both of us freeze for a moment before I speak. The contact we've been having with one another growing more intimate by the day.

"Don't do that," I say. "Don't pretend that sharing your emotions is lame or that I didn't want to know. I asked, Chase. I asked because I care. And it means something to me that you're comfortable enough to share with me. I know we don't exactly have the best history."

He snorts. "Understatement of the century."

I grin. "True, but things change, people change. And our dislike of one another was slightly irrational. We instantly clashed and I think it was because we're pretty similar. You use humor as a deflection while I use dismissal. But maybe because neither of us likes being vulnerable, it's okay that we are with one another? I know it sounds crazy, but sometimes I think it's easier to open your soul to a stranger than a close friend. Easier to take the burden off your heart as their reaction will be unexpected or they'll have none at all. With friends or family, we know how they will react. Whether it be comfort, dismissal or anger. Sometimes all we need is an ear to talk to, someone to simply listen."

"I don't really know what else to say, besides I think you hit the nail on the head there."

"I can be pretty profound when I want to be."

"Thanks, Monroe."

"Anytime, Mathews."

Georgia

I go to bed that night thinking of Chase Mathews. But instead of going over the things that annoy me the most about him, my mind races back and forth over the things I like about him. And these thoughts alone are enough to make me want to run. I'm not supposed to be thinking like this, picking apart what I like instead of hate.

Our relationship, if you'd even call it that, is centered around driving one another crazy. Him relentlessly calling me names while I purposefully think of ways to inconvenience his day. Sure, it's been a while since we laid down our swords, but I've still managed to keep these thoughts away. Feelings that I know are only going to lead me down a path to hell.

We're having fun. That's all this is. It's supposed to be easy and carefree. So why do I suddenly feel so overwhelmed and confused?

"I think I need to go see my parents," I tell Chase as I flop down on the sofa, wiggling my body into the soft fabric beneath me. A few weeks here and I can see why Chase made this place a second bedroom for so long.

His eyes leave his phone. "Sure, when should we go?"

My body slightly jolts with a laugh I can't contain. It's short, almost as if it just jumped out of my body without warning.

"You want to come?" My tone is filled with disbelief.

His eyes revert back to his phone as he lifts a shoulder. "Why not? Not like I can do anything here while you're gone."

With his focus now back on himself, I peel myself away from the comfy oasis.

"Uh, okay. Sure. I was thinking of leaving in half an hour?"

"Sounds good," he replies without looking up.

I nod to no one in particular, my teeth chewing on my bottom lip as I go back to my bedroom. Sure, I've brought a handful of guys home to my parents before. But Chase and I aren't dating. I'm not even sure if we're friends.

Who knows what is going to happen when I leave here in two weeks? Will we speak again? Hang out? They aren't really questions of necessity, but now they're all I can think about. Chase and I have had some deep moments, but did we only have them because it's easier to confide in someone who doesn't truly know us?

But maybe that's just a copout. I'd argue I know him pretty well now.

"Stop overthinking everything," I mutter to myself as I dig through my disheveled suitcase, attempting to find my blue jeans. I've been in a uniform of sweatpants and hoodies since I've been here. My usual attire of heels, pants, and blouses has been easily discarded to the bottom of the suitcase I never finished unpacking.

I hastily apply a layer of makeup, opting to forgo my usual routine. Not because I've grown out of it, but I just don't have the time. Job or no job, fashion and beauty matter to me. And I refuse to indulge those who think less of me because of it.

A rattle on my door stops me mid eyeliner. Chase is dressed for once, a clean white tee shirt topped with a fuzzy-lined denim jacket and jeans. Dark brown boots pull it all together. And dare I say, he looks fucking good.

"Looking good, Monroe," he says as I stand up. I wave my hand at him but mentally take the compliment.

"Shall we?" I ask, grabbing my black bag off the bed. Chase pulls open the door, a small smirk lining his lips.

"Ladies first."

"Mathews," my father says as he looks Chase over. "You wouldn't be related to Daniel Mathews by any chance?"

Chase's eyes light up at the name.

"Yes, sir. Daniel is my father."

My dad claps his hands together. "Your father and I are members of the same country club. I've known Daniel for years, surprised I've yet to meet you before, Chase."

I keep my perfectly pasted smile on my face. Yet my mind can't help but think how that country club membership is probably going to be a thing of the past for my father soon. I know there is nothing to be done about it now, but the crowd my father runs in will drop him as soon as word is out about the bankruptcy.

My dad is a good man and I can only hope people like Chase's father see beneath the dollar bills and Rolex.

"Georgia, darling, could you help me in the kitchen." My mother's sugary sweet voice seeps into my ears. I absentmindedly agree before making sure Chase is okay to be left alone with my dad. Appearing to be enthralled in conversation with my father, or perhaps the opposite way around, I take my leave.

"He's cute," my mom says as we walk into the family kitchen, I've known all my life. Sure, the house has had its fair share of makeovers, but this has always been my favorite spot.

"He's just a friend, Mom."

"A handsome friend."

I take the iced tea out of the fridge, noticing real estate brochures on the counter as I pass. They're haphazardly tucked into mail, like, somehow, they wanted to hide the inevitable from me. No matter how old I get, I think I will always be a child in their eyes.

"So you're selling the house?" I say, my head tilting to the counter.

A slight tint of red creeps up on her cheeks.

"We didn't know how to tell you, Georgie. You've been in this house since you were a baby."

"Mom," I cut in, "I love this house. I'll never forget it. But this is the right step." I move forward, taking her warm hand in my own. "This house isn't special because of the floral wallpaper or the sparkling chandelier. It was special because you and Dad put so much love and joy into it my entire life. You could decide to move into a shoebox and it would still be the best fucking place on the street."

Her eyes are slightly misty as she blinks. "Oh, Gigi, don't swear."

I smile at her. Because she's my momma and she will be telling me not to swear till we're both old and gray. "It's gonna be okay, Momma. I promise."

Pulling her into me, I make a promise I can't keep. But one I'm going to try with everything I have to do so. Because they've looked after me my entire life and I will be damned if I can't do the same for them.

No one ever likes to start over, let alone in your fifties. The world views you as expired goods. But that's just because the world is full of assholes.

"Why don't you go sit down next to handsome Chase and I'll bring in the food."

She beams. "So you do think he's handsome."

"If you tell him I said anything, I'll deny it!"

"Your secret is safe with me, my Gigi."

She begins to walk out of the room before I call her name.

"I love you; you know that right?"

"Always, my girl."

"So I'm just gonna say it."

I turn to Chase as we pull out of my parents' house, after spending the afternoon with them. In all my wildest thoughts, I'd never have imagined bringing Chase home to meet Mom and Dad. Let alone them loving him.

"What?"

"Your dad and I are best friends."

I nearly choke on the fry in my mouth. "Best friends, huh? Who is going to break the news to Logan?"

"I guess we will have to get Ash to do it."

I roll my eyes. "You're an idiot."

"I'm serious!" He momentarily takes his eyes off the road to grin at me. It sends a pang of something through me.

Oh god. Bad mind, ignore the hot guy.

"Well, I'm sure you can be his friend, he's probably going to lose a few so..." I don't finish the sentence. It's depressing and has totally killed the mood.

"Fuck, sorry, ignore me."

"Hey." Chase's hand reaches across the console and briefly lands on my leg before pulling away.

"I'm just so fucking worried about them. I've been so self-focused for the past month because they told me they were going to be fine. But if I'm being honest, I was just avoiding the truth."

"And that is?"

"My parents are in their fifties and are losing everything they've ever worked for. They're selling their house and Mom didn't tell me because she was worried about me. They're always worried about me. Even when this all went down, they kept reassuring me that they'd be fine and what did I do? I thought about myself."

"Georgia, it wasn't just their lives that were turned upside down. You're allowed to be upset."

"But am I? I mean, sure, I lost my job and had to move out of my apartment, but big fucking deal. I'm twenty-five and have a decent resume. I'm going to be fine. My dad, on the other hand? Who is going to hire a fifty-five-year-old who just lost everything?"

My voice cracks at the end. I screw my eyes shut before refocusing my gaze on the trees that pass us by as we drive. I'm thankful that Chase offered to drive, because clearly, in this state, I can't be trusted behind the wheel.

"It's completely normal to be worried about your parents. But have some faith in them. Your dad has gotten this far for a reason. He's clearly intelligent, and the same goes for your mom. Things have a funny way of working out for people."

"I can just see it now," I go on, dismissing his words. "His asshole friends at the country club will pretend they don't know him. I know he will say it doesn't matter, but it will hurt him. All of this will hurt him, *it is* hurting him."

Chase is silent and it's then I remember his parents are in that club. I've essentially called them assholes. And from what he's told me, they sound like great people.

"Fuck, Chase, I didn't mean how that came out. I'm sure your parents are the best. I'm just angry. I'm sorry."

Chase being Chase just smiles. "That place is full of assholes. In fact, besides my parents and your dad, I don't think I've ever met someone there I liked. Once Ms. Rodgers tried to proposition me to give her a full body massage." His body shakes at the memory. His words have a way of taking me out of my own head, my scowl now gone.

"You're just trying to make me feel better."

He sharply turns to me; thankfully, we're stopped at a red light. "Am not! You should have seen her, trying to get her claws into eighteen-year-old me! I ran so fast out of that place I left tire marks behind."

"Okay, maybe I believe you." No longer holding it in, a giggle escapes, and I sound like a child again. But that's the thing about being with Chase, he manages to bring out your inner child. And not in the bad way. He's got a playful youthfulness inside of him that so many disregard as they get older. It's something so many people would benefit from, if you ask me.

"Okay, maybe I didn't leave marks behind, but I made you smile."

"You made me smile," I confirm.

And in this moment, that is the only thing I need.

Chase

Despite previously loving getting a rise out of Georgia in the past, seeing her upset after being at her father's left a knot in my stomach. So, I told her the story about Ms. Rodgers in an attempt to cheer her up. It was my luck that it worked, but I know it is only momentary.

Our parents are our core family, neither having siblings. So when they're hurting, we hurt by extension. Just like it is for them with us. I know when Georgia lies down at night, she'll worry about her mom and dad. Worry about them financially but also socially. Because despite attempting to assuage her fear, the people at that country club and in their social scene are pretentious assholes. They only want what you can give. And if it's this week's latest gossip, they'll eat their own friends to get it.

So, as we pull back into Ash and Logan's house, I now know, more than ever, that our time here has an expiration date. And it's never felt more real than today. When we had what felt like endless weeks together, it was easy to ignore the clock running against us. But now that our time is almost up, I can't help but wonder what happens after this. What's next? And the one thing that scares me more than anything.

Why am I so desperate for more time with her?

"I thought we said no resumes."

Georgia's head shoots up, eyes wide as her gaze connects with my own.

"I'm just teasing, I'm not actually going to stop you from applying for a job. I want us to have fun, not ruin your future."

She lets out a breath, her shoulders sagging. "It's just another round of rejections. This one company did ask me to send over some more of my work for reference so that's hopeful, I guess."

"You can be pretty dedicated when you want to be. Don't give up and you'll find the right fit."

"Ugh!" She throws her head back, loose strands of hair dancing with each movement. "I feel like I've got no dedication. I'm just over this."

"Hey, you were dedicated enough to annoy me for five years. I think you can pull a bit of that into charming your way into a workplace."

"Hey! You were just as bad!" She smiles at me, her head titling backward, so it looks more like a frown from this angle.

"Eh, what can I say, I don't like to lose. And I know you don't either. That's how I know you're going to be fine."

She heaves her small frame, spinning around on the desk chair to face me. "So, since we're being adults for this moment in time, have you given any thought to what you're going to do? I mean, I feel like we're always talking about my bullshit, can I give any help with yours?"

I internally recoil at the question, because as much as I'm pushing Georgia, I have yet to figure out what the fuck I'm going to do when our time together ends. Only one thing is for sure, I'm getting my ass off this couch and out of this house. I've been an imposition on Ash and Logan for far too long.

"I don't know. I mean my condo will be done anytime now, so I'll at least have a place to go. But at the end of the day, I need something to keep me motivated. Something that I'm passionate about and so far in my life, all that has been is hockey."

"Have you looked more into coaching?"

"Yeah, I have. I've contacted an old coach of mine and I'm going to go see him next month."

"That's a positive."

"Yeah, I guess I can only view it as a step in the right direction. I just know I can't stay here forever, nor would I ever do that to Ash and Logan."

"They don't mind. I mean yeah, there may be a hole shaped like your perfectly sculpted torso on their sofa, but I'm sure it will be something to remind them of you once you're gone," she teases.

"I'm moving suburbs, not dying."

"Eh, for some people moving suburbs is like moving countries."

I laugh, appreciating Georgia's attempt to find humor in even the shittiest of situations.

"So, what about you? Where will you go next?"

Her eyes briefly gaze around the room, like perhaps it could give her the answers she so desperately seeks.

"I'm not sure, to be totally honest. Despite us planning to dedicate this month just for fun, I'll admit I've been looking for somewhere to live. I don't want to be totally fucked when our time's over."

"Understandable."

"But I'm not sure. I think maybe it's time I get out of Seattle for a while. I mean, I've been here my whole life, didn't even leave for college. Perhaps this is my sign to try somewhere new. I've always wanted to live in New York."

My stomach tightens at the mention of her potentially leaving Seattle. I guess I just figured when all of this was over, I'd still see her.

Wanting to actively see Georgia is a weird thought, considering I used to do all I could to avoid her.

"New York, huh?" I reply, voice calm and cool.

She elevates her shoulders slightly. "It could be fun. A fresh start, maybe that's just what I need, ya know?'

"That could be good."

"Elaine will miss you like crazy," I add in.

Her lips tilt upwards, but it doesn't meet her eyes. "She'd probably kill me, but I like to think, deep down, she'd be happy for me. You'd have to keep her company for me."

It's not lost on me the enormity of what she's asking. Elaine is like family to Georgia, and telling me to look out for her means a lot.

"That is if you don't end up leaving Seattle. Would you?"

"I'm pretty used to travelling, but I'll admit, I like having my quiet little bit of peace here. Away from the game, and all the cameras."

"I forget sometimes that the country, even the world, knows you and your face."

"Yeah." I let out a breath. "It can be a lot."

"Is that why you stayed here for so long?"

"I guess. I mean this place is so secluded for a reason. Logan and Ash need their time away from the public eye, I get that now. I used to be all about the parties and the people that came along with the fame. But that shit turns on you as quickly as it starts. Now when they look at me, all they see is the injured player, and they're always asking the same questions, what's next?"

"That's why you needed to get away."

Her words are not a question, merely a statement.

"I needed to get away. But from the looks of it, our time's nearly up."

"You don't have to have it all figured out at the end of the month, Chase."

"I know, but I want to be on the right path at least."

"I get that."

We're quiet for a few moments, both of us going back to our respective phones. I'm mindlessly scrolling back and forth before I speak again.

"So, I've been thinking," I start, briefly pausing until I have her attention.

"Yeah?"

"Um." I rub my hands over my mouth, the bit of stubble there sharp against my hands. I've always been clean-shaven; I guess recently I just haven't cared. "I was thinking about potentially going to see my birth parents."

Her eyes widen slightly, along with her mouth, as she leans forward. "Really?"

"Yeah, I mean why not, you know? I haven't really been able to get them off my mind recently." *Since our talk*, if I'm being honest, but I don't add that in. "I don't know, maybe there's no time like the present."

"Wow, that's awesome, Chase. When are you going to go?"

"Well, that's the thing. I was sort of hoping you might want to come with me?"

"Really?"

"Yeah, I mean I'm just coming to terms with the idea of going, so it won't be soon, but eventually."

"Well, when you want to go, you just let me know."

With that, we return our attention to our phones, pretending I didn't just make a major life choice and what it means that I asked her to be a part of it.

Chase

I can't sleep that night. My mind continuously thinking of Georgia. Thinking of how she understands me, how she lightens me. Her mere presence makes the rest of the bullshit going on feel like white noise. All I want to do is be present when I'm with her.

She was right when she said we were the same, that's why we fought like cats and dogs all these years. Instead of taking the time to actually get to know one another, we used it to bite one another's heads off.

And now that we've put down our armor, we're actually friends.

But do friends think about one another at night in bed?

Yeah, that's what's got me worried.

Not wanting to overthink it, I haul myself out of bed, in search of the one person I probably shouldn't be thinking about.

I find her typing away on her laptop, brows furrowed as her sole focus is given to the screen. Her presence is a daily occurrence in my life now, and the thought of not getting to see her guts me. But how do you tell the person you're supposed to dislike the most that the concept of not seeing them every day is slightly suffocating?

I guess in this case, you don't. You just enjoy the time you have together.

"Whatcha doing?"

"One second," she mumbles, her fingers speeding up as she continues to type away. I throw myself down on the space next to her, waiting until she's finished.

"Okay, sorry," she says, closing her laptop. "The New York agency wanted me to send over some more stuff. If all goes well, I might have a Skype call with them next week!"

Her smile is contagious, and despite not wanting her to go, I reciprocate, knowing it's what is best for her.

"I told you that you'd be okay, Monroe. Look at you, less than two months and you're back on your feet. Better than ever."

She bites her bottom lip, an action I've come to associate with her being nervous. "Maybe, but I don't want to jinx it, so let's pretend it's not happening until we know for sure things will work out. I don't have it in me to get my hopes up."

"Fair enough, so in another day of avoidance, what do you want to do?"

"I don't know, I wouldn't mind getting my nails done. We haven't really left the house this month and I'm a high maintenance girl, Mathews. I like my nails looking good."

I glance down at her hands. They look totally normal to me, but I say nothing.

"Okay, let's do it."

Her eyes light up. "Really?"

I lift a shoulder. "Why not, I'm sure it would do us some good to get out of the house. I'm surprised we haven't gone stir crazy by now."

"Me too. I think I've just been having too much fun to notice."

My insides light up at her words.

"Yeah?"

Her cheeks slightly redden as she turns to me, never shying away. "You know, if I'm being honest, my time here has been some of the most fun I've had in a long time."

I smile openly at her.

"Me too, Monroe. Me too."

"I guess you're really not so bad, Mathews. I mean, you still drive me around the bend, but now I don't mind being in the passenger seat."

"You know, I really thought one of us would be dead within the first week of being here. Me being the one in the body bag."

A laugh escapes her small frame. "I did too. I don't think anyone will be more shocked than we are that this has worked out."

"We are big personalities, maybe we just weren't ready for one another until we'd been knocked down a few pegs."

"What, so we had to wait for life to smack us in the face, to humble us a little?" The upward tilt of her mouth tells me she agrees.

"Seems to be."

She nods. "True. But now I've had enough humbling and I need some pampering. So get your coat, Mathews. We're going to the mall."

Georgia

I smile as I watch the manicurist file Chase's nails, having just done his cuticles. From the relaxed nature of his frame, I can tell he's loving every second of this.

And he calls *me* high maintenance. I'm sure this guy could give me a run for my money.

"Are you sure this isn't about to become a monthly ritual for you?" I ask him as I catch his eyes closing.

He cracks open one eye to look at me but doesn't reply.

I keep a small giggle to myself as I continue to sort through the selection of colors. I know I want pale pink, but there are 40 shades of that at this place.

After finally narrowing down the shade, Chase's light snores tell me he's far too relaxed, garnering the attention of some other patrons. A few people give him a double take when they walk in the door, yet again reminding me he's from the universe of the rich and famous.

It can be so easy to forget when we're locked away from the world together. But the reminder is always there when we go out, whether it's stares from strangers or the attempt at a sneaky photo. It doesn't bother me like I thought it would, it seems to get to Chase more than me.

I can only imagine the pressure he's under. Going from NHL player, one of the best at that, to out of the game in for good. I internally grimace at the thought of not only losing it all, but it happening in front of millions of people, forever on constant replay with just a few clicks on YouTube.

I initially thought he was lazy for taking up residence on Ash's couch, but now I question if I'd even want to leave the house ever again after what happened to him. My mind flashes back to watching him watch the clip of his accident. It was the first and only time I've seen it, but it was enough to be burned into my brain.

I grimace at the memory, my insides twisting up like a knotted shoelace. It would be disingenuous to deny my feelings for Chase, to say they haven't grown, but it would also be childish to think that anything could ever come from them.

"Georgia?"

I feel something poking my side, my head clearing of its fog.

"What?" I say, turning back to Chase, who is prodding me with a cane. "What is that?"

"I borrowed it from Janise," he replies, seemingly pleased with himself. "You were stuck daydreaming and couldn't hear me. Plus, I didn't want to get up mid-pedicure."

"Who?" I ask, my face scrunched up, confused by the whole thing.

He turns to his left, handing the walking stick back to the older woman next to him. Her expression is a mix of adoration and surprise as Chase says a smooth thank you. I don't miss the reddening of her cheeks.

"You really are something, Chase Mathews."

He just gives me a cocky smile before launching into a story about Janise's cat or was it her dog? I'm too lost by the entire scenario to follow along. All I've gathered is she's a big fan, they bonded over pedicures and now Chase thinks he should get a dog.

I'm still trying to catch up when we pay, so much so that I don't notice he's already paid for me.

"You really don't need to do that," I cut in as we exit the salon. Chase

gives a final wave to Janise and we're walking through the mall, my feet scurrying to keep up with his pace.

"It's not a big deal."

"I can pay for myself," I insist.

"Monroe, I know you can. But we're friends and friends do shit like this

for one another. You can get it next time if you feel like it."

"Okay," I reply, my mind thinking I've never had a friend I wanted to kiss before. Ah shit, I gotta get these thoughts out of my head. They're not going to do me any good. "Uh, thank you, I'll get you next time," I quickly reply.

He winks in response.

My insides dip.

"Where to next?" he asks, seemingly up for anything.

"Honestly? I think I'm ready to head back home."

Home.

I use the word, but upon reflection, it's not really my home. It's more a safe haven where I'm hiding out. But for this moment in time, that's okay. I'm happy to be there, and more than that, I'm happy to be there with Chase.

"Then let's go home," he says.

Georgia

"Can I ask you something?" I peer at Chase over my beer. A drink I used to hate, but recently have become more accustomed to.

He's leaning against the island in the kitchen, shirtless, grey sweatpants hanging far too low for my corrupted mind.

"Shoot," he replies before taking a sip of his beer, the bottle sitting casually in the palm of his hand.

"What happened to all the guys you played hockey with?"

"What do you mean? They're all still playing."

"No, I get that, I guess what I mean is, why haven't they come to see you?"

I'm walking a fine line here, the question could easily have an answer he doesn't want to give. But with Chase and me, there is no bullshit. So he will either tell me the truth or tell me to fuck off. Either one I can accept without hurt feelings.

He lifts his head, understanding dawning on him. "You mean why haven't you met them yet? Why has no one has been by in the month that we've been here?"

I nod.

"They're all still on the team, the team travels. There isn't any bad blood between us, if that's what you mean. Initially, when it all happened, they came by, but I wasn't in a good headspace to see them. It's only recently that I've come to really be ready."

"Do you guys text or message?"

"We check in, but I don't think any of them really knew how to navigate the situation." He rubs his jaw, leaning forward. "I don't think any of us did."

"That makes sense, Chase. I'm sure a lot of them felt guilty. It could have been anyone to take that hit, to be sitting in that hospital bed, but it wasn't. The sad reality is that it was you. Maybe that hits too close to home for some."

He eyes me thoughtfully, like my words are a revelation he's never once pondered. "You can be pretty wise when you want to be, Monroe."

"I try." I laugh, shrugging off the compliment. "But in all seriousness, you should call them. I'm sure they miss you. Guys aren't as good as girls at displaying their softer emotions. It wouldn't be the worst thing to put yourself out there for them. I mean you always talk about the game and how the team was like a family."

"You're right," he replies on a whisper. Expelling a breath, he looks at me. "I'm gonna miss you if you get that job in New York."

My fingers that were pulling off the beer label freeze. His comment is not one to easily ignore. I risk meeting his eyes, a sort of sadness lingering in them.

"Really?" My voice is wistful, breathless almost.

"Really, Monroe. You've become sort of a staple in my mess of a life. Thinking about you not being in it every day, well, it's shit."

"You really mean that, don't you?"

"I don't say shit I don't mean."

I gulp, despite having an empty mouth.

"I think I'm really going to miss you too."

"Yeah?" His voice is filled with surprise, like the thought of me being sad that he's gone, is a foreign concept.

"Yeah. I really never thought I'd say this, or even feel this way, but the thought of not seeing you feels weird, you're like a third arm I'm not sure I want or need, but have anyway."

He barks out a laugh. "Is that a compliment?"

"It is," I confirm. "I don't think I fully realized it before we were here, but I guess you could say I was lonely. I mean, I'm never really alone, constantly being surrounded by others, but it felt hollow. It doesn't feel that way with you."

Chase

I'm putting away the last of the dishes when the doorbell rings. I peer over at Georgia who is playing on her phone, still dressed in her pajamas from this morning.

"You order something?" I ask her.

She shakes her head back and forth. "Nope."

I walk to the door, assuming it's a delivery for Ash and Logan. Opening it, I'm nearly taken out by the three hockey players barreling into the entryway.

"Mathews!" Chapman yells as he pulls me in for a bear hug, his size notably larger than my own. My head spins as I take him in, with Taylor and Weston at his sides.

Taylor and Weston waste no time, clapping me on the back, each of them sporting jovial expressions.

"What are you guys doing here?" I finally manage to ask, closing the door behind them.

"We had a home game this weekend and after you texted us the other night, figured it would be better to see you in person," Chapman says, as captain, always the one to speak for the group.

"Thanks for coming, brother. I really appreciate it. Especially after everything."

He cuts a hand through the air. "Don't mention it."

I turn to Taylor and Weston, whose attention is no longer on me, but rather locked onto whatever is behind me. Or should I say *who*.

Georgia stands outside the kitchen, still dressed for bed, like myself, a soft smile tracing her rose-colored lips.

I want to smack them upside their heads, but what would be the point? Georgia isn't mine, despite how badly I might want her to be.

"You go and get yourself a girlfriend, Mathews?"

I wish.

Even from across the room, I see Georgia's face blush slightly, but as usual, she squares her shoulders and walks right into the lion's den.

"Georgia," she says, sticking out her hand to all three of them.

Eager to accept, Weston and Taylor both battle to introduce themselves first, the latter winning.

"A pleasure to meet you," Taylor says, laying it on thick. I jam my elbow into his side.

"No use, Bud. Georgia has seen *all* the tricks, hell, I'm sure she invented half of them."

That earns me a grin from her.

"Why don't you guys come on in? Chase and I can put together some food, you hungry?"

A round of yeses sound out as Georgia spins on her heels back to the kitchen.

I lead the guys in, motioning to the sofa, then follow her, grabbing some beers from the fridge.

"So, you texted your teammates." It's a casual statement, her focus directed at slicing the bread, but I hear the satisfaction in her voice.

"I texted my teammates," I confirm.

"I'm glad, Chase."

"I wouldn't have done it without you," I admit. I risk moving slightly closer to her, my body feeling the warmth of hers next to me.

"I'm sure you would have eventually."

I rest my hands on the granite countertop, attempting to cool my warming body temperature. "I wouldn't have, Monroe. You're changing things for me, and you don't even know it."

My words are raw, open, but more than anything, they're honest.

The truth.

"I know it," she whispers, her hands no longer fiddling with the bread, but her stare still focused ahead. "I know it because it's the same for me." I don't realize her hand has moved until it rests on top of mine.

The action itself is small, but emotionally, it's monumental. Like a deep bond has been woven between the two of us, yet we are only now realizing it.

"Chase," she begins in a whisper, before Taylor comes barging in, ruining the moment.

"Can I help with anything?"

I want to tell him the best way to help would be fucking off, but I'm not that much of an asshole.

"Yeah, can you take this out?" Georgia turns, handing over the plate of food she's put together.

"I need to shower and send some emails, so I'll see you all later," she tells us before exiting the room. She looks me in the eye briefly before disappearing.

With a sigh, I follow Taylor into the living room, wondering why the hell I can't seem to figure out what is going on between Georgia and me.

Chase

"So how did you all know where I was staying?" I ask the guys, taking another sip of my beer. My eyes continuously flicker back and forth between them and the doorway. Georgia's been gone for over an hour. I'd like to think she's just giving me time with them, but I can't help but wonder if she's freaking out about holding my hand.

God, even saying it in my head sounds stupid. Who overthinks a hand hold? Apparently, me.

"Logan told me," Weston says. "I saw your place was under construction, so figured if anyone knew, it would be Saunders."

I nod in understanding. Despite not being on our team, all the guys know Logan. He's the guy to beat in the NHL.

"I can't tell you guys how much I appreciate you coming here. I know time is limited, especially with having families, so it means a lot."

Taylor leans forward, tapping me on the back. "You're part of our family, Mathews, even when you didn't want to be."

I bite my lower lip, the emotion behind it all not lost on me. Despite months having gone by, the wound occasionally feels fresh.

"So, how's training going? Coach still trying to kill you?"

Taylor and Weston groan while Chapman grins.

"You know it, Man, he's a ballbuster, but that's why we're doing so well. We've got a game against Saunders next month; you should come if you're up to it."

"Yeah, for sure," I reply, knowing full well it's too soon.

I hear footsteps in the hall, and then Georgia appears, freshly showered. She's in jeans and a white tee shirt, her blonde hair in waves down her back. She's a natural beauty in every way. My attention's on her now more than ever.

"Georgia, grab a beer and join us," Taylor calls to her.

"Don't mind if I do," she says, pulling one out of the ice bucket and coming to sit next to me. She smiles at me; it's not forced or awkward, so I take that our earlier encounter was nothing. I try to ignore the pinch it causes.

"So, Georgia, tell us about yourself, how did you get stuck in a house with this asshole," Weston says.

She grins at the comment before replying, "Well, a string of bad luck led me here. But Chase may have been the reason I stayed."

"Wow, Mathews, Georgia seems to think highly of you."

I shake my head. "It wasn't always that way."

"Hey, the feeling was so mutual," she interjects. "Chase and I have known one another for years. Ash, Logan's wife, has been my best friend since we were kids."

"What are we missing?" Taylor asks.

"We hated each other," she states bluntly. "Like to the point Ash and Logan would plan to hang out with us separately because we always bickered. I think it drove them around the bend."

"I'm sure it wasn't that bad," Chapman says.

"Nah, Man, she's right. Georgia and I couldn't be in a room together without biting each other's heads off."

"Why? What happened to make you two hate each other."

Georgia and I look at one another, both coming up empty.

"Honestly," she starts, "nothing really. I just remember the first time I met Chase, he was next to Logan and everything about him gave off 'fuckboy' vibes. Plus, he definitely gave me the eyes, so I think his fate was sealed from first glance."

"Whoa," I cut in, "I did not give you the look."

"Oh, come on Mathews, you so gave me the look."

"The look?" Weston asks.

"Oh, you know, the look," she replies. "You're all big famous hockey players, you know the look."

I glance at the guys; Taylor and Weston are grinning.

She isn't wrong. We do know the look.

"See, you're grinning," she says to me. "You so know you gave me the look."

I totally gave her the look that day.

"I don't know what you mean," I lie.

She throws a pillow at me that I easily dodge. Her blue eyes sparkling. "Anyway, I decided I *really* didn't like him and I guess ever since then, we just butted heads."

"So, what changed?"

Our gazes connect again, a silent conversation between us. What changed is we created a deeper connection from our shared experiences. We opened up to one another when no one else was around. But there's *no way* we're telling these guys that.

"Not sure, now I can't get the asshole away from me," she jokes. The boys grin, eating up every one of her words. She's got a charm that draws people to her. Not only her physical beauty, but her confidence and her wit.

They all continue talking, one beer turning into four. Georgia gets along so easily with them all, like she's always been a part of the fold. Soon enough, the sun sets into the night, and Georgia decides we have to pull out Rock Band.

Taylor and Weston follow her around like a puppy as she sets up the game, all three of them deciding to play first. I can't wipe the grin off my face as I watch them together.

I grab another beer, a light buzz invading my system. If I'd have known reconnecting with the guys would be this easy, I'd have done it months ago.

Chapman pulls himself off the couch, heading my way, pulling out another beer for himself.

"You sure there is nothing going on between you two?" Chapman asks, voice low as he watches Georgia sing with Taylor and Weston. Her hair flails as she shows her best moves, my gut clenching as I catch Taylor and Weston's eyes lingering a little too long.

"Nah, Man, just a friend," I reply. In reality, I want to say the opposite. I want it to be more, but there is something stopping me, us. I can't place what it is, could be timing or circumstance, but I'd bet money Georgia feels it too.

"Okay," he replies, clearly not believing me. "So, any thought to what's next?"

"What do you mean? I can't live on my friends' couch forever?"

He rolls his eyes at me, leveling me with a look.

"Not sure yet. I'm gonna look into coaching. I may not be able to play the game anymore, but that doesn't mean it all has to be in my rearview, you know?"

"Of course, man. It's been your life for forever, you don't have to give it up just because your knee gave out on you. If it means anything, I think you'd be a great coach."

"Thanks, that means a lot. I'll keep you updated on what happens. I won't go dark again. I know I've said it already, but I really am sorry for just fucking off. It wasn't personal, I just couldn't deal."

I'm being honest here with Chapman, not only as his teammate, but him as my captain. I feel that, out of everyone, I let him down the most.

"Nah, man. What happened to you, fuck, it was the worst thing that could happen, the nightmare of any and all players. No one blames you for taking time."

I turn to him, patting him on the back. "Thank you."

"No, thank you, brother. I can't tell you how happy it made us all when you reached out. More of the brothers wanted to come tonight, but I thought bringing these two lunatics would be enough for anyone."

"Yeah, as much as I want to see everyone, this is perfect for tonight."

While I'm close with my entire team, I've always held a special bond with these three, especially Chapman.

"Now let's go show those two idiots how Rock Band is really done, because Weston's singing is doing my head in."

We head on over as they're finishing the final verse of a Journey song, Georgia, of course, ending with the high score.

"Wow, you two are shit," she says, reaching for her beer.

"Blame Weston, he sounds like a dying bird," Taylor replies.

"Oh, you're no better. You are practically butterfingers on those drums, it's a wonder you can hold a hockey stick," Weston shoots back.

"Okay, okay, boys, it's time Monroe and I show you how it's done."

Beaming, she picks the next song, grabbing the mic from Weston and putting it in the stand.

"Buckle up boys." She grins as I sit behind the drum kit.

Although both of us have had a few drinks, we still manage to crush the other twos' score, Georgia letting out a howl of triumph before throwing herself into my arms.

I spin her around, our faces so close they could touch. She seems to sense it too, but doesn't pull away, instead tilting her head forward, leaning it against my own.

I swallow, trying to stop myself from breaking our invisible barrier that appears to be on shaky ground. Yet, I won't do it. Not in front of the guys. Whatever is happening between us is intimate, private, not for any other eyes.

I put her back on the ground, both of us turning as the oblivious trio attempt a Radiohead song.

We stay like this for a few more hours, the five of us hanging out, simply having fun. It's unlike any feeling I've had before. A sense of wholeness overtakes me. And if I really dig deep, I know it's because Georgia is at my side.

I've been avoiding the nagging thoughts in the back of my mind for weeks now, but tonight, it became clearer than ever that she's become a part of me. Whether it's something she wants to accept or not, our time together has bonded us in a way I never thought possible. So, having my old world collide with my current, it's an overwhelming experience to say the least. Sure, seeing my teammates, just like old times, meant a lot to me, but having Georgia here made it mean the world. I had the ability to truly be in my own skin, no longer hiding behind the cocky playboy persona or bullshit facades of being single and playing the game. Tonight, I was simply content and it was all thanks to one person.

And that thought alone is both terrifying and comforting.

Chase

I wake up the next morning feeling better than I deserve to. The guys left around midnight, all having to be at the airport at seven this morning. Georgia and I went to bed soon after, but my mind wasn't ready to rest.

Every time I closed my eyes, I saw her. I wanted to go to her. It was crazy talk, but it also felt so natural. Yet I knew walking to her room to talk after our night wasn't a good idea. That's why when I woke up today, I knew we needed to speak about what's been happening between us. It's time I'm honest with her and myself.

"Hey, Monroe," I call as I enter the TV room, knowing full well she will already be awake. "There's something I want to-" I cut myself off mid-sentence when I see her sitting on the sofa wide-eyed.

Her fingers are clasped around her phone, mouth slightly open.

"Georgia?" I ask, walking over to her.

She shakes her head, her eyelashes fluttering before looking at me.

"I got offered that job."

I pause, taken aback by her statement. Since initially mentioning it, she had been tight-lipped about the whole thing.

"Are you serious?"

She nods, a smile breaking out across her face. I waste no time rushing over to her, lifting her up into my arms. It feels far too natural as my arms wrap around her waist, hers circling my neck. It's too intimate, too familiar, so we both pull back. I set her on the floor gently, before moving away.

"So, I guess this means you're leaving?" My stomach plummets as I say the words out loud, but manage to keep a smile plastered on my face.

She bites her bottom lip, her eyes creasing as if the thought is only now occurring to her.

"I guess so. In all the excitement of getting another job, I kind of forgot I'd actually have to leave this house to start it." She lets out a humorless laugh.

"Hey," I say gently grabbing her arm, "this is going to be great for you, you've worked so hard to get here."

She smiles, but it doesn't reach her eyes.

"But what about your birth mom? They want me to start next week and the job's in New York."

I push away the feeling of disappointment entering my system. I've been selfish a lot throughout my life; I won't ruin this moment for her.

"That can wait. I'm not ready anyway. This job, on the other hand, can't."

She bites the side of her cheek, her face clearly telling me she's unsure of which emotion to stick with.

"I need to call my parents and Ash," she finally says.

"Go." I motion my head to the door, winking as she skips off. There's already an air in her step, one she didn't have before getting the call. Now if I can only channel her energy into my own life, I might not feel so fucking lost all the time.

Georgia

I get off the phone with my parents, feeling slightly more confident in my choice to move states in less than a week. It's a huge step and a rushed one no less, but I can't pass on this opportunity.

A boutique real estate agency in New York needed a new hire in marketing for their social media team and this girl got the job. So now I've got a week to find a suitable Airbnb that won't break the bank until I find an apartment. Thank god I sold my furniture before I moved into Ash's; otherwise, I'd be fucked.

Speaking of Ash, she's the other person I need to call.

It rings a few times before I hear her familiar voice.

"What did I do to deserve a call from my best girl in the world?"

"Well, I've got news for you," I reply.

"Hold on one second."

I hear murmurs and movement before she's back to me.

"Sorry, I wanted to give you my full attention so I gave Henry to Logan. What's up?"

"I got a job."

The squeal through the other end nearly bursts my ear drums. Ash has never been one to screech so this says something.

"Where? When? Tell me everything, G."

"Well, it's at a boutique real estate agency. It's in social media marketing, so something I'm comfortable with and have experience in, which is great."

"I'm sensing a but. Where's the hesitation coming from?"

I pause, taking in a breath. "Well, it's in New York."

"And that's a bad thing, honey?" Her tone is warm, one a mother would use when comforting her child.

"Not a bad thing, just a new thing. It starts next week and I'm just a little scared with all this change."

"I've never known you to be scared, Georgia Monroe. Is there more to this?"

My idle fingers begin to pick at the notebook in front of me, tearing off little strips as I think.

"That's the thing, Ash. I'm never usually scared, and don't get me wrong, I do want this. But I guess the thought of leaving you all behind is a lot."

"That's understandable. Moving is a huge change, but don't worry about the rest of us. You know Henry and I are going to take any chance we get to visit you."

"Oh, I do believe that." I laugh, knowing full well Ash isn't lying.

"Can I ask you something without you going off?"

"I don't go off!" I say, audacity coating my tone.

All I hear is her familiar chuckle through the phone.

"Oh G, you so go off."

I lift a shoulder, despite her not being able to see me. "Okay maybe I go off a little. But that's beside the point, ask away."

"Could some of your hesitation be due to a certain injured hockey player?"

"What? No." My response is too quick and I realize I've now given her more reason to doubt me.

"It's okay if it is."

"Ashley Ashford, there is nothing going on with Chase and me. We're friends. Nothing more."

She hates it when I call her by her full name. She is so not an Ashely, and as she says, it sounds like a bad sorority name Ash Ashford. God, she's right. What were her parents smoking when they named her?

"Okay, I just had to ask." She isn't convinced, but it doesn't matter because she drops it.

"So, onto other things, when are you leaving?"

"I'm looking at places to stay now and then I guess I'll book my ticket as soon as that is settled."

"I'm bummed I won't get to see you before you leave, but I'm happy for you. You deserve this, G."

"Thanks, Ash. I couldn't have done this without you. I can't thank you enough for letting me stay here."

"You know you're welcome anytime. You're family."

We talk for another twenty minutes before I have to go, my to-do list getting longer by the second.

Surprisingly, I find an Airbnb for the next two weeks that won't bankrupt me, along with a plane ticket. With everything seemingly falling so easily into place, I'm beginning to wrap my head around the fact that this is really happening.

But with that comes the realization that I'm leaving. Tomorrow.

For some reason, I thought I'd have more time.

"I don't do FaceTime."

Elaine eyes me from across the table, sitting in the antiquated green chair. My insides twist as I take in her face. I try to commit every line, every spot to my memory, as I'm not sure the next time I'll see her. Chase opted for me to visit Elaine alone, clearly sensing I needed some one-on-one time with her.

"I'd rather just see you in person."

"I know," I reply, voice soft. "But I won't be able to be here in person. So, the next best thing is talking on the phone, as opposed to not talking at all."

"I think I'll just wait for you to return."

My throat tightens and I try to dismiss it with a cough.

"Chase will still come by to see you. We can all FaceTime when he's here."

She shakes her head. "He can come, but only if he wants to. I don't want to be a burden to you all."

I take her hand in my own. "You've never once been a burden. Seeing you is what makes my week. And Chase loves you too. He told me he's going to bring Joyce by in the next month or so."

At the mention of Chase's grandmother, Elaine perks up.

"I'm so sorry to have this visit be so short, but I've gotta get going." Standing, I take a deep breath.

This is only goodbye, it's not forever.

"I fear I'll get far too emotional if we talk on the phone my dear Georgia. I'd rather you remember me happy, and we can just cherish our times together when you visit.

I nod, not fully understanding her reasoning, but deciding to respect it.

Taking her hand in my own, I look into her eyes. "I love you, Elaine. I really mean it."

"You're my special girl, Georgia. You always will be."

With a parting hug, I leave, quickly wiping away my tears before she sees them. With each goodbye I have, I begin to question if I'm making the right choice.

I guess only time will tell.

Chase is waiting for me when I get in the car. It's then I finally let my tears flow freely.

He rubs my back as I cry.

It makes me cry more.

"So tomorrow?"

I look down at my spaghetti, unable to keep eye contact with Chase. It's ridiculous, but I can't seem to look him in the eye.

"Yeah, it's just easier to get over there and get it all sorted."

He mashes his lips together and I look longer than I should. Small things like this have been happening to me more and more lately. Admiring the way he looks, how he laughs, him confiding in me. But I know, deep down, this isn't a path I can go on.

Chase doesn't do serious relationships and I have vowed to no longer do casual. Plus, this is Chase Mathews we are talking about. I'm chalking all of it up to cabin fever. As soon as I'm back in the real world, I will realize that this was just a passing moment. A phase.

Regardless of how many times I tell myself this, though, I'm struggling to believe it.

"Georgia?"

"What?" My head snaps up.

Ah fuck, I've been caught staring at his mouth.

"Just some pasta sauce," I lie.

He picks up his napkin and wipes his mouth. I give him a thumbs up, letting him know the imaginary sauce is gone.

"So, I guess this is the last night. When the clock strikes midnight, do we go back to hating each other?"

"Why don't we just finish our movie and we can figure that out tomorrow."

He grins at me, but it lacks his usual vivacity. "Sounds like a plan."

"Stop hogging the blanket," I grunt as I pull the soft woolen throw back to my side. But Chase, who has years of hockey on his side, is quick to pull it back.

We scuffle back and forth before he finally relents and stands up.

"We're literally doing what we've been doing for weeks. I have an idea, but I want you to just go with me on it."

I turn to face him, eyebrows raised. "What kind of idea?

"Can you just go with it?"

"Fine, can I have a clue at least?"

"Nope. Go put on some shoes, we're driving."

My eyes widen. "Chase, it's ten p.m."

He laughs. "Really, Monroe. I didn't take you as the boring type."

"Whatever," I mutter as I pull myself off the sofa. "But you're driving."

"I'm the only one who can drive, you don't know where we're going."

I roll my eyes despite the fact he can't see me. "I'll meet you in the car."

Ten minutes later, we're on the road. Chase grinning as his hands tap against the steering wheel.

"So, when do I get to find out where we're headed?"

"You'll see soon enough," he responds, staring straight ahead.

"Okay," I mutter.

Soon enough, we pull up to the grocery store, Chase telling me to wait in the car as he runs in. I fiddle with my iPhone, not really having anyone to call except Ash, but not this time of night.

The driver's side door opens, and Chase reappears, hoodie up. It's when I spot the carton of eggs in his hand that I start to become suspicious.

"Let's go," he says, starting the engine and pulling out of the empty parking lot. We drive through the suburbs in silence, Chase still wearing that mischievous smile.

"Chase, I hate surprises, can't you just tell me?"

"We're here," he says, pulling up to a large residence in an upscale neighborhood.

"Remember this place?" he asks, turning off the engine.

"No."

"Are you sure? Think back, Monroe."

I study the cream-colored two-story home, with its white fence and lush green shrubbery. Brown brick steps lead up to the grand double-front door with two white pillars at its side. It's a nice house. An expensive house too. I study it one more time, but it's hidden in the shadows of the night. It sparks a glimpse of familiarity, but not enough to trigger a memory.

"Whose house is it?"

"Brad Wilcox."

"Oh my god!" I screech. "Chase, what are we doing here?" Suddenly I'm taken back to seventeen-year-old Georgia. I only visited this house, maybe once or twice, but the grandeur of it clearly stayed with me.

"We're having fun. And also getting a little revenge for seventeen-year-old Georgia."

"Chase, I don't even know what to say." I'm filled with panic and curiosity, and they're both fighting for dominance.

In truth, I'm completely touched. The act of throwing eggs at his house might be completely immature, but I think, deep down, both of us are a little childish.

"How do you even know he still lives here? This was his parents' house back in high school. They didn't exactly do anything to me and they wouldn't hesitate to call the cops on adults egging their home." I pull at the sleeves of my sweatshirt enough so they're covering my hands.

"His mom and dad live in Florida now, left the house to him. From what Ash tells me, he's still up to his old ways."

"Ash?" I ask, confused what she has to do with this.

"Apparently, he was hitting on her a few months back at the supermarket. She ran into him and he kept trying to take her out, despite knowing she was with Logan. Ash's answer was to run over his foot with her cart, but yeah, the guy is still a prick."

"She didn't tell me that," I mutter, curious as to why I missed out on that little tidbit. Probably because so much happens in our lives, and with Chase and I refusing to hang out one-on-one with Logan and Ash, we were bound to miss things. If they could only see us now.

My head spins back to the house, a flood of ugly and humiliating memories hitting me like a tidal wave. "Fuck it, let's go."

I reach for the eggs in his hands before unbuckling my seat belt. If I don't do this quickly, I know I'll chicken out. I'm one to have fun and push a boundary here and there, but getting arrested is more Ash's style, or it was. But that's a story for another time. Okay, now I'm just stalling.

"Let's do this," I whisper more to myself than Chase.

"Fuck yeah!" he hollers into the night. I shush him, but the smile on my face betrays me.

"Oh, you're loving this," he teases from next to me in a hushed whisper.

I don't reply, opening the brown carton and pulling out the first egg. I roll it around in my palm, before deciding this one will go straight at his front door. I'm avoiding windows at all costs.

I want to have some fun, not spend the night in jail.

Pulling my arm back, I use as much force as possible before launching it at his front door. A satisfying smack hits my ears.

"Nice aim, Monroe."

"I actually used to be semi-athletic back in high school, believe it or not."

Chase flings his own egg at the house, hitting his target. "It doesn't surprise me. I know you're a blackbelt, remember?"

"You remember that?" I think back to the conversation where I swore to kick his ass over three years ago.

"You may be small, but I know a weapon when I see one."

I laugh before throwing another egg. It hits the left side of Brad's house, on an angle that will be awkward to clean up tomorrow.

We continue on, only the sound of splattered eggs and our hushed midnight whispers lingering through the air.

We're both grinning like village idiots when a light turns on in the room on the upper right, the one where our second to last egg just hit.

"Shit," Chase whispers, "we gotta go."

"We only have one more," I say back, quick to pull it out. With all my might, I heave the thing onto the brick before more lights begin turning on in the house.

"We're going," Chase now yells, grabbing my hand and pulling me toward the car. I'm practically buzzing with adrenaline at the thought of being caught. Chase wastes zero time, starting the car and peeling out down Brad's street.

My chest won't stop heaving up and down, the thrill of it all so tantalizing. I want to do it all over again.

"You do know when the lights come on, you're supposed to run," Chase finally says. With his free hand, he leans over grabbing mine to pull it in the air. "Ladies and gentlemen, we have a real daredevil on our hands!"

I just start laughing hysterically in response. "That felt so good!" I yell into the car. Chase returns his attention to the road but keeps taking peeks at me as he drives. I roll down all the windows, my long hair getting swept up in the wind, small bits of it dancing out the window. The midnight air is brisk against my hot skin, soothing as we drive back home.

"Who knew you had such a wild side, Monroe."

"Who knew," I mutter, feeling better than I have in a long time. This time with Chase has freed a side of me I didn't know I'd buried. And now tomorrow, I have to leave him. Leave all of this behind. Unable to think about it, I focus on the music he's turned on, Third Eye Blind, the wind in my hair, and the fact that I'm only just realizing that he's still holding my hand.

"I don't want to go to bed," I say as we enter the house. The clock against the cream-colored wall tells me if I don't go to sleep now, I will hate myself when I get up tomorrow. But apparently, I've thrown all reason in the trash tonight.

Chase throws his fleece-lined denim jacket on the sofa before turning to me. I greedily let my eyes rake over him in blue jeans and a white tee shirt. It should be a fucking crime for such a basic outfit to look so good on someone.

"Georgia?" His voice comes out on a rumble. Deep. Low.

"I-" I start, stuttering my words.

Chase slowly begins to walk toward me. "So what *do* you want?"

"Tell me now, Monroe. Am I reading into things? Should we just go to our own beds."

My feet halt right in front of him.

"I want to," I whisper. "But this," I pause, "this would be crossing a boundary I don't think we can come back from." My head rests against his chest. My senses eager to soak up every little bit of him.

"I'll make it easy for you." His voice is soft, considerate, as he pulls away from me. "I'll see you in the morning. Goodnight, Monroe." His eyes graze over me momentarily before he turns away, exiting the room.

"Goodnight, Mathews," I whisper into the dark night, regret coating each word.

Chase

After our last night together, I wake up early, no longer able to sleep in. I know in a few short hours Georgia will be out of here and our time together will feel more like a dream than anything.

"All packed?" I ask as I poke my head into her room, noting the two zipped suitcases on the floor. I have to admit, I'm surprised by how little she has.

"I guess so? I'm sure I've probably forgotten something, but if I can't remember it now, I guess it doesn't matter that much then."

She takes a spin of the room one last time before finally stopping in front of me.

"Can I grab these for you?"

"I'll help," she insists, but I take them before she can. How she will get either of these into the airport alone I have no clue.

"You know I would have dropped you off, right?" I offered last night, but she was adamant to do it solo.

"I know, but calling an uber is just easier. Thanks, though."

"Anytime."

I lug the suitcases that feel like they're filled with bricks to the front door. One is so stuffed it wobbles, threatening to crash against the hardwood floor at any moment.

"You called your uber?"

Looking down at her phone she nods. "Yep, he's five minutes away."

"Okay, I'll take these out front, so they can load them into the car." I'm out the door before she can reply.

"Thanks," she mutters as I walk back in. The air between us is awkward and I hate it. I'd even take our old jabs at one another over this.

"So, I guess this is goodbye?" She swallows a few times, her eyes looking everywhere but at me.

"I guess so," I reply, suddenly feeling uncomfortable.

I have to wonder, does this hurt her like it hurts me? Nothing physical has happened between us, but there is an emotional connection I can't ignore.

"Is this where we go back to hating one another?" I tease, but hope like hell she sees what I'm really asking her. Is this the end for us?

"I don't know if I ever really hated you, Chase. Was I annoyed by you, yes, but did I hate you? Hate is a pretty strong word." She shakes her head, my eyes unable to look away from her.

"I'll miss you, Mathews."

Well shit.

Her eyes well with tears. "Fuck," she mutters, her fingers quick to wipe them away.

"Hey," I say softly, my hand clutching her arm. She comes to me easily, our bodies surprisingly comfortable with one another.

"We will still see each other."

Despite my words, my gut tells me it won't be the same. The look on her face confirms my thoughts.

"Well, I better go." Georgia repositions her purse on her shoulder before leaning in for the world's quickest hug. She's gone in an instant, already walking to the door.

I want to call to her, ask what happened to change our dynamic overnight, but she turns at the last minute, coming back to me.

"Thank you, Chase."

"For what?"

"For everything, for nothing in particular? I needed this month of fun with you and despite how badly you can annoy me and I'm sure vice versa, I wouldn't have wanted to do it with anyone else. In a surprising way, you've calmed me." She pauses and I stay silent, knowing she's not yet finished.

"I was running from my problems when I moved in here. And sometimes the world makes you think that's a bad thing. But from being here, I've learned how wrong that is. Sometimes it's okay to run away, just for a little bit. Just to rediscover what you're missing. Being with you, I feel like I'm seventeen again, and not in a bad way. I feel free, youthful. A feeling you really can't buy. So thank you for helping me find that."

I go to open my mouth, to tell her it's the same for me. That our time together not only helped me heal my soul, but irrevocably changed me. That I want her in my life, *need* her in my life. But before I can say a word, I see her phone light up.

"My uber is here." Her voice is full of reluctance, but I know we can't stay in this house forever, no matter how badly we want to hide away from the world. As Georgia said, it's okay to hide, but only for a little bit. And our little bit is over.

"Who would have thought the asshole and the princess would have so much fun together?" I say to her as she goes for her designer bag.

"You're not always an asshole, Mathews." She smiles at me, and I'm desperate to eat up every last bit of our remaining time together. For my mind to memorize the way her lips tilt upward and how she looks at me.

"And you're not always a princess, Monroe. Looks like we were both a little wrong."

"That we were," she confirms. Her stare leaves my own, briefly connecting with the floor.

"I guess I'll see you soon," I tell her, deciding I won't accept this awkward goodbye. I step forward, pulling her into me. Her arms wrap around my middle as my face breathes in her hair. Neither of us says anything as we take this one final moment.

I pull away first, running my hands down my side. But then she shocks the hell out of me by reaching up on her tiptoes, briefly connecting our lips. It's sudden, and completely out of left field, but everything about it feels right. I want to deepen the kiss, run my fingers through her hair as I hold her close, but she's gone before I can react.

I watch her with a thoughtful regard, my eyes roaming every plane on her face as if it's going to give me clarity.

"I better go. I'll see you around, Chase."

She wastes no time with those parting words, collecting her things and practically running out the door.

One minute she's here and the next she's gone.

And even after I hear her car pull away, I'm still standing here, my mind attempting to take in everything that has happened over the past few months.

Georgia may have stood here and said I'm the reason she's moving forward, but I never told her how I feel. How when it comes down to it, she has helped me more than I ever helped her. Because at the end of our time together, one thing is clear. She's the reason I got off the couch.

1 day later…May 23rd

Chase: Did you get to New York okay? I didn't hear from you yesterday.

Georgia: Yeah, I did. Sorry I forgot to call, jetlag!

Chase: Is the Airbnb okay?

Georgia: Yep, it's good! Still want to get my own place ASAP

Chase: Yeah I get that. I went to see Elaine today, she said to kick ass in the big apple.

Georgia: Of course she did, tell her I miss her already!

May 25th

Georgia: How are things? Still doing your PT?

Chase: Things are good. Keeping up with the PT. I saw Elaine today, she refused to FaceTime, sorry.

Georgia: I'll keep trying, I have to wear her down eventually.

Chase: if anyone can do it, you can.

May 28th

Georgia: My new boss is like Samantha from sex and the city!

Chase: Who?

Georgia: Shit, that was meant for Ash! But in simple terms, it means she's awesome!

Chase: I'm glad it's all working out for you.

June 1st[th]

Chase: Henry definitely said my name today.

Georgia: Hmmm, don't want to kill your vibe but he's not even one yet… lol

Chase: Eh, he's a baby genius

Georgia: I won't debate that haha

June 10th

Georgia: Ash told me you moved out?

Chase: Yeah, it was time. I moved on from that place.

Georgia: I get that, maybe I'll see you in New York soon, Logan has a game coming up.

Chase: I don't think I'm going to make it, but hopefully next time.

Georgia: Yeah, for sure.

June 20th

Chase: Saw a kid dressed as Captain America today, made me think of you. Hope everything is going well.

June 22nd

Georgia: Sorry, work has been crazy and I totally forgot to reply. The kid has good taste lol. Maybe we should dress Henry up as a little superhero next time I'm in town haha.

July 1st

Georgia: Happy birthday

July 2nd

Chase: Thanks, Monroe.

July 4th

Chase: Happy 4th
Georgia: You too!

July 13th

Georgia: Hey, how is everything going?
Chase: Yeah, pretty good. You?
Georgia: Yeah, good.

July 20th

Chase: Elaine misses you
Georgia: I miss her too…

186

Four months later

September 2019

Chase

"So, you're leaving me too?"

I eye Elaine from across the chess table. Yep, chess is something I play now, apparently. A lot about me has changed in the past four months, to say the least.

"I'm not leaving you, don't be like that. I have a new job in Boston. You should be happy for me, I'm no longer a loser sleeping on his friends' couch."

"You were never a loser," she says quickly.

Despite her words, it's hard to believe them. All those months I spent wasting away at Logan's didn't exactly put me in the best position, literally or mentally. But if these past five months have shown me anything, all it takes is something, or *someone* to offer you another perspective. After my time with Georgia, I was quick to get back into the world. What I didn't realize was every day I spent with her, I found myself coming back to life a little more. Day by day, I put more effort into my PT, I spent less time on the couch, got a little more excited for the future.

Then when she left, I had to face the reality of the situation I was in. I could go back to being a hermit or pull myself together enough to start fresh. I went with the latter. I just hate that I lost her in the mix of it all.

Elaine rolls her eyes at me. "They all leave."

I tilt my head forward, giving her a look. "It's okay, I know deep down you're happy for me."

The corners of her lips twitch. "As long as you bring back our girl next time you're here, then I will be happy for you."

My stomach twists at the mention of Georgia.

"She's not our girl," I remind her. "She's your girl, she *was* my friend, but that's over now."

Elaine scoffs. "Horse shit. She's our girl. I saw you two together."

I level her with a look. "It seems my swearing is rubbing off on you."

"I've been alive long enough to know how to swear, stop deflecting."

"Well, we haven't seen one another in four months. Haven't spoken since July."

"Don't get me started on that, Chase Mathews. I should call up Joyce and get her to come sort you out right away."

"What do you expect me to do, Elaine? She lives in New York. I'm moving to Boston. We haven't spoken in months, don't even live in the same city."

"So?"

"So? Well, that kinda puts a roadblock up in your plans."

"I'm not wrong, boy. I've seen things in my 77 years. I know a connection when I see one. You've just got to go see her. Once you see her again, things will go back to normal."

What I don't say is I'm not sure what our normal is. Things were murkier than ever when she left. Sure, I wanted more, still do, but when you haven't spoken to someone in months, that kind of makes things hard. But it would be a fucking lie to say I don't miss her.

"I'll be in New York this weekend," I find myself admitting.

Her wrinkled hand comes out to smack me.

"Now you tell me! Why have we been wasting our time playing chess? You're going after our girl!"

"I'm going to see Logan and Ash while they're there for the weekend. Who knows if I'll see Georgia."

"Don't bullshit me, Chase. You have to see her; this is your shot to finally tell her how you feel!

Another problem with Elaine becoming a permanent fixture in my life. She's also become like a therapist. At times I've been painfully honest with her, especially about Georgia. Now I'm slightly regretting it.

"She's a good girl, my Georgia. She likes to put on a brave face for the world, act like nothing hurts her, but she's a sensitive girl. A huge heart too. And when she gives you the privilege of having a piece of it, it should always be treated with care."

I pick up the chipped wooden chess piece, turning it around in my hand.

"Don't you go closing back up on me. It took months for you to open up. Remember Chase, real men talk about their feelings."

I smile at her. She isn't wrong. I've never been romantic or lovey dovey, but after Georgia left and I started spending more time with Elaine, I've managed to be more open, more honest about how I'm feeling. I guess my doc was right when he said I needed a therapist. I'm sure he didn't' expect it to be a 77-year-old woman, though.

"I know," I tell her. "But I also know I can't make you any promises. I'll see where the weekend takes me and if it leads to Georgia, then so be it, but if not, you're going to have to let this go."

"I don't think I'm the one who needs to let go, Chase."

I try not to allow her words to get to me, despite how true they ring.

Her eyes widen as she leans forward. "Checkmate."

Georgia

"Georgia, we need you to get those posts up by the end of the day," Monica, my supervisor, tells me as she shuffles by my desk. Her Prada skirt brushing it as her heels carry her past me.

"I've just gotten them up," I reply, attempting to finish the task and respond.

"Good, since it's a Friday and I'm not an asshole, you can clock out for the day." She winks at me.

"Thanks, Mon." I take the time to look up briefly.

"Your friend from Seattle is in town this weekend, right?" Mon's manicured fingers fiddle with the chunky gold charm bracelet on her left hand.

"Yeah, she and her son got in this morning, so I will meet them at her hotel when I get off."

"Ah, now I see why you've finished the job so quickly," she jokes. I grin, knowing it's all in jest. Since day one of getting here, I've been dedicated and committed to everything they've thrown at me.

"But yeah, I don't know if they'll make it to the farewell. A bar isn't exactly the best spot for a baby."

Mon, who has probably never held a baby in her life, nods. "Yeah, I didn't even think about that. Not really a kid person, if I'm honest. My friend's daughter once used a permanent marker on her new pair of Manolos'. That story was enough birth control for the rest of my life. God, imagine a small little thing that you pushed out of your vagina ruining a $1200 pair of shoes." She visibly shivers. "Absolute nightmare."

I laugh, because I know, for Monica, there would be nothing worse in this world. And truthfully, if that's how she feels, more power to her. To each their own.

"You want any of them, Georgia?"

"Um, maybe? I mean, I've always just assumed I'd have at least one or two, but not anytime soon. I want to meet the right person."

Her head moves up and down, but it's clear from the squint of her eyes she doesn't get the appeal. Of the man or the kids.

"So I take it the New York dating scene isn't as exciting as you thought it would be?" She bends down, pulling a bottle of Moet from the mini fridge. It's Friday afternoon, so we're the only two left in our department, everyone hightailing it out of here already.

"Champagne, you spoil me." I beam as I eagerly take the glass from her.

"It's been a week, plus, if anyone deserves this, it's us." She pours herself a generous glass before leaning forward, clinking her glass with mine.

"To the weekend."

"Cheers to that," I reply before taking a hearty sip of the cold bubbles. It's like a million little dance parties in my mouth at the same time. It's delicious.

"So, back to dating, no one?"

I lift a shoulder. "Not really. I mean, it's not like I've really been trying too hard to begin with."

"Someone back home?" She leans forward.

My mind all so briefly flashes back to Chase, before pushing him out as quickly as he came in. I don't like to think about him too much, especially seeing how these last four months have played out.

"No one," I lie.

"Eh, you're not missing out. Men are only good for one thing." She gives me a devious grin. Monica is the closet I've come to meeting a real-life Samantha from Sex and the City. She's epic.

"Is that why you keep Elias around?"

"Elias has many skills, if you know what I mean, but being a boyfriend is not one of them."

"Noted."

"Okay," Mon says, downing the last of her glass, "get out of here before I try to pull you into date night with Elias and me.

I can't help but laugh, knowing full well their date night would involve handcuffs, feather boas, and blindfolds, not dinner and drinks.

"Okay, I'm out." I blow her a kiss as I pick up my black Prada tote, throwing it over my shoulder.

"See ya, sweetie. Have a good one."

"See you tomorrow!" I call as I exit the building, thrusting myself onto the hectic sidewalk that is New York City. People push and shove past one another, anxious to get to their next destination. It's one of the things I love most about the city. The constant movement, a city that never sleeps.

"Stupid Motherfuckers! The world is ending!" Lenny, the man who sits outside my building, screams as I walk past him. When I left work the first day and he screamed at me, I nearly shit myself. Now he's just a familiar part of the city.

I waste no time walking to Ash's hotel; thankful I don't have to catch the subway. Sure, every New Yorker uses it, but I'm not about being crammed into a moving tube filled with other humans. That shit activates my claustrophobia.

My footsteps are lost amongst those of the city dwellers around me with each stride I take, excited to finally see Ash after all these months.

Despite her initial promise to visit all the time, real life gets in the way, as it did for both of us. My first few months working were harder than I ever imagined, fitting into not only a new workplace, but also a city. But fit in, I soon did. And finding my footing never felt better. For the first time in my life, I really felt like I was on my own, and it was liberating.

But despite it all, I still miss home and the people I left behind. Unfortunately, that
includes Chase Mathews.

Our goodbye feels like forever ago. Me impulsively kissing him before hightailing it out of there. Do I regret it? No. Should I have done it? Probably not.

I'm not sure if that's the reason we haven't spoken much since I left. Sure, we had a few texts here and there, him making sure I got to New York, me asking how his leg was feeling. But eventually, it all just stopped.

I wish I could say our friendship fizzled out, but that's never the case with us. If anything, it's that we have too much energy zapping between us.

But all that energy needs to be released at some point, and with us, it would be epic, I just know it. But then the comedown would be the worst. Him in Seattle, me here. Plus, we'd probably kill one another if we ever attempted to give it a try.

Yep, that's just what I continue to tell my deluded self as to the reason why we are no longer in contact.

Before I know it, I arrive at The Carlyle. The doorman is quick to open the doors.

A sparkling lobby greets my eyes along with the movement of guests, all smelling of one thing. Money.

Being a bestselling author and wife to a professional athlete has its perks.

I spot Ash and Henry instantly. She sticks out like a sore thumb with her silver hair and tattoos. A shock she always loves to give people when she first meets them.

"Long time no see."

With Henry snugly positioned on her hip, she walks over to me. He gives me a gummy smile as I pull them both into a hug.

"Uh, I missed you, Ash." I tell her as I pull away, running my hand over Henry's outrageous blond curls. I swear the kid has better hair than most. Hair goals all the way and he's not even one yet.

"Way too long," she agrees, her hand squeezing my arm. "Let's get upstairs so I can put Henry down for the night and we can really catch up. I feel like it's been years since I've seen you."

We waste no time heading to her room, or should I say, her beyond stunning suite.

"Wow, this is-" I can't even get the words out before her face reddens.

"Ridiculous. It's totally ridiculous, but you know Logan." She shakes her head, thinking about her husband.

"I mean, if you don't want him, I'll take him," I joke.

"Why don't you take this one instead," she says, passing Henry my way. I gladly take him, wrapping my arms right around him for a big bear hug. He's nice enough to let me have a moment before beginning to wiggle, clearly having had enough of my antics.

"Okay, Handsome. Time to say goodnight to your aunty Georgia because you've gotta go to bed."

"Night my little lovebug."

Ash leaves the sitting room, closing the door to her bedroom behind her to get him to sleep. I play on my phone until she comes back out fifteen minutes later.

"Sorry, his sleeping schedule is way out of whack from all our travel so a five-p.m. bedtime is as good as I'll get before he's up at nine for a feeding."

"Don't be silly, you're a mom now. You go by his schedule."

"That I do. But enough baby talk, I need a drink."

She hustles over to the minibar, squatting down as she rummages through the stockpile. I lean back into the plush cream sofa that probably cost more than my monthly salary.

"God, this place is nice, Ash. I could get used to this."

"Couldn't we all," she mutters as she eyes a mini bottle of Jack Daniels and Absolute.

"Can we not die tonight?" I say, eyeing what's in her hands.

"Eh, you're no fun." I know she's kidding as she once told me having a hangover with a child is worse than torture.

"Vodka soda or vodka Redbull?" she asks before standing and tossing everything we need on a tray.

"Soda, thanks. I don't have it in me to be up till five a.m."

"Agreed."

Ash quickly makes our drinks before handing one my way. I can already tell it will be vodka with a dash of soda, but at this point, I'll take it. It's been a while since I've had some time with my girl.

Ash kicks off her combat boots, wiggling her black painted toes.

"Ugh, there is nothing like when the kid is asleep and I can just veg out on the sofa. Plus, I've got you with me, heaven."

"It's good to be here." I tilt my drink toward her before taking a gulp.

"So, tell me all the things, Georgia Monroe. What have I missed in the past four months?"

I raise my eyebrows, giving her a look. "Bitch, we talk practically every day! You know my life."

She waves a hand through the air. "Yeah, but talking on the phone only takes us so far. I want the juicy face-to-face gossip."

"I don't think I've got any." I laugh. "My life for the past four months has been work, work, and uh, more work."

"So you're loving it then?" Her words are hopeful. Ash is as much a sister to me as anyone. Our happiness matters to one another greatly.

"I'm loving it," I confirm, sounding like a McDonalds ad.

"But?"

"No buts. I love the city, the job, the people. Only downside is you're not with me. I feel like we haven't really been in the same city since we were twenty."

She nods. "Yeah, I get that. First I moved away, then when I actually came back, Logan's job kept us moving until you up and left. It's hard, but we make it work."

"That we do."

"Any new men I need to know about?"

I shake my head back and forth.

"Georgia Monroe. You've had a permanent boyfriend since we were thirteen and you got boobs. Yet for the last six months, there has been no one."

"And your point is?" I ignore the truth behind her words. Unfortunately, the downside of having a best friend like Ash is that she knows me better than I know myself.

"And would it potentially have anything to do with a certain blond hockey player you roomed with in April?" My smile evens out at the mention of Chase. "Seriously?"

"Hey, I'm just being honest." She finishes her drink before pouring herself another.

"I just haven't had time to date."

It's the truth, well, part of it.

"Have you spoken to him recently?"

I shake my head. "Nothing since July." Ash being my best friend already knows we initially spoke when I left.

"Why?"

Blunt. Straight to the point. That's Ash. It's also one of the traits I like most about her, just not always when it's directed at me.

I down the last of my drink, signaling her to slide the bottle my way for a refill. This time, I skip the soda all together. I'm only twenty-five, I don't need to be acting like a geriatric.

"I've got no fucking idea. We went from enemies to friends in a matter of days. From seeing one another every few months, to being around one another 24/7. Maybe our friendship was just a product of our environment."

"You don't really believe that," she says, calling me out.

I groan. Of course I don't believe it. It would be an insult to our connection to deem it a product of our environment. "I don't know what to believe, Ash. It's been months and our lives have just reverted back to how they were before we really knew one another. It's like that time at your place didn't even happen."

It hurts to say those words because, deep down, I know they meant something to me. The hurt comes from the reality that maybe they didn't mean as much to Chase.

"I don't think either of us believes that. It had to have been real, G. Chase and you used to be at one another's throats all the time then suddenly you're acting like bffs. That isn't nothing."

"Guys and girls can just be friends and nothing more, Ash."

Her dark brows rise as she tilts her head forward. "No shit, Sherlock. But I also know you and I know Chase."

"I didn't lie to you when I said nothing happened between us. I gave him a peck when I left, that was the extent of it."

Mouth slightly open, she gives me a what the fuck look. "Yeah, the kiss you totally tried to downplay!"

"Oh my god, I kept if from you for like a week, big deal! It was embarrassing, Ash! I don't let boys make me feel embarrassed! And I did with Chase, without even knowing if he felt   the   same   way!"

"Ah!" She points a hand at me. "He does feel the same way! How could he not!"

"Ugh," I groan, throwing my head back onto the feather pillows. "I don't want to like him. He's Chase for god's sakes, he's annoying and an asshole and pushes all my buttons."

"Yet you do."

"Yet I do. I really fucking do," I confirm for the first time aloud. It feels almost liberating, finally being able to put my cards on the table. After I moved to New York, I filled Ash in on my time with Chase, but I don't think I've ever really been upfront with how I feel. Of course Ash already knows this, but there is suspecting, and then there is confirming.

"You want the truth, Ash? It felt like an emotional affair," I quietly confess. "Nothing physical ever really happened, but emotionally, I felt myself connecting with him more and more every day. It was unlike anything I'd ever experienced. I don't know how to explain it. But it feels like one day I went to sleep constantly annoyed by him, then the next, I couldn't imagine not seeing him each day. I mean, how does that shit happen?"

"Oh Georgia."

"It scared me; it still scares me. And to be straightforward, I think it scared him too; otherwise, I think I would have heard from him. I'm not putting the silence on him, I know I've contributed, but if he felt as fiercely as me, I think he would have called. I know it was only a short time we were together but the shit that happened during it, how can it not link people?"

"Honey, I may not have the best track record on love before I met Logan, but anyone with eyes could see the connection between you two. Deep down, you have to know it wasn't just close proximity that brought you together."

I lift a shoulder. "I think at first, yeah I convinced myself the distance would show me that it was just the environment we were in that brought us together. But it's been months, and I still think about him."

"Why don't you reach out to him, G? What's the worst that could happen? You said you two were friends." It's the same thing she's been begging me to do for months. The same thing I've avoided. Now that she's right in front of me, I can't exactly run.

"It's not that easy, Ash. I can't start anything with him. For starters, I don't even know what I'm feeling. And I know for sure I don't want to start anything with someone who doesn't live in my state, let alone someone who has never been in a committed relationship."

"I'm not saying anything about a relationship. Just reach out, rekindle the friendship and go from there."

"I don't even know what I'd say. It's all so awkward now."

"Start with hi."

I level her a look. "Thanks, smartass."

"That's what I'm here for."

Eager to change the subject, I pick up my phone and begin to show Ash photos of my apartment. She's easily swayed, grabbing the device and swiping. Soon the burst of laughter that comes out of her is unexpected. I think nothing of it until the familiar tune of "Ms. Jackson" starts playing. I don't know how, but my gut is telling me it's the video of Chase and me.

Rushing from my seat on the couch, I dive to the spot next to her, my visual confirming my suspicions.

How the hell did she find this?

"Georgia, what is this?" Ash's lips are tilted up in a smirk, her body shaking as she tries to hold in a laugh.

Despite how much I miss Chase, I can't help but laugh at the video in front of me. Chase is singing the chorus of "Ms. Jackson" by Outkast while I rap the chorus. Both of us decked out in feather boas and neon glasses. I should be mortified, but I can't help but laugh at the memory. Both of us look like idiots, but we're smiling idiots. We were having fun.

"You don't even want to know." My body shudders along with hers.

"So, this is what you two did while Logan and I were gone?"

"Yep," I say quickly.

"I won't lie, I'm kinda jealous of you guys, but I'll get over it."

I nudge her side and she wraps her arm around me.

We watch the rest of the video, a bittersweet feeling coming over me.

"You know it's okay to miss him, Georgia. It's not like he's in another country, he's in a different state is all."

I shake my head. "Of course I miss him, but Chase isn't one to do serious, he said so himself. Plus, he's a hockey player. He gets more ass than a toilet seat."

"Uh okay, Eminem. Did hanging out with Chase change your vocab?"

I lift a shoulder, my eyes roaming over my freshly painted nails. Something I've recently become very good at.

"I don't know what it was, Ash. But being with Chase, it felt like being a kid again, and not in a bad way. I felt… free?"

"And you want to run from that why?"

"I don't want to get hurt. Being with Chase is a risk."

She gives me a pitying look, and my insides cave in on me. Standing from next to her, I rush back to my drink, downing the last of it.

"Enough about all that, tell me about the new book you're working on." I change the subject with ease, Ash eager to tell me about her latest adventure. I know she can tell I'm diverting her attention, but she lets me. We stay up late into the night, talking about everything and nothing at the same time.

Chase

"Are you coming tonight?" Logan asks as I shove a pile of pancakes into my mouth. He eyes me from across the diner table, taking a sip of his black coffee. He and Ash are in New York for the weekend, Ash having spent the whole day with Georgia. I try not to let my mind think about how we're both in the same city for the first time in months.

I swallow before taking a sip of my shake. "Yeah, I'll try and stop by. I've got to meet with Robbins this afternoon, so depending how that goes, I should be there around seven or eight."

Logan tilts his head back slightly, his eyes trained on me as he continues to drink. Robbins is the head coach of the new Division 1 college hockey team I'm assistant coach to in Boston.

"What's Robbins doing in New York?"

"His daughter lives here, he's visiting for the weekend. We have a few things to discuss about the team so figured we might as well do it here."

Logan nods thoughtfully, still staring at his shitty cup of coffee. I've known the guy long enough to tell when something is on his mind.

"Yes?" I finally ask, already knowing where this is going. I take another bite of my breakfast, it suddenly tasting all sorts of bland.

"Have you spoken to her?"

I put down my fork, leaning back into the plastic booth.

"I'm assuming you mean Georgia?'

He says nothing and I run a hand over my face. It's back to its usual stubble-free ways.

"We haven't spoken in months; I don't know what to tell you."

"Why aren't you two still friends?"

It's the same type of question I've been getting since she left all those months ago. After she was gone, I rushed back to my finished condo to get my shit together because I couldn't bear living in that space without her there. Not that I tell Logan that.

"We're not, not friends," I reply.

"Dude, don't bullshit me. You sound like I did when Ash and I started dating."

"Really?" I give him a blank look. Ash and Logan's history is far from perfect. Their infatuation with one another started instantly when they became roommates, but it was so much deeper for them than that. I'm still shocked they found their way back to one another after all the shit they went through.

"You know what I mean, all the denials."

"It's isn't like that. We were friends and then she left and I followed suit not long after."

"Chase, I'm your best friend and I was always honest with you about Ash. I think I deserve the same courtesy. I know your condo was finished in early May."

I laugh, but it lacks all humor.

"So, what if it was? Is it so bad I wanted to spend more time with her?"

"No, Chase. That's the whole point, it isn't bad at all. What I have with Ash, Man, I want you to experience that. And if there is a possibility that person is Georgia…"

"You don't think I know that? You don't think I want to find my person? I get it, back in college, hell back last year even, I was a walking one-night stand. But after my injury, everything changed for me and it's taken the last seven months for me to realize that change was for the better."

"It took Georgia." He says it as a statement, a matter of fact.

"What can I say, she got me off the couch."

"So, call her. From what I'm understanding, nothing bad happened between you two."

I shake my head. To be completely fucking honest, when it comes to Georgia and me, I've got no fucking clue what happened.

Exhaling, I push my plate forward as I no longer have an appetite. "I don't know what to tell you, Logan, because I've got no clue what happened. It was like living in a bubble with her all those weeks. She drove me fucking crazy half the time, but we still had fun. And sure, did I think we'd be friends when she left? Yeah, I did. But things just got awkward. Not being in the same city made it all just sort of fall apart."

"You're in the same city now."

"For less than a week, dude."

"If she really matters to you, a few days should be more than enough."

I constantly find myself thinking back to my time with her. Georgia and I became something deeper than friends. We shared things with one another that we hadn't told others and perhaps that bond and those secrets stayed in the house when we both left. It's the only thing I can think of to numb the feeling that gnaws inside my chest when it comes to the fact that she never called.

"I'll think about it. But, if anything, it would be to restore our friendship." I'm a huge liar, but it cuts too much and too deep to talk about right now; her departure still fresh in my mind.

"Okay, Man. Well, if that's what you need to tell yourself."

I toss a packet of sugar at him and he just grins.

Idiot.

Georgia

I take a gulp of my rosé, ready for a fun night with Ash and Logan. It's been far too long since we've actually gotten to act our age and relax. I have to say, the past day with Ash has been exactly what the doctor ordered. We've spent the entire day together, shopping, talking, and just spending time with Henry. Ash's brother Asa, who lives in New York, is babysitting him tonight, so we can have some adult fun.

I step away from the overcrowded space, smiling at the bartender in thanks. It's a Saturday night in New York City, what could be better? The movement and life in the city make me feel alive.

I spot my silver-haired friend pushing past strangers, her combat boots and black dress making her look like a kick-ass action hero.

"Okay, don't kill me," Ash grabs my arm, pulling me away from the endless supply of alcohol.

"What?" I ask, eyeing her warily.

"Chase is coming tonight."

I nearly spit out my drink. "What the fuck, Ash? I told you I might reach out to him, not invite him to dinner and drinks! Plus, what's he even doing in the city?"

"I didn't invite him, Logan did. Chase is in town for work and we couldn't not invite him."

Work? I push down the curiosity to know where he ended up.

"Okay, you're right. This isn't a big deal." I down the rest of the clear liquid in my glass, anxiously needing another.

"Right," Ash says, trying to convince, not only me, but herself.

"I'm gonna get another," I say before slipping away. It's at that very moment I see two familiar builds walk into the bar. Logan in a button-up and jeans while Chase is rocking a white tee and dark denim.

This is okay. I can do this.

But it's the skinny feminine arm that quickly encircles Chase's arm that makes me stop in my tracks. Manicured red nails pet his bicep as the blonde in stilettos leans into him, clearly whispering in his ear.

And suddenly I'm pissed. I've been thinking about this dude for months, feeling like a dick while he's clearly moved on. Georgia Monroe does not wait for men. Especially men like Chase Mathews. When I left and kissed him, the ball was clearly in his court. And he's made his move. It's just not with me.

I am a strong, badass woman and I can accept this and move on.

Putting on my best bitch smile, I walk over to where they've found Ash. Logan has his wife pulled into him; his arms wrapped around her waist. While Chase and his new girl are standing next to them, doing what I'm assuming are introductions.

I smooth down my white dress, happy I decided to go all out with my black Prada pumps.

"Georgia," Logan beams as he sees me, momentarily breaking away from Ash to pull me in for a hug. How the hell he can wear a long sleeve shirt in the middle of summer in New York, I will never understand. But I won't deny he looks good doing it.

"Hey handsome, long time no see."

He pulls away, gently squeezing my arm before returning to Ash's side.

I bite my teeth together before turning to Chase. I push down the familiar way my body warms to his presence, my eyes greedy to take all of him in.

He's back to the clean-shaven face and buzz cut I knew him to have for all those years. He's noticeably bulked up, clearly back in training mode. It gives me hope his leg isn't giving him too much grief.

I finally reach his eyes, his stare digging into me.

"Hey, Monroe." He speaks first.

"Hey, Mathews," I respond, keeping my hands at my side.

I swear a look of hurt briefly flashes across his face at my lack of enthusiasm. The entire interaction confuses the hell out of me.

I look away from him, smiling at the girl at his side.

"Hi, I'm Georgia," I say, deciding that making her feel like shit isn't on my agenda for the night.

"Lindsay," she says back, her tone and demeanor bubbly. Big blue eyes shine as she leans her hand out to shake mine, and I already know this Bambi-eyed girl isn't a bitch. She's genuine, sugary sweet.

"Nice to meet you."

"You, too. I love your shoes." She looks down, pointing to my Prada pumps. I can't help but like her for the compliment.

"Thanks, they're old, but they've done me well."

She continues to beam so intensely about everything, I feel as if I'm standing in front of a Chucky doll. I turn to look at Ash and Logan, both attempting to hide their amusement.

"I need a drink," Logan finally cuts in, "anyone else?"

Lindsay agrees to accompany him, with Ash hot on their heels. I'm left standing with Chase, in the hectic bar I no longer want to be in. I move side to side on my heels, the sticky public floor attempting to hold them down.

"So-" I begin, not really sure how to proceed. The back and forth between us was easy all those years he drove me mad, but now I have no idea where we stand.

"She's my boss's daughter," he finally says, my gaze shooting to his. "Lindsay, I mean, my boss asked me to take her out for the night, couldn't exactly say no."

My teeth are pulling on my bottom lip as I nod, the faint taste of vodka no longer in my mouth. God, I hope Logan gets me another one.

"Boss?"

"Yeah, I'm working as an assistant coach with Bill Robbins for the Tigers. It's college hockey, but you've got to start somewhere."

"That's amazing, Chase. I have to say I'm impressed."

"It clearly took time for me to get my shit together, but I got there in the end." He continues to look at me, those green eyes not darting away.

"I'm really happy for you. I mean that."

I can't help but keep my focus on him, the unsaid words between us saying so much more than either of us ever could.

"Georgia, I-"

"I've got drinks!" Lindsay's voice pierces through our uncomfortable silence, my feet instantly stepping back.

"Great," I mutter as she hands Chase a beer, before resting her hand on his chest. I ignore the pang in my stomach seeing them together.

Stop. It. Georgia.

I waste no time slipping away from them and finding Ash at the bar. She gives me a sympathetic look I choose to ignore.

"Vodka on the rocks," I call to the bartender.

Fuck this night.

The night drags on and I continue to wish I had stayed home, a feeling I'm not familiar with. I'm always the one pushing to stay out, to have fun, but tonight is anything *but* fun.

I've had to watch sweet Lindsay paw at Chase all night, my anger and sadness only continuing to grow. Which is pathetic because I didn't even realize how intense my feelings were until I saw him tonight.

I guess that's the thing about time. You manage to convince yourself things don't matter as much, that is until they're staring you in the face again.

After dinner, I excuse myself from the table, making up some bullshit excuse about having to work tomorrow. But my issue? Tomorrow is a Sunday, so I'm sure they all see through it. Chase is thankfully in the bathroom, so it's the perfect time to escape.

Ash and Logan give me hugs with promises made to meet for breakfast with Henry tomorrow. I just can't be around Chase and his flavor of the month anymore. I mean, it's appalling; he churns out women like I change outfits! He's ridiculous, I'm ridiculous, this whole fucking thing is ridiculous. He's Chase Mathews for god sakes, I shouldn't be surprised he's with someone. Just because we spent that month together, that doesn't mean anything. So why am I so angry?

"Georgia!"

Oh fuck. And here I was thinking I'd made a quick escape.

Plastering on a smile, I turn around, finally facing him alone for the first time tonight. Sure, we've been in the same room, but I've avoided him like the plague, unsure how to interact or proceed with us. And what even is us? Are we truly friends? Or, was it just cabin fever and misery that brought us together for that month?

I don't say anything as our gazes collide. It's intense and it hurts and I want to look away.

"You're leaving?" he finally says, his voice catching in the night air.

"I've got a big day tomorrow for work," I lie.

His stare is blank, eyes hollow, and I know he can tell I'm lying, but thankfully, he doesn't call me out.

"You weren't gonna say goodbye?"

I bite my lip, unsure how to reply. What do you know, Georgia Monroe is out of words. Someone grab a camera. This is a once in a lifetime moment.

"Is it because I'm here with someone?"

His question catches me so off guard that I flinch.

This isn't territory that we've ever entered. His statement alone is opening up a door to something I'm not sure I'm ready to deal with.

"No," I say all too quickly.

"Are you sure? Because from the look on your face, you're pissed at me. Hurt, I'd even say. And to have those types of feelings toward someone means you care about them. But I wouldn't know how you're feeling because you haven't called in four months. Did something change in the short time we've been apart? Tell me what I missed because I'm going crazy trying to figure it out."

Been apart.

Even the words sound romantic.

"Let's not forget you didn't call either. Don't put this all on me."

"You're right, I didn't call. So let's talk about it. Let's talk about something, anything, with fucking meaning and depth, because the bullshit we're giving one another in there? That isn't us, that doesn't work for us."

"Us?" I say, looking him up and down. "There isn't an *us*, Chase." I shake my head, wondering why of all places this has to come out on the grimy sidewalk of a New York bar. But then again, I know this city has seen worse. Our conversation is probably child's play.

"Look, I need to get home. I don't have the energy to deal with this right now." I angle my body away from him, ready to escape into the night.

"I really thought you had more guts than this, Monroe. You're always calling me out on my shit, but the second I do it to you, you run with your tail between your legs."

"I'm not running," I snap, facing him again.

"Really? Because coat on, bag in hand, it sure as shit looks like it to me."

"You want to talk about running? You're the one who hid on his friends' couch for months because he was too scared to face the world!" I spit back at him, the words tasting bitter.

He lifts his arms to his side. "You're damn right I did. I ran from everything until you came into my life and ripped me away from all of that. So tell me, Georgia. Why run now? You've always been the one to face your fears head on. Let's talk. No bullshit, no fake smiles or pleasantries, let's really fucking talk."

I shake my head, trying to focus my attention on the flickering streetlamp behind his head. His words are too real, too raw and honest to accept. Because I know the moment I do, the moment I take it all in, it will be too much.

"Ugh, you drive me mad!" I say, frustration coating each word.

"Yeah, well you make me insane!" he yells back, but I hear the laughter in his voice.

"I don't know how to process all of this, Chase! I don't understand what I'm feeling! We're supposed to hate each other, but I find myself constantly confused more than ever in your presence." My admission slips out; yet, I can't seem to regret it.

His face softens. "I get it. Don't you think it shocked the hell out of me too? We wasted years harboring pointless grudges against one another. Then in a matter of weeks, it all changed. Going from nothing to something to pure radio silence in a span of two months, no shit we're both confused on how we're feeling."

I stare at the dirty New York sidewalk, littered with old gum and grime from the city. "So, what are you saying?"

"Spend the night with me."

My eyes widen at his audacity.

He laughs. "Not like that. I mean, let's hangout like old times, spend the night just being friends. Let's actually talk. Who knows what's going to happen? I sure as shit have no idea. But I care about the friendship we had enough to want to fix things, to want to understand them."

"Since when is this you?" I ask him. "Suddenly you're so keen to talk about our feelings?"

He lifts a shoulder. "A lot has changed for me in the past few months. I'm sick of being afraid."

His words hit me, and from the widening of his eyes, he sees it.

"So, what do you say?"

This is what I've been wanting, isn't it? Time with Chase to figure it all out. We're fire and gasoline, but sometimes you've got to let them burn together.

"I say okay."

Georgia

I'm leaning against the side of the grimy terra-cotta colored brick building when Chase emerges five minutes later. His head whips around as he searches me out in the crowd, like I somehow could have vanished in the short time he was gone. Hiding out in the shadows, I let him squirm for a moment longer before calling out to him.

"Funny," he deadpans as he walks over to me, stepping around all the city night owls.

I grin, feeling slightly pleased with myself. "So, what's happening inside? How'd you get away?"

"I just told them the truth."

"Which is?" I lean my head back, the hard brick digging into my hair.

"That I wanted to spend time with you."

"Okay," I reply, attempting to keep my words light, but inside I'm buzzing. "What about Lindsay?"

"She's actually having a great time talking Logan's ear off. Ash may kill her by the end of the night, but she didn't even give a shit I left. Even offered to catch her a cab, which she declined.

"Okay, so we're good to go?"

He nods. "After you."

We begin walking in no direction of importance, the movement of our feet giving me something to focus on.

"Can you promise me something, Chase?"

"I can try."

"Honesty. Complete and utter blunt honesty between us tonight. And if shit is awkward, we push through it and lay everything out. And tomorrow, when we go back to reality, we can part ways if tonight is too much. But tonight, we lay all our cards on the table."

"What if we hear things we don't like? Sometimes that's a can of worms you can't close once opened."

My finger fiddles with the loose thread on my dress as we walk. "True. But I'm not one for secrets and I think at this point, could it really do more harm than good?"

"I guess we are going to find out." He chuckles before adding, "And yes, I promise to be honest."

"Good." I begin walking, not really sure where we are going. It's ten p.m. on a Saturday night, so the city is as vivacious as if it was the middle of the day.

"So, with this pledge of total honesty, does this mean we can ask anything we want?"

"I guess it does," I reply, knowing full well we are asking for vulnerability from both sides.

"Good," he says, repeating my earlier words. "So why did you kiss me?"

My eyes widen slightly, but I attempt to keep my expression neutral. "Wow, jumping straight in, are we?"

I turn to look at him, his familiar face illuminated by the glowing stores we pass.

"I mean, why not? We've never really done anything with caution when it comes to one another, so why start now?

He has a point. One of the reasons we can hate and like each other so well is because we don't hold back. And when we do, shit gets weird and awkward like tonight.

"Okay, well, I kissed you because I wanted to. I don't actually have any solid reasoning behind it. I was in the moment and I was scared of what the future would hold, what it would mean to leave that house behind. Leave you behind."

His head moves up and down, but he manages to keep an even expression, not giving anything away.

"So, it was fear-based?"

"No, not fully. If you haven't noticed, Chase Mathews, I don't do anything I don't want to. Yes, it was random and unexpected, but in the moment, it felt right."

"Okay," he says, giving me nothing.

"Okay? That's all you're gonna say?" There is a very good chance he could proceed to tell me he didn't like it or want it, but my gut tells me otherwise. His actions and words tonight say it meant something to him.

"I wanted to grab you by the waist and kiss the shit out of you. But you pulled away and left so quickly. I didn't really process what had happened until you left."

My steps halt at his words. They're not flowery or romantic, but there is a raw truth behind them. He, on the other hand, continues on in front of me with what I can assume is a Cheshire grin.

"I wish I could tell you my thought process behind it all, but there really was none. It just kind of happened and the next thing I knew, I was in the car headed to the airport. If you haven't noticed by now, I can be sort of impulsive."

I hasten my steps, slightly regretting wearing these heels as I'm not sure either one of us has any clue as to our next destination.

"Oh, I've noticed." He laughs, still staring straight ahead. "Anywhere to get a good burger around here?"

"Didn't you eat before coming to the bar?"

His head tilts to the right. "Georgia, my stomach's ability to ingest food is endless."

"There is a diner around the corner we can go to. I've never been, but a girl at my office says it's good."

"Speaking of your office, I am curious as to how all that's going."

"Can we just save honest time until we're sitting down. My feet are killing me in these shoes and if I'm being real with you, that's all I can really think about right now."

I take his silence as agreement. Leading the way, the neon sign directs us to the land of pancakes and deep-fried food. It's got the odd person inside, but I know in a few hours, after everyone is done at their club or bar, it will be packed.

The worn sign at the front tells us to seat ourselves, Chase picking the booth in the back. It's something I've only recently started noticing he does. My mind now understanding he's a public figure, so it makes sense he doesn't want to be right by the door.

A gray-haired woman, probably in her sixties, waltzes on over in her yellow and white outfit and apron. Deep circles mar her under eyes, yet she still smiles at us, attempting to show joy at being here and not in bed.

Placing two menus on the table, she looks over each of us. "Coffee, tea?"

"I will take a black coffee, please," I reply.

"Chocolate milkshake, thank you." Chase smiles at her, her eyes slightly lightening from his look alone. She shuffles away to put in our order.

"Guess your charm really does work for everyone."

"What can I say."

I grab a sugar packet from the muted silver holder, my fingers calmed by having something to fiddle with.

"Back to truth time?"

I look up, nodding. "Sure, what do you want to know?"

His green eyes connect with mine from across the table, my gut clenching as I realize just how much I've missed looking at this idiot.

"Why didn't you call?"

Straight and to the point.

"Why didn't you?" I shoot back.

His left hand reaches across his chest as he crosses his arms. I try to ignore how his biceps have only gotten bigger in the months since I've seen him. But stupid Chase, he looks great, in and out of shape.

"Touché," he replies.

Our waitress comes back, placing our drinks in front of us and Chase orders some food in the process. I pour the crinkled-up sugar packet into my drink, before taking a deep sip. My gut tells me tonight will be a late one, so I'm going to need as much caffeine as I can get.

"Well, I'll go first," Chase begins, "I didn't call because I didn't know what to say. When you initially left, I thought we would keep in touch, but then after those initial text messages, I guess I just kind of felt like you wanted a clean break."

He clearly sees my mouth about to open, so he quickly finishes his sentence. "I didn't mean it like that. I'm not putting this on you. I'm a big boy, I could have called, but I don't know, it just felt awkward. And I don't know why."

"I get it, Chase. I felt it too. I probably didn't help the situation by kissing you then running off. And no, you're not fully wrong. It would be a lie for me to say I wasn't developing some sort of attachment to you and I think a part of me thought leaving Seattle meant I had to leave you behind too."

His head moves up and down, his stare thoughtful. "I think four months of guessing could have been avoided if we were just honest with one another."

"We used to be good at that. I think we need to channel our old selves moving forward."

"I can do that."

Chase's burger soon arrives, and I sneakily swipe a fry in the process. He turns the plate around, so they're facing me, his way of sharing without saying it.

He wipes his mouth on his napkin before leaning back. "When you saw me tonight with Lindsay, you looked pissed."

I feel my walls going up at the line we are about to cross but force myself to shove it down. Honesty was my idea after all. So instead of snapping or getting defensive, I stay silent to let him finish, but he doesn't say anything.

"Is there a question in there?" I finally ask.

He takes a breath; his eyes leveled with my own. "Why did it bother you?"

He doesn't ask if it bothered me, no, the question is why *did* it bother me. Clearly, the look on my face was all the confirmation he needed.

"You know why," I reply.

"I want you to tell me." His body leans slightly forward, elbows placed against the table.

"I was jealous," I admit, the words coming out short and to the point. The tips of his lips tilt up slightly, although he tries to hide it.

"I'd have been jealous too."

"What?" I ask.

"If you showed up with someone tonight, I would have been jealous too."

I rub my hand along my face, unsure how to handle all this new information. Inside, I feel all shaken up. Bits of excitement mixed with worry coat my stomach. It's like we went weeks ignoring our feelings and now they're being placed out on the cutting board.

"I could feel things changing," I say, looking away from him. "With us, I mean. I got attached to you, Chase. Far more attached than I'd been to anyone in a long time. It all felt far too natural, too easy."

"And that's a bad thing?"

"It's a scary thing," I say. "Tell me you didn't feel the same way. I'm not the only one who tried to ignore it. You may want to talk about it now, but five months ago, that wasn't exactly the case."

His eyebrows crease. "You're not wrong, it was scary. I don't think either of us have ever been in a stable relationship, so how were we supposed to know any better?"

His admission takes me back. "Yeah," I whisper.

"That feeling you're describing, I felt it too. Half the time, I had to convince myself it was all in my head, that these feelings I was feeling for you weren't real. I mean, we'd hardly even hugged before and now all of a sudden, these romantic feelings are here. Georgia, you have to understand, my life, my relationships with women were never like that. Everything revolved around having fun. In my mind, it wasn't even possible to have feelings for someone you hadn't messed around with. I think it's the rationale I used after you left. I managed to convince myself I had made it all up. I even went as far as denying it all to Logan."

I let out a humorless laugh. "Yeah, I might have tried that route with Ash. She didn't buy it for a second."

Chase chuckles, the familiarity of his laugh bringing some calm to my tumultuous insides.

"Neither did Logan. But I stuck to it, went as far as to convince myself I could be cordial with you tonight and move on. But the thing is, Georgia, the second I saw you tonight, it all flew out the window. All those feelings I'd been trying to bury for months just came flooding back."

Our waitress comes to refill our water glasses, effectively pausing our conversation. It feels like forever until she leaves again.

I reach for my water, suddenly feeling all kinds of parched.

"I wanted you physically, Chase. But the way I wanted you emotionally was what scared me. That hasn't changed, but I can't deny that this all feels like a huge fucking gamble. I've got whiplash over the entire situation."

"It wasn't exactly a conventional situation."

I smile softly. "One could say that."

"I think after everything that's happened between us; it would make sense that even trying to navigate something as simple as our feelings is fucking complicated."

I bite my lip. "My feelings have never really been that simple, and if the last six months have taught me anything, it's yours aren't either."

His eyes glimmer softly. "I think you're right, Monroe. Our feelings for one another are anything but simple. But if it's okay with you, I'd like to spend more time understanding them."

Letting out a breath, I sink into the booth. My hair parts, my bare neck connecting with the sticky laminated surface behind me.

"I want to spend the night hanging out with you, but I also want you to know I can't promise anything. I know that might sound selfish or crazy, but you scare me. This whole thing scares me."

"And all the odds are stacked up against us," he whispers.

"They are," I confirm.

His eyes drift off momentarily, a slight vacancy slipping into his stare. I begin pulling apart a napkin in front of me. There are not many situations in this life where you can be one hundred percent honest, so I'm trying to embrace the moment.

"Let's just take each moment as it comes. It's been so long since we've seen one another; we don't want to spend four hours dissecting our feelings. No matter what, we will walk away from tonight as friends, right?"

"Right," I am quick to confirm, despite my mind knowing how hard that will be.

"So enough of the heavy shit for now? Friends catch up with one another, and we've got a lot to fill one another in on."

"Fair point. So, how have you been surviving without me for the past five months?" I grin at him, happy to know our easy conversation is still alive and kicking.

"Elaine," he deadpans.

"Oh god, I miss her so much. I've managed to get her on the phone a few times, but it never lasts long. I hear her and Herb are back on."

"Oh, you have no idea. The in-house drama has been off the charts. But yeah, they're an item again, which I guess works out in my favor as I won't be in Seattle for a while."

"God, she probably hates us, both of us leaving her."

"Deep down she doesn't, she just likes to tease us. She was actually a very big champion of me seeing you this weekend, so at least we will have this good news to report back to her. Surely that will make her take our calls."

"One can only hope." I grin. "Besides our fabulous Elaine, what else is happening?"

He wipes a smear of ketchup off his face. "Well, I got my shit together and left Logan and Ash's house soon after you. It didn't have the same appeal without my favorite Rock Band buddy."

"Obviously." I toss my hair in jest.

"Anyway, so I left and spent the next two months getting back to my old self. I'm back to physical therapy, I mean, my leg will never be NHL ready, but I'm still capable. I ended up getting in touch with an old coach based in Boston, and I've been shadowing him for a while. He coaches a Division 1 college hockey team, so it's a great place for me to start. He recently offered me an assistant coaching position."

I can't help but smile, my heart less heavy with the knowledge Chase is finally finding his way. "You've got no idea how happy that makes me, Mathews."

"Thanks, Monroe. That means a lot. I don't know if it would have happened without you. I was in a pretty deep black hole before you came along. I don't even think I realized it until you pulled me out of it. My doctor recommended I see a therapist, but to be honest, Elaine happily took on that challenge."

"Yeah?" I'm so fucking proud of him.

My throat tightens at his words. He doesn't know it, but that means the world to me, because he saved me from falling into any real hole at all.

"I'm really glad things worked out for you, Chase. So, you're in Boston now?"

He nods. "It's new. Otherwise, I really would have called sooner. I only moved a week ago. Looks like we're neighbors."

I push down the sparks of hope that bloom from the prospect of us being so close to one another.

"I could think of worse things," I joke. I take a gulp of my coffee as it cools, the amber liquid already less appealing than before.

"So, what about you? How's the Big Apple treating you?"

"I'm loving it. Don't get me wrong, it was a huge change when I first got here, but it's home, for now anyway. My job is great, I'm finally able to explore more creative fields than what I was limited to when I worked for my dad, plus my boss, Monica, is amazing."

"So it all worked out for you, Monroe."

"I wouldn't go that far, but I'm getting there."

"And what about your dad, how is he holding up?" His question is filled with genuine concern, my mind drifting back to the day they met.

"He's doing okay. The house sold and he's gotten a new job this week at a big real estate company. It's crazy, really. I was so worried about him not finding work and it feels like this opportunity just fell into his lap. But I'm not complaining. I think it's an adjustment for him not running things, but life is all about changes. Mom's looking for work. They're taking it day by day."

"If I can do anything," he offers.

"I know, thank you, Chase, but I think they're going to be okay. It took me a while to see it, but I can't fix their problems, no matter how much I want to. And I've come to understand, they don't want me to either."

"Ah getting wise in your old age, Georgia." He flashes those pearly whites at me and I can't help but warm to him.

"What can I say, I'm wise beyond my twenty-six years."

His eyes flash briefly. "I'm sorry I missed your birthday."

I look down, lifting a shoulder. "I missed yours too."

"Eh, we'll have more."

I steal another fry before he polishes them off. Finished with his burger, he pushes the plate my way. I take the remaining few and munch on them until nothing's left.

"So, have you given any more thought to seeing your birth mom?"

It's a bold question, especially considering the last time I saw him he asked me to go with him. For all I know, he could have gone without me; that thought hurts more than it should.

"Still the same as when I last saw you. I'm ready, it's now more just about timing than anything else." He pauses, finishing the last of his shake, the straw calling out when nothing is left in the glass. "You still want to come with me?"

"You still want me to come?"

"I do, when the time comes. If you want to, that is."

"I do," I say far too quickly. "I do," I repeat once more, this time slower.

"Good," he replies, shaking his head up and down. Slowly, longingly.

"Want to get out of here? Just because Ash and Logan are parents doesn't mean we need to be. There's a killer club I want to take you to."

He lights up, Chase never being one to turn down a good time.

"Let's do it."

Chase

We walk into The Jane, the dance floor packed with sweaty bodies, all of them probably looking for an escape from their real lives, whether in a stranger or themselves, who knows.

On instinct, I grab Georgia's hand, not wanting to lose her in the crowd. Her head snaps around, the glow of her wide eyes tells me she's shocked, but she says nothing, quickly giving my hand a squeeze.

Weaving through the swarm of bodies, we find the bar. I'm thankful for the dark room, no one able to interrupt our night for a photo. It's shit I used to not mind, still don't sometimes, but time with Georgia isn't guaranteed and I'll be damned if it's interrupted tonight.

I order us some drinks, already knowing what she wants. She could easily pull her hand from mine, but to my surprise, she inches closer. I slip my hand from hers, sliding it around her waist. It's a bold move, but one she doesn't reject.

I quickly pay for our drinks, Georgia downing hers in a few sips. I follow suit, placing my empty glass on the dirty bar.

"Wanna dance?" she asks.

Instead of replying, I take her hand and drag her onto the dance floor. We push past sweaty bodies until Georgia starts dancing, I follow her lead. We're thrust into the mindless movements of dozens of others. Georgia lets loose, her body swaying back and forth to the music. I can't help but take all of her in, my mind drifting back to our conversation earlier.

I don't have any expectations for Georgia and myself, but it would be a lie to say I didn't have hope. If tonight has proven anything to me, it's that I want her more than I previously knew. Being around her again has lit a match inside of me. Hell, even my thoughts are turning more romantic as the seconds go by and romance hasn't exactly been at the top of my list in life.

Shaking off my thoughts, I refocus on the moment. "Do What U Want" by Lady Gaga and Christina Aguilera comes on; Georgia throws up her hands as she dances to the music, her body dancing up against mine.

I move along with her, letting her lead the way, and set the pace for whatever does or doesn't happen tonight.

People bump into us as we move, but I don't think either of us notice, too caught up in the movement of one another. It's hard to ignore how badly I want her when she grinds her ass into me. Quickly, she spins around, her eyes connecting with mine, even in the dimly lit room.

"We shouldn't do this," she whispers in my ear, her breath fanning across my face.

"A terrible idea," I confirm, my hand resting on her hip.

"Terrible," she mutters.

"The worst," I say, before closing the gap, our lips connecting with one another.

She pulls away, whispering into my ear, "Just for tonight." Then her lips are back on mine, a shot of adrenaline coursing through my body.

I waste no time, pulling her closer. Our tongues tangle in a war for dominance, neither one of us willing to submit.

Bodies continue to crash into us, but neither of us pulls away. Her nails dig into my side as I close the remaining distance between us.

Eventually, she pulls back, her breathing labored and face flushed. I'm sure if I looked in a mirror, mine would be the same.

We look at one another, as the world goes on around us, my gut twisting at the thought that she might run. But to my utter surprise, she laughs, a full blown, teeth-showing laugh. It's contagious, so I reciprocate, an immense sense of relief overtaking me that we didn't ruin everything before it even began.

Georgia, once more, links our fingers, our bodies fusing together as we continue to dance.

This sort of scene isn't new to me. As an NHL player, I'm used to the parties and the women and while it was fun for a while, it's lost its shine in the past year.

Until Georgia.

We spend the next two hours at The Jane until Georgia complains of sore feet and an empty stomach. I take her purse for her, leading us out of the blaring club.

"Uh!" Georgia pulls away from me, spinning around in the street, her forehead still beaded with sweat. "I don't think I've had that much fun in a long time, Chase."

"Me neither, Monroe."

She stops her street-wandering, coming back into step with me as we wander the 2am streets of the Meatpacking District.

"I'm starving, what do you say we get a slice before heading back?" She turns to me as we continue on, her eyes crystal clear.

"Let's do it."

"There is this amazing place that does a $1 slice near my apartment, we could get a cab?"

I nod, before stepping onto the main road, the faint glow of other vehicles deceptively keeping the real time hidden. I hail us a cab and we quickly get in.

Before long, we're outside 2Bros Pizza, Georgia chatting with the man behind the counter. Her familiarity with him tells me she's been here before.

"Thanks, Tim!" she calls out as we exit, Georgia already having half the slice down her throat.

"Uh, so good." She moans, enjoying every bite.

I finish my pizza quickly, Georgia already having inhaled hers before the restaurant was in our rearview.

"This is me," she says, finally stopping in front of a brown brick building. It blends perfectly with the rest of the street.

I pull out my phone to call an uber. She sees the app and puts her hand on my wrist.

"Chase…." she starts, "I had a really good time tonight."

"Me too, Monroe. And if I'm being honest with you, I don't want it to end with tonight. Tell me you don't feel it?"

Her head looks to the ground. "I feel it, Chase. But can you honestly tell me you think this is a good idea?" Her voice wavers.

"I've never been one to follow good ideas."

"Yeah, I've gathered that but what if it all goes wrong? For starters, we don't even live in the same city, Chase. That isn't exactly a sensible way to start dating."

A laugh stumbles out of me. "Sensible. Georgia, we're twenty-six not ten, why do we have to be sensible?"

"Because we're not kids anymore. You can't throw ragers and drive motorbikes into the pool without consequences."

My lip tilts at the side. "I mean I feel like I could."

She levels me with an annoyed look.

My hands go up. "Sorry, I'll be serious."

"I just don't see a realistic way this could work."

"Georgia, what is really holding you back? Because I know it isn't just geography."

Biting down on her lip, she rocks back and forth on her heels. "We argue with so much passion, we became friends under the same circumstance. We're not tame people, we're fiery and I'm scared of what will happen if we ignite at the same time."

"It will be epic," I answer genuinely

"Or catastrophic."

I turn, my hands gently taking her arms and pulling her into me. "You telling me you're afraid to fall in love with me, Monroe?"

My heart speeds up at the prospect of love. A concept I don't think either of us has ever really experienced before.

"That's exactly what I'm telling you. We're intense, too intense. I don't know if I'd make it out alive." She tries to lighten her voice, but I see through the façade.

"All I see is your fear of me breaking your heart, but I've got to be real here. I think I'm the one who should be scared."

Her lashes flutter as she stares down, but her hold on me tightens.

"We're really doing this?" she finally asks.

"We're doing this," I confirm.

Georgia

"Chase."

I poke his side as I stare at him from the left side of the bed. My elbow holds up my head as I use my free hand to attempt to wake him up.

After last night's unexpected turn of events, I woke up feeling surprisingly light. Like months of unacknowledged worry had finally dissipated with a single conversation.

It was past three a.m. when we finally made it back to my apartment, so no sexy time for us. But that didn't mean I didn't take full advantage of using his six pack as a pillow.

But it was far too comfortable, hence why I'm attempting to wake him up. A gargled snore escapes his mouth as I push against his bare chest once more. I see a brief flutter of eyelashes before they open, Chase's sleep filled eyes connecting with my own.

"Took you long enough," I say as a good morning. "You snore."

Somehow, his crinkled eyes look adorable as he eyes me. "Do not."

"Eh, agree to disagree." I pull myself up, settling myself on top of him. Strands of my disheveled blonde curls fall as I look down at him, risking morning-breath death to peck him on the lips.

"Get dressed. We've got breakfast with Ash and Logan in 20."

With that, I get off him and skip from the room, reveling in how easy it feels to be with him. How easy it feels to be happy.

It's only twenty minutes later I want to kill him. I am turning on my hairdryer when a burst of white powder hits me in the face.

"Chase!" I scream, "What the fuck?"

He pokes his head into the bathroom—his lips turn up at the sides when he sees me.

"Oh my god, you better not be laughing at me right now. What the actual fuck? We ended this months ago!"

He tries to keep a straight face but cracks. "I'm just trying to keep things interesting, babe."

"I'm so getting you back for this. When you least expect it!" I yell as he walks into the living room, his laugh ringing out in the hall.

If Chase wants to keep things interesting, then he better buckle up, Baby.

After having to re-wash my hair, we're beyond late for breakfast. Yet, I've already got a slew of ideas on how to get him back.

"So how do you want to play this? Should we trick them into thinking we hate each other again? Or maybe we overwhelm them with PDA?" I throw the suggestions at Chase as we near the restaurant where Ash and Logan are waiting.

He chuckles, his chest moving up and down. "Any other day of the week I'd go for either of those ideas, but today, why don't we just be ourselves."

"Ugh, you're so boring, but fine, let's do it." I wink before taking his hand. It's such a small gesture, but it means everything. I see the occasional stranger take a second look at

Chase, like they might know him from somewhere, yet no one stops to say anything.

"It's weird, don't you think? How natural this all feels? I mean it was literally only yesterday we hadn't spoken in months, now look at us. Holding hands in public, being civil."

"But it's a good weird," Chase replies. "It's fast, but at the same time, it feels right."

That it does.

Chase pulls open the door to the brunch spot Ash and Logan picked. I spot Ash's silver hair instantly. Her attention is on Henry, so Logan spots us first. His eyes widen, and I know he's seen Chase and me holding hands.

"Well, here goes nothing," I mutter. Chase laughs before walking toward them, pulling me with him.

"Well, look what the cat dragged in." Ash's words die on her lips when she sees what Logan's already spotted.

"We're together," I blurt out, having zero tact.

"Clearly," Logan says, his voice full of questions.

Ash's mouth is still on the floor, her head ping ponging between Chase and me.

We take her moment of silence to sit down, the sticky vinyl of the booths squeaking as we slide in. Ash sits directly across from me, while Logan faces Chase.

"Ugh, so yeah, what Georgia said, we're together," Chase says casually, leaning against the table to take a menu from Logan.

"What's good here?" he asks the table.

I peer over his shoulder, attempting to get a look at the options. Seeing my movement, he tilts it to the right, sharing it with me.

"Thanks," I reply as I scan the menu items. "I might get a crepe. Ash, what are you getting?"

"Food?" she says, finally finding her voice. "You two who hated each other more than life itself then became bffs then had a falling out, are suddenly together? Logan, what did we miss? I mean, don't get me wrong, this is great, and it will make it a lot easier for you two being godparents to Henry, but like, why am I the only one confused here?"

"She's rambling." Logan turns to her. "You're rambling, Ash," he says, his hand moving under the table to her leg.

"I know, I just really can't believe it. To hear about it is one thing, but actually seeing it is another. Wow." Her words aren't said with anger, rather awe and disbelief. But I know my best friend, once it sinks in, she will be over the moon.

"Logan, nothing to say?" Chase chuckles as he looks at his best friend.

"Nah, Man. I can't exactly say I saw it coming, but in a weird way, it makes sense. People don't have such a strong disdain for one another if there isn't some underlying tension."

"It's always the sexual tension," Ash mutters. "That's what got us."

"And the fact I pretty much fell in love with you after our first conversation," Logan tosses in. Ash's cheeks redden as she leans into her husband.

"I'm ravenous, can we order?" Chase interjects.

"Worked up quite the appetite, huh?" Ash grins. Logan gently nudges her side, but she swats him away.

"We'll talk later," I whisper to her. She grins like she's gonna get some hot gossip.

I bet she's expecting all kinds of details later, but unfortunately for her and myself, that won't be the case. After the night Chase and I had, sleep was the only thing on the agenda.

Logan gets the waiter's attention and we all order, Henry attempting to grab the silverware with his pudgy little fingers. Logan is quick to move it away, instead replacing it with a green baby spoon from their diaper bag. His big blue eyes light up as he turns it over, still attempting to gain control at his young age.

We all quickly order, my mind desperate for a cappuccino. I'm a girl who needs eight hours of sleep at all times or I can be a bit of a nightmare. But considering my best friend, her hubby, and beautiful little boy are only in my city once in a blue moon, I will pull my shit together for them. And for Chase.

Chase who I guess is now my boyfriend? I've had boyfriends from the moment I got my first bra, but, somehow, this all feels so different. And it being with Chase of all people. It is bizarre to say the least, but aren't the most interesting and exciting things in life the craziest sometimes?

"Monroe." Chase's voice gets my attention, my eyes widening at the sight of my coffee.

"Thanks," I reply, taking it from his hands and pulling it straight to my mouth.

"So, what's the plan for the day?" Chase asks.

I look at Ash and Logan, leaving the ball in their court.

"I was thinking we could take Henry to the park. Then maybe grab an early dinner? It's not exactly what you'd call exciting, especially after the late night you two had, but kids change things."

"Don't be ridiculous," I interject. "We all know Henry is the real MVP. To be honest, I'd rather hang out with him than the rest of you."

"She isn't wrong there," Chase adds, before turning to Henry, still enthralled by his spoon. "You want to go to the park with your favorite godfather?"

"You're his only godfather," Ash says, but Chase pays her no attention.

He continues his cooing, Henry also garnering Logan's attention in the process.

"Oh no, I think someone shit themselves."

I knock Chase in the ribs. "Don't say shit, he's a baby."

"But you just said it!"

I ignore him as Ash hands Logan the diaper bag.

"Come on, man, I'm gonna need a second pair of hands for this." Chase looks terrified as he follows Logan to the bathroom. I don't bother to hide my laughter as they go.

I give my attention back to Ash, happy to be around my friend, even just for the weekend.

"So, you two have really done it," she says. Her dark eyebrows are raised, as she leans back, her pale complexion stark against the black seat.

"I guess so. I mean we're going to give it a shot, whatever this is. It could epically backfire, and we will never be able to have lunches like this again, but we didn't really have them from the start with Chase and I always at one another's throats."

"True."

I grab a packet of sugar, my fingers moving around it before dumping the contents into my cappuccino.

"You know, I always wondered if something happened between you two."

My head lifts up. "Between Chase and me?"

"Yeah, back when him and Logan were in college. There was this one night, when you were visiting, and you two didn't want to kill each other. It was brief, but I did wonder."

"You never asked about it."

"I figured you'd bite my head off if I did. I know we can talk about anything, but Chase always seemed to piss you off."

"Yeah, I might have bitten your head off," I confirm with a grimace. "Sorry."

"Eh, I don't care. If it really mattered, I would have asked."

I look down at my drink, my thumb wiping away the chocolate on the rim of my cup. "Yeah, I know the night you mean. We had a moment, I think we both set down our weapons for the final days at Breslin, but it never came to anything more than that. When we woke up, we simply hated each other again."

"But did you really hate one another or was it just twisted foreplay?"

I burst out laughing, bits of my cappuccino foam flying from my mouth. "It wasn't foreplay. He really did drive me around the bend, but as I said the other day, we are so similar, and I think that played a huge role. Plus, it's Chase, pissing him off can be entertaining."

"Very true." Taking a sip of her iced coffee, she peers at me over the glass. "So, have you talked about what will happen after this weekend?"

"No, but truthfully, I'm not worried. We didn't really talk out logistics last night, it all happened so quickly. It's crazy and impulsive and potentially reckless for my heart. But I just want to jump in with him. He makes me feel like a kid again in the best ways. Feel a freeness I haven't felt in years."

"That makes me so happy to hear, G. I think you two will be good for each other."

"I hope so," I reply just as the guys bring Henry back. Our food comes moments later and we dive headfirst into talks of the past, present and future, Chase's hand on my knee the whole time. And for once, everything just feels right.

Chase

"I'm staying till Tuesday."

Georgia spins around in my arms, her blue eyes livelier from my words. The summer heat beats down as children pass us by. Logan and Ash are pushing Henry on the swings while we look on.

"Really?" She beams.

"I don't have to be back till Wednesday morning, so I can stay a few extra days. Give us some time together, sort some things out."

"I'd like that. I know we have a lot to figure out, but for now, I just want to enjoy it."

I lean forward, briefly connecting her lips with my own. "Me too, Monroe. Me too."

We pull apart at the sound of Henry's laughter. Georgia takes my hand, leading me over to the swing set. He gives us a toothless smile, his cheeks looking like they're storing chestnuts for winter.

"We might have an adrenaline junkie on our hands," I joke as he goes higher and higher.

"I'm going to miss you, little guy," Georgia says as she watches Henry kick out his little legs, still unsure how to manage the swing at his age.

"He's going to miss you both, I think we all are," Ash says, leaning her head against Logan's arm.

We spend the rest of the afternoon together, experiencing a peace I'd yet to know existed in this life.

Before long, Ash and Logan are heading back to the airport, little Henry in their arms. I pull Georgia into my own as we wave off their taxi, before dragging her back up to her apartment.

Somehow, all our built-up frustration explodes the moment we step inside. Our movements are frantic as we pounce on one another, hands rushing to remove our clothing.

"Don't get me wrong," she says to me through scattered kisses, "I'm thrilled to spend the weekend with them, but I'm glad we finally have some more alone time."

"Me too," I reply quickly.

I back her into the living room, her front matching up with my own as we move together. Her back hits the side of the couch and she grunts before laughing.

I rip off my own shirt before pulling her white tee over her head. Her chest heaves up and down, her black lace bra now on full display.

"Less looking, more moving," she says, her voice airy and breathless.

I chuckle under my breath before reaching around, unclasping her bra. Her hands go to my jeans, quick to drag them to the floor.

"Commando?" she asks before laughing.

I lift a shoulder. "I don't think you laughing at me is going to help our current situation.

She shoves my shoulder until I fall on the couch. Climbing on top of me, she scatters kisses down my stomach, my abs clenching at the movement.

"Thank god for hockey," she mumbles between kisses.

"Condom?" she asks, pulling back. Her lips are red, cheeks flushed. I take all of her in. Who would have ever thought I'd be seeing Georgia Monroe like this? Not me, but thank fuck for being wrong.

"Wallet," I quickly reply when I realize I've gotten lost in the sight of her.

"Of course." Her voice is raspy, an underlying amusement hidden between her words.

"What? Better to be safe than sorry. Wrap it before you tap it!"

Her head turns to me as she fiddles with my jean pocket. "Chase, don't kill the mood."

I stifle another laugh as I think to myself that maybe I've lost a bit of game since last year. Yep, it's been that long. I'd never usually crack jokes during sexy time, but with Georgia, it's just so easy. There is no need to put on the playboy persona or façade. When you're in the public eye, people always expect so much from you, but with Monroe, it's always 100% real.

Before long, Georgia has that familiar silver wrapper opened and is rolling the latex down my length. "Do you -" My words are cut off as she lowers herself on top of me in one swift movement.

My eyes close on instinct as I suck in a breath.

"Hold on, Mathews. I'm about to rock your world."

Oh, I have no doubt about it.

I open my eyes, not wanting to miss a single second of this moment. She's on top of me, eyes shut, her teeth biting down on her bottom lip. We move in sync, like somehow the universe created us just for one another. Like all the mindless faces and forgotten bodies were leading up to this one moment.

Shit, I've heard sex can be a religious experience, but this is something else.

"Chase," she says, grabbing the side of my face to bring me back to her. I connect our lips, biting down on that bottom lip that's been teasing me all night. She moans into my mouth, her hands roaming up and down my chest. I rake my free hand through her tussled hair while the other latches onto her side, my fingers sprawling out against her hot skin.

It feels like mere seconds before we both go off. It's epic, each of us so worked up that we're pawing at one another, breathing labored, skin covered in sweat.

The two of us have always been at each others throats, but who knew the culmination of the two together would be so epic.

Georgia

"Well, that was -" I pause, unsure how to put it into words.

"It was okay," Chase jokes with a shrug. I shove his face with my palm, as he takes the opportunity to pull me closer to him.

Thank the universe for central air conditioning because summer in New York mixed with sweaty naked bodies is a recipe for sticky discomfort.

"I'm kidding," he whispers against my cheek, before his teeth go to nibble on my ear. "It was epic."

"I guess Ash wasn't wrong when she said we had years of built-up sexual tension between the two of us."

He laughs, it's a deep rumble in my ear, sending goosebumps across my already exposed skin.

"I think I could just lie here forever," I tell him.

"Forget about the world and all our problems."

"We could become recluses like that girl from ABBA."

"Who?"

"You know, the band ABBA. Didn't one of them become a recluse."

"I have literally no clue," he replies.

"Never mind. My point being, we would never have to leave this apartment again, or this bed."

"You'd get sick of me."

I turn, my head facing his on the pillow we're sharing. "You're right. You can be very annoying."

He grins at me. My insides swirl with contentment, happy that despite it all, we've kept our banter.

My stomach takes our moment of silence to let out a deafening grumble, alerting everyone in the East Village that I'm hungry.

"Food?"

"Starved," I reply, reluctantly pulling away from him.

"You shower and I'll order us some Chinese."

"How do you know I even like Chinese?" I say, unable to resist poking him.

He levels me a stare. "Do you like Chinese food, Georgia?"

I smile. "I love it!"

Shaking his head, he walks out of the room, but I see his shoulders move with laughter. I stare unabashedly at his ass.

"And I thought Captain America had a good ass," I mutter to myself.

I waste no time running to the shower to clean up. As I'm washing my hair, I can't help but think about how the old me did just about anything to get away from Chase, and now I'm rushing through sacred personal routines just to get an few extra minutes with him.

"All I'm going to say is if you eat all the orange chicken, I think I'll have to go back to Boston tonight."

I laugh in Chase's face as I pretend to take the last few pieces, before passing the container his way. Relief floods his face as he takes a bite and then splits the final two pieces on each of our plates.

Mine is already overflowing with noodles, rice, eggrolls, and now more orange chicken.

"This is fucking good," he says, leaning back into my leather sofa. It doesn't have the charm or malleability of Ash and Logan's, but I like it. Chase's abs are on display as he rocks low hanging sweats. I know he's done it on purpose to distract me, but he doesn't yet know the power Chinese food holds.

"Right. I can never get all these dishes because I'll never eat them on my own, but now that I've got you, I can have it all."

"I hope I'm good for things other than ordering an entire menu."

I lift a shoulder. "Of course you are! The sex is also a huge benefit."

"You're incorrigible, Georgia Monroe."

I wink before slurping a noodle into my mouth.

"So, how's the coaching gig going?" I know we spoke last night, but I want to know more. We can't possibly catch up months' worth of information in a few hours.

"Surprisingly, I'm really enjoying it. I was a bit apprehensive at first. You know, it had been a while since I'd been on the ice, I'd let myself go a bit. But after some time and routine, it really feels like it was meant to happen. Like if I had to be doing something else, this is it."

"And your leg?" I look toward his pant covered leg like it will give me the answers.

"It's okay. The occasional pain, but that's expected. It will never be what it once was, but I already knew that. I'm at peace with it now. Plus, Coach Robbins has been a mentor to me through it all."

"I'd like to meet him, eventually."

His smile widens at my comment. "I'd like that."

"I've just started at work, but maybe in a few months, I could get some time off to see you."

"I'd love that, but don't push yourself. I know you're new and want to stay in good graces with the higher ups."

I grin. "You know me too well. But we also have weekends. Where there's a will, there's a way."

"It will be okay. Sure, the timing probably couldn't be worse, both of us trying to impress at our new jobs, but we can do it. From what I've gathered, you're close with your boss?"

"Monica? Yeah, she's amazing. We clicked instantly. I'm lucky it all worked out as well as it did. Lord knows in the short-ass time frame I had; I'm surprised I landed on my feet."

"I'm not. I knew you'd be okay."

I say nothing.

"So, you'll be travelling for the next few months?" I try to be casual with the question, but I know Chase catches it, his eyes dropping from my own.

"Yeah, we will. I know it isn't exactly fair on you to ask you to be in this with me when I'm always on the road, but I'm selfish when it comes to you. I want to have my cake and eat it too."

"We can make it work, Chase. As whirlwind and crazy as this entire thing has been, I know if anyone can do it, it's us. I can come visit you on my time off and vice versa. We can handle a handful of months."

"I don't know what I did in this life to deserve you, Monroe. But I'm not going to think twice about accepting all you have to offer."

"The feeling is entirely mutual, Mathews."

Chase and I spend the next day in bed, before I have to go to work on Monday. It's hard to say goodbye, even knowing I'll be seeing him in less than eight hours. I can't imagine how it will be when he really leaves, the thought alone cuts up my insides.

We spend our two final nights together tangled up in one another's mind and body, learning things we didn't get to during our time at Ash and Logan's. Everything is different this time around. An even more intense vulnerability has been exposed between us, an intensity that's hard to describe. In all my years of dating, I've never felt an intimate connection with someone this fast. But then I have to question, is it really that unexpected? We spent weeks in the same house together, only leaving a handful of times. We got to know one another without the pressures of dating, so perhaps, our feelings are not so unusual at all.

"What are you thinking about?" Chase whispers into the night-filled room, his hand rubbing up and down on my uncovered hip.

"Us. This. It's all so unexpected, but when I really think about, it feels like the most natural thing in the world.

"I know what you mean. All my life I've never felt like this about someone, never let myself, if I'm being honest."

"It's scary," I admit, letting my words be swallowed up by the darkness. Sometimes it's easier to admit the truth when no one can see you.

"Fucking terrifying," he confirms. "But also fucking exhilarating. Like freefalling."

I kiss his chest; it's warm against my lips. "Well, if we're going to fall, there is no one I'd rather jump with."

His arm tightens around me, neither one of us speaking until sleep carries us away into its comforting embrace.

Chase left Tuesday night. I kissed and hugged him goodbye. Both of us ignoring the fact we didn't know when we would see one another next. My heart carries a slight ache, mourning the already disrupted start to our relationship. We're supposed to see one another multiple times a week. Call and have the other there in a short period of time. Show up at the other's word. I'm envious of other relationships that get to start out like most should. But I've done that before and I don't want any old love. So I will take this chance with Chase, despite our limited time together.

I'm so slammed at work I don't have much time to sulk, Mon throwing task after task at me. It comforts me, letting my mind be set alight by each and every job.

At lunch, I check in with my parents, having yet to speak to them at all this weekend. I mention Chase, because he is no secret to be kept. In the months following our separation, my father would ask about him, clearly having taken a liking to him. I know it will thrill them both to know he's now my boyfriend.

Ash and Henry are back in Seattle, having opted to spend some time with her mom while Logan has an away game.

I, of course, have been texting with Chase since the moment he left, the idiot continuously sending me memes he thinks I'd like. I'm not one to partake in meme culture, but I laugh at what he sends because I know he thinks of me as he does it.

My phone rings when I'm shoving half a cream cheese bagel in my mouth.

"Hewo," I answer, trying to talk and swallow at the same time.

"You okay over there?" Chase asks, humor filling each word.

I quickly wash my mouth out with water. "Sorry, just on my lunch break. How was the ride back?"

"Yeah fine, just getting set up for practice this afternoon. Coach has had the guys training like crazy while I was away, so he gave them the morning off."

"Big game this weekend?"

"Yeah, playing against Seattle so we'll see what happens. I have faith in the team. How is work going?"

"Not bad. I'm busy, which is good. Keeps my mind occupied."

"I was thinking, I could fly you out to our game next month if you want. Give us a little time together."

"Awe, you missing me already, Mathews?" I tease despite loving the idea.

"Since the moment I got into the car."

"Yeah, well the feeling's mutual. When am I going to see you next?"

"Soon," he promises. "Hold on a sec. There is a delivery here for me to sign for."

I grin, hoping it's what I've sent him. Although time has passed since the flour in my hairdryer incident, I didn't forget.

I hear distant chatter over the phone, but not enough to make out what they're saying. That is until I hear a deep voice roar, "Mathews, is that a fucking dildo?"

Unable to contain myself, a bit of my bagel comes shooting out of my mouth mid-laugh.

"Georgia, you sent me a chocolate dildo?" Chase's voice comes out in hushed tones as he speaks into the phone, clearly mid-way through evacuating his office.

"What, I'm just keeping things spicy, babe."

"What am I going to do with you?" his voice is soft, clearly finding the humor in the moment with me.

"Oh god, I didn't even think you'd open it in front of your boss, but this makes it so much better. I thought your neighbors would laugh at you at most, but god, this is great."

"Aren't these things supposed to have discreet packaging?"

"Oh, babe, not these ones. That's the whole point."

"You know I'm going to get you back for this?" He says.

"Bring it on."

Chase

"You speaking to that new girlfriend of yours, Mathews? I hope she isn't sending you any more dildos."

I turn at the sound of Coach Robbins' voice, as he enters the rink. His dark green eyes filled with humor, constantly busting the balls of anyone around him. I watch him skate over to me, my mind can't help but imagine if he still feels like he did all those years ago when he won the Stanley Cup, three years in a row. It seems like a lifetime ago, but you wouldn't tell by looking at him.

Just shy of fifty-five, he's tall with muscles he's clearly cared for and built his entire career. Sporting a military haircut, he's a scary motherfucker for many, myself included back in the day.

"Yes, Sir, uh, no Sir." I reply, the words naturally falling from my lips.

"You aren't my player anymore, Mathews. Robbins is fine."

"Sorry, habit."

He says nothing, coming over to help me unpack the equipment.

"The boys have been working hard since you left. I reckon we will take it all the way this year with you by our side."

"That means a lot. I know I haven't been here as long you or have even a sliver as much experience, but it's important for me that you know I'm all in. I'm not that kid I was all those years ago."

Back in collage, my university, Breslin, played against Robbin's team. We beat them by a hair, but I was arrogant about it then. Most might not guess it, but I've grown.

"You wouldn't be here if you were still that cocky little shit." He laughs, a deep belly rumble before dismissing the conversation. "Now let's get this shit out so we can finish on time for once and I can go home and see my wife. If I'm late one more time, she might try to divorce me."

I'm quick to get everything done, selfishly also wanting to finish on time. Despite just having spoken to her, I already want to call Georgia again. It's obsessive, like I'm a needy little puppy dog. Or maybe it's romantic? At this point, who the fuck knows; as long as I'm with her, I will take any name given.

Georgia

My days continue on in a daze. Work, speak to Chase, eat, sleep and repeat. They say absence makes the heart grow fonder, I'm tempted to agree. He's coming back to the city this weekend, only having Friday and Saturday night to spend with me. But I have zero doubt we will make the most of it.

I'm hastily putting away my things in order to make it home before Chase arrives. We've got less than 48 hours together and I don't want to waste a second of it.

I yell out a rushed goodbye to Monica, always the last one in the office. She waves farewell, her crystal-encrusted cat eyeglasses focused on an email she's reading.

My feet fly me out the door, immediately pushing against the flow of heavy foot traffic. Each person clearly desperate to get to their next destination, whether it be a bar or the comfort of their own home. After a week at work, it's anyone's guess how people let off steam.

Being in such a rush, I forget to swap my nude pumps for my Adidas sneakers, my pinky toes screaming out with each step I take. I'll pay for it tomorrow, but I can deal. There is nowhere for me to stop now and I'm almost home.

I grin as my building comes into view, a familiar figure with a duffle bag sitting on the front steps.

"Hey, handsome," I call out, breaking into a sprint when his head spins to his left, spotting me.

Chase wastes no time opening his arms, meeting me halfway. I jump into him, my lips instinctively finding his. Pine and peppermint invade my senses, the familiarity of his scent causing me to pull him closer.

"What a welcome," he husks against my mouth before pulling away. His green eyes shine, greedily eating up every inch of me.

I pull away, linking our fingers and walking to the building. He grabs his bag, following me up the cement steps to my tiny little West Village apartment. My feet scream against the pressure of each stride we take, but soon enough, we've reached the third floor and I'm home.

Chase, already familiar with my place, walks a few feet to my bedroom, dropping his bag at the foot of it. I waste no time in pulling off my shoes, immediate relief flooding me.

"Jesus, Monroe, your feet are really red," he says as I massage them.

"No shit, Sherlock. Pain is beauty," I reply.

He just shakes his head, walking over to my open kitchen, if you could even call it that, and pulling out two bottles of water. The space in here is limited to say the least, my mind having contemplated pulling a Carrie Bradshaw and using my oven as shoe storage, but even I couldn't go that far. A girl's gotta eat and only fictional characters have the ability to order out every night on a marketing salary.

"Thanks," I say as Chase passes me a bottle of water before sitting down, pulling my feet onto his lap.

"Stop, they're all sweaty!" I say, mortification lacing my tone.

"I train 20-year-old athletes, now *they* are sweaty. Your little feet are just adorable."

"You're a weirdo," I reply, but accept the free massage. Especially when it starts and I realize how incredible it feels. Okay, he can do this anytime he wants.

"So how was work, honey?" he says in a dated voice.

I burst out laughing. "What is this, the 1950's?" I pull my head up slightly, spotting the grin on his face, before resting it back on the pillow. "Well, darling, work's busy but we like that. Keeps me on my toes and stops my mind from missing this certain someone that I'm dating."

"Well, whoever he is, he sounds like a lucky guy."

"Eh, he's okay. He does have America's ass, though."

"You didn't tell me you were dating Chris Evans."

I burst out laughing as he wears a grin to match my own.

"Well, speaking of this lucky guy, how would you like to meet his parents in two weeks? I've got to go back to Seattle to see them; I thought you might want to come for the weekend?"

My head snaps to him. "Really?"

He nods. "I've met yours; it feels only right."

I bite the inside of my mouth. Meeting the parents is a big deal. This is a big deal.

His face seems to look slightly uneasy at my pause. "Only if you want to. I totally get if it's too soon. Shit, did I jump the gun?"

"Of course, I want to meet your parents, Chase," I add in quickly, trying to reassure him.

I take a sip of my drink before turning back to him. "Can I ask you something?"

He nods.

"That night we went to the bar, you let me win."

His eyes monetarily open, as his head tilts backward. "That's a random question."

"I know, but I always wondered and never asked. So I figured, no time like the present."

"How did you know I let you win?"

"I found the number in your pocket when I was doing laundry," I admit.

"Truthfully? As silly as it may sound, I thought you needed some type of victory, no matter how small."

I don't fight my smile. "That's strangely sweet."

"What can I say, I'm a romantic."

"Pulling out your best moves, huh?"

"For you? Always." He winks and damn if it doesn't make me swoon.

I don't hesitate to pounce on him, forgetting about the food we need to order, the things we need to do.

Because right now, all I need is him.

Our two days together go by in a blur, and before I know it, I'm watching Chase leave again. It's bittersweet: the knowledge that we're not living in the same state and may not for a long while, but also the excitement of what is to come with us.

We spend our time together, locked inside my shoebox apartment. On our third attempt, Elaine finally answers our calls. She tells us she's in love and it must be in the air. I don't disagree.

I watch Chase leave my apartment; my weak ass not strong enough to take him to the airport. It feels like I've just gotten him. Really gotten him. Like the time we spent together in Ash's house was completely wasted not being together.

But it's at these moments I have to remind myself, it's because of that time that we are here. If not for all the horrible events that took us on the path to staying in our friends' Seattle home, we wouldn't be here. Who knows, we'd probably still be spending the rest of our lives biting one another's heads off.

Chase

"I'm nervous," she whispers, her hand clenching mine. It's been two weeks since my weekend trip to New York. Now we're on the way to meet my parents.

"Georgia Monroe, nervous?" I tease, knowing I feel the same as her on the inside.

"What if they don't like me?"

I scoff. "Trust me, they're going to love you."

"What if they compare me to your other girlfriends? I have resting bitch face sometimes, what if they think I'm being rude?"

"You need to calm down, Monroe. For starters, your face looks great, and second, I've never brought a girl home before, so there will be no comparison."

Despite having my eyes glued to the road, I see her head snap to the side. "What do you mean?"

I shrug. "You're the first."

"I'm the first," she whispers to herself, suddenly silent. I lean my free hand across the console to rest it on hers.

We drive the rest of the way in silence, but I don't miss the small smile plastered across her face.

As I predicted, Georgia meeting my parents goes better than I could have expected.

"It's clear she matters to you," my father says, watching Georgia and my mother through the kitchen window. They're sitting on the patio, leaning in to what one another is saying.

"She does," I confirm.

"I've never seen you like this with anyone, Chase."

"It's never been like this."

He nods, his gaze thoughtful as he looks into nothingness.

"I told her about Marie."

At the mention of my birth mother, his head snaps to the side like a whip, surprise etched into his features.

"You told her about Marie?"

"It was before anything even happened between us, but yeah, I did. I guess that should have been the first indicator that it meant more with her."

"I'm proud of you, Chase. I know it is never easy to open up old wounds, let alone share them with others... but I have to say, if there was ever a girl to help you with this burden, it would be her."

"I asked her to go with me. You know, down the line when I'm ready."

My parents have always supported my choice to meet my birth mother. In fact, they used to encourage it before I told them I wasn't ready.

My father's hand comes down on my shoulder, squeezing it.

"I can speak for your mother and myself when I say that sounds like a great plan.

"Would you tell Mom for me? I know she won't be upset with me, but I don't think I will have the time before Georgia and I leave."

"Of course."

"Who wants more cake?"

I turn at the sound of my mom's voice and see Georgia's arm linked with hers. Mom took to her instantly. Both of them having far more in common that I thought.

"I think I could do with a little bit more," my dad says, a grin on his aged face. His previously blond hair has darkened to a salt and pepper, while Mom still rocks her platinum blonde locks.

"Why not," I reply, going over to stand by Georgia. Mom walks away to get the dishes but mouths "I love her" behind me. She's clearly forgetting the mirror in front of her. Georgia sees every word, and the smile on her face tells me everything.

She loves it here as much as I do.

Georgia

The weeks continue on, summer drifting away as the leaves of fall scatter in. If feels like I blinked and we're in September. It's been over two months since Ash and Logan last visited. To say I miss them and Henry is an understatement, but I know my place is here in New York, for now anyway.

When Chase and I went to visit his parents, Ash and Logan were away, yet again, our paths never seeming to cross. I know our distance is just a part of life right now.

As much as I'd like to say fuck it and go be with Chase, he isn't stagnant himself. Plus, I can't live my life following him around.

Unlike Ash, who can write when Logan is on the road, my job has a base, and that base is New York. And for that I'm happy. For the first time in forever, I finally feel at peace, all elements of my life seemingly coming into place.

It's coming up on the final few months of Chase's season as an assistant coach. So I do what any good girlfriend would do. Go behind his back to surprise him. I made up some bullshit excuse on why I couldn't make it out to the game. He told me it was fine, but I heard the disappointment in his voice.

"Is it all set?" Ash asks as I throw my purse over my shoulder, darting around the hundreds of bodies that fill the hotel lobby.

"Yep!" I say with a pop.

"I've got the key to his room, thanks to you and Logan. Let's just say Chase is going to be one happy guy when he finds me in his bed."

"I still can't believe you checked into the hotel naked," Ash says through the phone.

"Hey, I'm not *naked,* naked. I'm wearing a trench coat."

"This is so very scandalous of you, Georgia Monroe."

"It will be worth it, seeing his face. We haven't seen one another in nearly a month. I wanted tonight to be epic."

"I'm sure with the two of you involved, it will be fireworks and all."

"Don't you know it."

I'm grinning ear to ear even thinking about it. His game is tomorrow, but everyone arrived yesterday to party their asses off tonight. But I know Chase. He's taken this position seriously; he'll be in his room for the night. My mind can't help but drift back to how he was before all of this. The old Chase would have partied until the early hours of the morning but still kicked ass on the ice. But people have to grow up sometimes.

That doesn't mean we can't have fun in the meantime.

My black stilettos call out against the marble lobby floor, one hand holding my purse while the other has my overnight suitcase.

I have to give them credit, this hotel is not too shabby at all. Not that I'll be seeing much of it if I have anything to say about it.

I wait by the elevator, the up arrow glowing as it lands back on the lobby level. A gentleman with silver hair holds the door open for me, quick to ask me my floor number.

"Ten," I reply as he punches the button for me before pressing his own. "Thanks."

He just smiles at me, before turning to face the doors. It feels like the ascent upward takes hours, the anticipation of finally seeing Chase killing me. It's crazy to think I went five months without seeing him once, but now even a few weeks apart cause my insides to twist like a tornado.

I'm exiting the floor when I hear raised voices coming from Chase's room. It's muffled, not exactly yelling, but it's clear he's agitated. I don't hesitate to slip my key into the lock, pushing open the door and finding a stern-faced Chase standing by the door.

His body is quick to turn to me, clearly ready to yell at whoever has entered. But to my surprise, all the color drains from his face at my appearance.

"Surprise!" I say, but it lacks conviction.

"Georgia?" He stays in place, eyes wide, his head quickly darting to the side of the room hidden by the wall. I'm no fool, I've dated enough men to know when they're hiding something. So instead of running into his arms and pulling off my coat like

I'd planned, I march past him, the sight on the other side not one I'd ever expect.

Sprawled out on his bed is a naked woman, her long blonde hair spilling down, practically covering her exposed breasts. A smile sweet as sin lines her cherry red lips when our gazes connect.

"And you are?" She has the audacity to ask.

"Now, Georgia, this isn't what it looks like." Chase's panicked voice says from behind me, but I'm having trouble hearing him from all the smoke coming out of my ears.

"I literally just got back to the room and she was here."

"Baby," the girl on the bed whines, "don't play shy just because this boring Betty is here. I'm sure we could make things interesting enough for her to join."

I'm silent, body stiff. Pure rage flowing through my body, seemingly unable to process what I'm seeing.

"Shut up," Chase snaps. "I swear to god, Georgia. You know me, I have no idea who this woman is." I silence him with a hand. Clearly sensing this woman's impending doom, he shuts up.

I walk over to the minibar, grabbing the knife from the silverware pile, clearly leftover from Chase's room service last night.

"I will give you five seconds to get your filthy slutty ass out of my boyfriend's bed, before I rip out those shitty extensions and jam a butter knife so far up your ass, it comes out your mouth." My voice is low, but each word said with grit. I don't need a mirror to see the fire behind my eyes, knowing full well I'm okay with going crazy girlfriend on this bitch.

"I'd listen to her," Chase says.

She looks between the two of us, the smirk no longer tracing her balloon lips. As if accepting this is a losing battle, she scurries off the bed, grabbing her black dress from the floor. I don't take my eyes off her as she exits.

"Now Georgia, I know you're angry, but can you put the butter knife down and talk about this?"

I look down at my hand. It's turning red from the grip I have on my weapon of choice. I let out a yell as I toss it across the room, out of Chase's way.

"Georgia." He says my name once more, taking a step towards me.

I shake my head, attempting to keep my tears at bay.

I will not cry.

"Don't," I whisper, "Just don't."

"I swear, Georgia, nothing happened."

"Shut up, Chase! Just shut the fuck up for once in your life." I snap, and along with that, goes my control over my emotions. My hands are quick to wipe away my escaped tear, but I know if I don't get out of here soon, there will be many more to come. And despite previously wanting to be around Chase, I can't think of anything worse right now.

"I need to go," I mutter, keeping my stare straight ahead. I simply can't look at him because I will crumble or say something I don't mean if I do. I'm just so fucking angry right now.

He tries to reach for me, but I shake him off. "Don't follow me. I mean it." My words are firm despite my voice cracking at the end.

Thankfully, he heeds my warning, not chasing me as I leave the room. My hands shake as I press the elevator button, yet I'm thankful that skank has vacated the floor. Otherwise, who knows what I would do.

I should probably call Ash, lord knows she would understand what I'm going through, but I stop myself. Because I don't want to be comforted right now, I just want to get my own room and sulk. Then I'll be on the first train out of here tomorrow.

Three hours and a shit ton of room service later, I decide to call Ash. Finally, I've slightly calmed down, the anger having faded into sadness.

"Oh, G, I'm so sorry."

"I don't know what to do, Ash. I know he'd never do anything, but I don't want to have to constantly worry about other women."

"I know, and as much as I hate to say it, it's part of the territory. Probably less for Chase now he's out of the game, but as today has shown you, it can still happen."

"I don't think I'm strong enough to deal with that. I mean, I nearly killed them both today, and I know it wasn't his fault, but I was just so fucking angry. Like how did he get himself into this position?"

"It's okay to be mad at him, G, but don't let it ruin everything you two have together. Plus, if the amount of calls

Logan and I have gotten over the past few hours mean anything, he clearly realizes how fucked up this is."

"He's called you?" I ask.

"Yep, at least a dozen times."

I sniffle, "He's been calling me too, but I've just sent him to voicemail."

"I can't force you to talk to him, G. But think about calling him back, let him explain before you leave tomorrow."

"I'll think about it," I promise her.

We hang up, Ash clearly sensing I'm in no mood to speak anymore. I pull the duvet over my head, hoping to block out the memories of this afternoon and all that came with it.

Yet no reprieve comes my way, as someone knocks on my door only moments after my eyes shut.

"Coming," I yell, already annoyed at whoever has disturbed me. Yet my annoyance is quick to turn into anger when I see Chase outside.

"How did you find my room?" I grumble as I eye him. His shirt is wrinkled, hair sticking up like he's run his hands through it a few times.

"The woman at the front desk is a fan," he admits with a weak smile.

"Ah, so that's probably how that skank got into your room. Good to know this will be an ongoing issue for us."

"Georgia," he says, reaching out for me. I rip my arm away, knowing I'm not ready for any sort of affection from him.

"Can we at least talk about this? You can't possibly think anything happened between the two of us."

I lift a shoulder.

Hurt splashes across his face.

Of course, I know nothing happened between them, but that doesn't mean I have to let him off easily.

"Tell me you're joking?" His voice is no longer soft, instead filled with what I suspect is a slight annoyance at me.

"You don't get to be annoyed at me," I yell. "I'm the one who gets to be upset here. I'm the one who walked in on you and a naked woman!"

"She broke into my room!" His hands wave in the air as he speaks, slight speckles of red dotting his cheeks. "I know how it seems, I get that. And trust me, if the situation was reversed, I'm sure I'd be as pissed as you are. But right now, Georgia, this is one of those times that will make or break a relationship. So even though you're angry and hurt, I need you to trust me. I need you to know I'd never betray you like that."

And that does it.

Like a small child, I burst out into tears in front of him. He wastes no time pulling me into his arms, his warmth instantly surrounding me.

"I'm sorry," he whispers into my hair. "I'm so fucking sorry."

I say nothing. Instead, I just let him hold me.

"You ready to talk about it?"

I peer up at Chase, both of us lying next to one another in bed. It's still only early afternoon, yet it feels like midnight.

"I know nothing happened. I've heard enough of these types of stories from Ash. But fuck," I run my hands through my hair, "I'm allowed to be upset by it. I mean, how did she even get in there?" I turn to him, his face ashen.

"I don't know. I was trying to find that out along with getting her the hell out of my room when you walked in." He tries to keep his voice even, but I hear the distress in it.

"This happens a lot, doesn't it?"

His head snaps to mine, fear coating his eyes, like perhaps I'm contemplating throwing in the towel.

"It has been known to happen. Not usually to assistant coaches, but I was a player before anything else. This kind of behavior is common from some fans."

"Great," I mutter.

He reaches out, brushing his hand through my hair. "Georgia, I'm sorry. This shouldn't have happened. I will make sure it doesn't again. I'm not that guy I was in college. I don't want you to have to worry about things like this when we're not together."

"I know," I whisper, annoyed that the bitch ruined my big surprise more than anything. It's hard to feel sexy when Slutty Barbie has just been naked in front of us. "I just want to find her and rip all her extensions out."

He stifles a laugh.

"I'm serious! You'd think that if she was going to seduce one of the hottest ex-NHL players, she would have put in a little more effort rather than 6-week-old extensions."

"Yeah, I have no clue what any of that means, but you know I agree. Now, can we finally have our proper hello that was so rudely taken from us?"

I'm quick to lean into him, meeting his mouth halfway. I don't have to wait long until I'm intoxicated by his scent. His warm hands wrapping around my waist, pulling me on top of him.

"I've missed you so much, Monroe," he says against my lips. I deepen the kiss in reply.

"And I hate to be a buzzkill, but I've got practice with the guys in an hour."

I grin against his mouth. "Then we better make it quick."

Chase

I walk down to practice, feeling much better than a few hours ago when I found that woman in my bed. When Georgia walked in, I thought for sure it was over. She would kill the girl then come for me. I just thank the fucking universe that isn't the case.

I didn't expect to see my little firecracker so soon. My insides were gutted when she told me she couldn't make it this weekend, but I didn't let it show. It's getting harder and harder as the months trickle by, not being in the same state. But the fact that my feelings for her only continue to grow, well, that tells me how real this all is.

I'm lingering dangerously close to a feeling I've only ever heard about, shit, perhaps I'm already there. But it's only been a few months, the last thing I need is to freak Georgia out with big words and feelings, causing her to run off.

"Hey Coach M, practice in five?" One of my players, Jenson, calls to me as he passes me in the hall.

"Yep, we're meeting out front for the bus, don't be late. And make sure to bring Colson with you, that kid can't make it on time to save his life."

Jenson just laughs, turning the corner. I continue on, out of the hotel lobby, spotting Coach Robbins outside by our bus.

"I spotted Jenson in the hall, told him to round up Colson," I say on approach.

"I'm doubling warmup if they're even a minute late."

I can't help but think back to when I was in their position. "Fair enough," I reply, situating my duffle on my shoulder. The amount of shit I've managed to jam into this one bag is astounding.

"Go sit down. I can make sure they're all on the bus," I tell Coach. He grunts in thanks before stepping up, taking the first seat on his left.

It isn't long until the players start spilling out, no surprise that Jenson and Colson are nearly late. They make it by one minute, clearly not wanting to get on anyone's bad side this weekend.

I'm quick to follow the guys onto the bus, my mind attempting to get my head in the game. Too bad it keeps drifting off to thoughts of the blonde bombshell in the hotel room.

It's late when I finally get back to the room. Practice ran long then we decided to get dinner as a team. No matter how badly I wanted to hightail it out of there to be with Georgia, these guys are my commitment this weekend.

"Someone's back late," Georgia remarks, voice low and sleepy. I attempt to tiptoe around the dark room, but for a bigger guy, that isn't exactly easy. As my foot smacks into the edge of her suitcase, I attempt to bite back every fucking curse word in the English language.

"You can turn on a light." Each word is slightly slurred, like she's fighting against sleep, her head still buried so deep into her pillow, I wonder if she will ever come out.

Slipping into the bathroom, I take the world's quickest shower before pulling on my briefs and sliding into bed next to her. She mutters something incoherently before turning, her warm face burrowing into my chest.

I waste no time, slipping my arms around her, pulling her into me. She's passed out to the world, just the sound of her small snores echoing in the room. I bury a laugh, thinking about how mad she would get if I told her she snored. Maybe I will save that for a rainy day.

I lie there with her in my arms, and everything feels far too natural, far too right. Like everything in my life has been leading up to these little moments with her right where she is, right where she belongs. I may not know a lot about life, but I know I'll do whatever it takes to keep Georgia Monroe in mine.

Georgia

I fight against the cheering fans to find Chase. I spot him next to Coach Robbins, face red from the game, but a smile due to the victory. Robbins, who I met and loved earlier, pats him on the back before walking over to the cheering players and fans.

Chase's head looks around before connecting with my gaze. He wastes no time pushing through everyone to get to me.

"You did it!" I yell, throwing myself into his arms. Despite not being one of the players, he's sweaty and worked up. I guess coaching is just as, if not more, stressful than playing.

He kisses me. It's deep and passionate, and despite being surrounded by hundreds of people, he manages to make me feel like I'm the only one in the room.

"You killed it out there, Mathews," I tell him pulling away. "I can see why you love this so much, it's a high."

He beams at me, clearly loving that I've finally been able to come to a game. "It is, right?"

"Yo, Coach, is that your girlfriend? You didn't tell us she was such a stunner!" A huge player tackles Chase, my mind instantly going to his knee, but Chase stands firm.

"Jensen, this is Georgia."

Jenson takes off his helmet, his black hair sweaty against his skin. He's handsome, yet his face is youthful, probably not older than twenty.

"Pleased to meet you, Georgia." He winks at me and I have to stop myself from laughing.

"Nice to meet you," I reply as Chase shakes his head.

"Don't you have a victory to celebrate," Chase adds in, moving to slide right next to me.

Jensen chuckles, before saluting us and returning to his friends.

"They clearly love you," I tell him, nuzzling into his side.

He tries to shrug it off, but I don't let it go. "I'm serious, Chase. You mean something to these guys. You may not acknowledge it, but you're shaping their lives. You matter."

His response is to pull me in closer, his head resting on mine as we're swarmed with other players whose lives are being changed by the guy right next to me.

*

Chase

I drag my hand up and down Georgia's bare side, appreciating every moment we get together.

"It's not fair that this isn't our regular," I say into the dark room.

"I know," she whispers to me, her breath warm against my chest. "But it's the reality we're working with. And isn't it better to have these small stolen moments together than nothing at all?"

I nod, knowing she can't see, but she can feel me. Despite not admitting it, the distance between us has been harder on me this past month than before.

Clearly sensing something, she pulls away from my side, looking me in the eyes, the dim lights of the city illuminating our hotel room.

"Hey, what's wrong?"

"Nothing," I reply, but the lie is weak and she can tell.

"Even when it hurts, you can be real with me, Chase. I always want that for us, so no matter what happens moving forward, let's just be honest."

"Even when it hurts?" I ask.

She nods. "Always."

"It's harder than I thought it would be," I admit.

"I know," she replies, voice gravelly. "But with us, I don't think it was ever going to be easy.

I pull myself upward, not wanting to talk lying down. My back leans against the headboard as she watches me, waiting for me to finish.

"I was so desperate to have you, I think I just assumed everything would be so easy, you know? And I don't want you to think for a second I regret any of this, I don't. But it's because of how well it's all going that I think it's harder."

I take a breath, grabbing her hand to have some form of an anchor. "It's the little things, like when I roll over in bed at night and all I want is for you to be there. Or waking up in the morning. Small things like going to the movies alone or going out to eat."

"It can be isolating," she replies, taking the words out of my mouth.

"You feel it too?" The thought that I'm not the only one overwhelms me.

"I feel it every day," she replies. "When I've had a bad day at work and go home to an empty apartment. Or even when I have a good day. Or when I catch your games on TV and you guys win, there is nothing I want more than to be in the stands cheering you on." Her eyes shut while her voice cracks.

"I wish there was some easy solution for all of this," I say, reaching for her.

"It won't always be like this. Eventually, we will figure all this shit out. For now, we just need to be thankful for moments like this one."

"You're right."

We settle back into the comfort of the bed, of one another's arms.

"Chase?

"Yeah?"

"Let's not keep these things from one another. If we're ever feeling lonely, we are only a phone call away, okay?"

"Okay, Monroe."

Georgia

It's been nearly a month since I've seen Chase. Again. While our time together at his away game was short-lived, I loved every second of it. Well, almost all of it. That naked psycho wasn't exactly great, but why dwell on the little things?

I'm thinking of him at my desk when I hear Monica's voice.

"Uh, Georgia, I think there is someone here to see you out front."

"Okay," I tell her, getting up. I rack my mind, coming up empty of who it could be. Despite having lived here for nearly a year, I don't know anyone well enough to visit me at work.

My heels click against the laminate floor as I round the corner of the office, heading toward the main entryway. The man standing by the velvet sitting chairs is the last person I expected to see this week, especially considering the state he's in.

"Chase?" I say, surprise coloring my tone.

He turns around, his eyes have bags under them, his hair slightly ruffled, like perhaps he's run his hands through it one too many times.

He wastes no time, crossing the room between us. I'm in his arms before I know it, his lips on my own. Warmth instantly washes over me, along with comfort, something I've only ever felt with him.

I manage to push my concern to the side, embracing his kiss, before remembering I'm in my place of work. I pull back, quickly glancing around to make sure no one else is in the room. When I know we're okay, I take his hands, pulling him over to the sitting area.

"Chase, what's going on?"

He bites down on his bottom lip, our hands still linked as he looks me over.

"I've missed you, Monroe."

I can't help but smile because I feel the same. Despite my initial attempts, it's clear how attached I've become to him. The L word appearing more and more in my mind as the days go by.

"I've missed you too, but I didn't expect to see you so soon."

He nods. "I know. I have the weekend off and was going to surprise you," he exhales, "I need to ask you something."

"Okay."

"I want to go see my birth mother, and I want to go this weekend."

My eyes widen, his panicked state making more sense. "And you want me to go with you?" I finish what I already know he's asking.

He pulls his hands back, his eyes closing briefly. "I know it's last minute and you're in the middle of work, I just -"

I cut him off by holding up my hand. "I just need to finish up here. I should be another hour, then we can go."

His head snaps around. "Really?"

"Always."

He opens his mouth like he wants to speak, but no words come out. He moves his mouth a few more times before a sense of realization seems to wash over him. An understanding.

"You'd really do it? Drop everything for me?"

"That's what you do for the people you care for." I look down toward my lap, my voice dropping slightly. "I mean, you'd do the same for me."

It's phrased like a statement, but inside, I'm desperate for it to be a question for him to answer.

"In a heartbeat, Monroe."

We stare at one another, an invisible link appearing to wrap around both of our hearts, tying us together in this moment. It's a bond that I don't think either one of us have ever felt.

The moment is broken when Monica exits her office, calling for me. I wink at Chase before slipping out of the sitting area, back to my desk.

"Hey, Mon," I say, catching her before she slips out for the weekend.

"Would it be okay if I left at four today?"

Since coming here, I've been a dream employee, not wanting to fuck up. That means coming in early and leaving late. So, I'm hopeful my request won't go ignored. Plus, Mon is a friend, and I've never asked for any favors before.

"Georgia, I'll get Mac to cover the rest of your day. Go spend the weekend with your handsome man now."

"Really?" I ask. "I'm really fine finishing up by four."

She smiles softly at me, her rouge painted lips curving upward. "I may not be actively searching for love myself, but I know it when I see it. You and that man out there have something special. I wouldn't waste a second of it talking me into letting you stay at work an hour longer than you need to."

She turns her attention back to her laptop screen. "Now scoot before I go out there and ask him out."

"Thank you!" I half-speak, half-squeal as I beeline to the entryway, my mind quick to ignore her mention of love.

I'm quick to pack up my desk, handing off the rest of my work to Mac. Thankfully, she doesn't seem to mind. But at this point, I'd still leave even if she did.

"Change of plans," I tell Chase, catching him off guard. "We can go now." His head shoots up.

"Really? What about work?"

"I just happen to have the world's best boss! Now come on before she changes her mind." I grab his hand, practically hauling him out of the office into the buzzing afternoon sidewalk.

We weave in and out of the pedestrian traffic, our hands staying firmly glued together. "I just need to go home and grab a few things. Do you have a bag packed?"

He nods his head. "Just this one on me."

I look down, finally seeing the small duffle in his hand.

"What about flights? Do we need to book?"

"I kinda already booked them."

"Presumptuous much?" I tease.

He grins, his hand squeezing mine as we continue on our way. It's not long before we're back at my apartment, and I'm packing. As I do so, I realize how crazy this all seems. Chase showing up at my work, me leaving early to spend a weekend in Vegas tracking down his birth mother. The whole thing is bananas, yet also very in character for us. Instead of overthinking it, I pick the few things I think I will need and place them in my duffel.

My mind instantly calculates how long this will all take. There is no way I will be back in the city by Monday morning. To be safe, I need to call Mon later and ask for a few days leave. I'm risking my ass for this, but I can tell Chase needs me.

"What time is our flight?" I call out.

"Not till seven."

I take a deep breath, the hysterics of the afternoon bleeding out of me. I know I need to get to the bottom of what has triggered Chase wanting to see his birth mother, but now is clearly not the time.

We arrive at the airport an hour and a half before our flight. I opt to grab a Starbucks while Chase gets a burger. His hand doesn't let mine go, only pulling away to eat. But even then, he lets one linger on my thigh. Like he needs the reassurance that I'm here. That I'm not going anywhere.

"Hey, it's gonna be okay," I say, finally breaking our spell of silence.

He turns to me, his usually vibrant eyes slightly dimmed, while bits of stubble line his jaw.

"Talk to me, Chase."

Taking a deep breath, he closes his eye before positioning his body toward me. "I don't even know what to say, G. I know how frantic this all seems. Me showing up in the city when I live in Boston and pulling you away for the weekend." He shakes his head, staring off into nothingness.

"Did something happen?" I ask, voice soft amongst the chatter and speakerphones of JFK.

"One of my players, Jenson, his mom died."

My stomach clenches, but I stay silent, my hand on his leg being both our lifelines.

"His mom died and all I could think about is what if that happened to me. What if my birth mom died before I even got to meet her? I mean, I've known where she is for years and I've just been too fucking scared to do anything about it. I'm still fucking terrified, Georgia. And I just thought to myself as I sat alone in my room last night. If you don't do this now, you're never going to do it. And I know myself, I'd always regret it."

My head moves up and down on instinct.

"So, I packed a bag and caught the first bus to New York. I just knew in my gut that I had to go this weekend. I texted her out of the blue, I'm shocked she even replied. I basically word vomited that I was her kid and I wanted to see her. She said okay, but not much else. I just had to get it out before I had the chance to overthink it all and run away again."

"I can't pretend to understand what you're going through, Chase. But I respect it. And I'm honored you wanted me to be on this journey with you. I want you to know I'd go anywhere with you."

He pulls me in close, his head resting on mine. It's intimate and personal. Saying everything our mouths can't say right now.

"It's going to be okay," I whisper to him. "I've got you."

Chase

I'm a ball of panic. It's the only way to describe my emotions. Thankfully, I've got Georgia with me to calm me down. Just being near her manages to tide over the frenzy of emotions I'm battling.

She's sleeping next to me on the plane, her head resting on my shoulder. The only sound around us is the faint humming of the plane and whispered chatter of those not wanting to sleep.

It's the first time in 24 hours I've managed to calm myself. It feels as if I've been on fast forward since yesterday. Since the thought of my birth mother popped into my head and I couldn't stop thinking about her. And when I officially decided I had to go this weekend, I knew I needed my girl by my side.

I don't know how to describe it, but since Georgia came into my life, it's like she's pressed play on everything. I was living in this permanent state of pause. On my career, my social life, my family. And her mere presence alone has jolted me into action.

I don't have the slightest idea what is going to happen moving forward, but I know having her next to me is all I need to keep going.

"Chase."

I feel a jab on my shoulder and hear a voice echo in my head. "Chase, wake up, we're here."

Slowly peeling my eyes open, I spot a wide-awake Georgia staring at me.

"We're here already?" I ask, sleep coating my words. It feels like just seconds ago I finally rested my eyes.

"Come on, sleepy head. The sooner we're off this plane, the sooner we can go to sleep at the hotel."

I stand from the tiny space, attempting to stretch my cramped muscles. Georgia already has both our bags in her hands, clearly ready to get out of here as soon as possible.

"I got it," I tell her, reaching for the bags, but she brushes me off, securing them on her shoulders before stepping into the aisle with everyone else. I'm quick to follow her, not wanting to be trapped, waiting for parents with kids and the elderly to get off first.

Despite my sleepy state, I'm quick to slip in behind her, thankful we didn't check any of our bags when we get off the plane.

"Uber or taxi?" she asks as we walk into the cool night.

"Taxi?"

"Agreed, let's just get out of here."

We waste no time hailing down the first one we see, both of us slipping into the back seat.

"The Bellagio, thanks," I tell the driver.

Georgia turns to me, her face illuminated by the swirl of traffic as we drive. "We're staying on the strip?"

"I figured we might as well be somewhere fun in case this all goes to shit."

"It's not going to go to shit. But either way, we're gonna make the best of it."

Her hand lands on my own, squeezing it as we dart through traffic.

I just sure as shit hope she's right. Because I don't know if I can handle the disappointment.

We arrive at the hotel, just in time to order some room service and binge mindless TV. Despite trying to stay awake, around midnight, Georgia eventually falls asleep in my arms. As much as I'd love to plunge into slumber like her, my mind keeps going over every possibility of how tomorrow could go.

I've waited twenty-six years for this moment and in less than 24 hours, it will finally come to fruition. I guess we never really know what the hell tomorrow will offer, we just have to take the leap and hope we don't fucking fall.

I feel far from ready, but perhaps in these situations, you never really are. With my racing thoughts, I close my eyes, hoping to get any reprieve sleep will offer.

Chase

"It's going to be okay."

Georgia's voice cuts through the silence that has filled the car like a thick layer of smog. It's the first thing either of us has said since we picked up the rental and started driving an hour ago. I know it isn't fear that's kept her quiet; Georgia doesn't shy away from speaking her mind, a little awkward silence won't stop her. So, when she finally says something, five minutes away from our destination, I know to listen.

"No matter how this turns out, it will be okay. It might be great, or it could hurt like hell, but either way, you will get through this."

I nod, while keeping my eyes on the road, passing the desert with each mile we drive.

"Georgia, I know I might not say it enough, but all of this, I couldn't do it -"

"You don't need to say it," she says, cutting me off, "there is nowhere else I'd rather be than here with you in this moment."

"Shit, there is no one else I'd rather have with me," I say back. Since being with Georgia, she's managed to unlock a part of my emotions I never thought I'd see.

Her response is to link her fingers with my free hand. I squeeze hers back, attempting to soak up every bit of her warmth.

Despite only being five minutes away, the rest of the drive feels like a lifetime, the weight of what's to come heavy on my shoulders.

"Umm Chase," Georgia cuts in as I drive right by the white house surrounded by an aged picket fence. "I think you missed the house."

"Just going to do a lap," I reply, continuing to drive.

"Do as many as you need."

I proceed to pass the house three more times before actually getting the courage to stop in front of it. I park our rental Volkswagen behind a beat-up Toyota, quick to make sure I don't ding it.

"I think I might be scared," I admit aloud.

"It's perfectly normal to be afraid. Doing this takes courage."

With the engine off, I finally turn to the house, taking it all in. Peeling white paint coats the outside, yet it's still incredibly homey. There's a lush garden full of roses and perfectly trimmed grass. It lacks the grandeur of the neighborhood I grew up in, but I think that makes me like it even more. Not having everything be so incredibly flashy all the time.

"I think I'm ready," I say, at the same time the front door is pulled open. A woman with short light brown hair walks out, wearing a tee shirt and jeans. Her hands rub up and down her sides as she gazes down the street, probably looking for our car. I doubt she knows what I look like, considering she's had no photographs, but looking at her now, even from a distance, it's hard to deny we look similar.

"She looks just like you," Georgia whispers from next to me. Her voice is thick, taking on the emotion I'm feeling.

"She looks so young," I find myself saying as I try to study her from afar. Her stare still off in the opposite direction to us.

"She can't be more than forty."

"In my head, I guess I just imagined her being older, you know? With gray hair and wearing an apron." I laugh at the ridiculous image of her that I had in my head, the reality being more than slightly different than I imagined.

"I guess I did too," Georgia says.

"I shouldn't leave her standing there; I think it's time to go in."

"Do you want me to give you two some time alone? I can wait in the car if you want."

My grip on her hand tightens. "I need you with me."

"Then let's go."

Marie's head turns in our direction when our doors slam shut, her green eyes mirroring my own as they widen.

Side by side, Georgia and I enter the gate, Marie not having moved from her spot.

"Uh, hi, Marie?" I say, suddenly feeling like a twelve-year-old boy again. No confidence or conviction in my movements.

"Chase." My name falls off her lips like a prayer as she attempts to take me in. Big green eyes tracking every inch of me.

"Yeah," I confirm, then quickly clear my throat. I bite my cheek, giving myself some form of distraction as I'm completely lost for words.

"I'm Georgia, it's lovely to meet you, Marie." Seemingly understanding how lost for words I am, Georgia steps in, extending her manicured hand.

Marie, clearly grateful for the interruption, is quick to shake her hand before stepping back, once again. "Would you both like to come in? I've made some sweet tea." There is an element of fear in her voice, like perhaps I will reject her and leave. It's in this instant I realize, I'm not the only one who was afraid. She probably has more to fear than I do.

"Um, yeah. That sounds great," I reply, voice finally gaining some control. I'm determined to make this as pleasant as possible, none of us should be on edge. Yet, I'm on the fucking edge.

"Let's go," Georgia says, linking her hand with mine as we follow Marie's retreating form up her small set of wooden steps.

I trip over my own foot as we begin to walk. "Shit," I mutter. Georgia shoots me a look. "Shit, sorry, I shouldn't swear."

Marie briefly turns around to face me, as she opens the door.

"Fuck, I did it again. Sorry, lead the way."

Upon entering the home, it's clear how cared for it is. The front door opens into a narrow hallway, its cream paint stark against the wooden floors. The occasional painting, all similar in style, line the walls. A mahogany staircase sits at the end of the hall while two open archways are on the right side of it. The first, which we enter, opens into a small living room, filled with similar art as before. I spot a paint splattered easel in the far corner, a detailed work of floral arrangements sitting upon it, clearly midway through creation. I surmise that the art has all been done by Marie, her talent clear.

A cream-colored couch sits in the middle of the room, a green ottoman in front with a silver tray on top.

"Please, take a seat, I'll grab the tea," Marie says, gesturing to the sofa before exiting the room. I'm assuming that second doorway leads to the kitchen when I hear clattering coming from the next room.

"She seems nice," Georgia says, her hand still linked with mine. Leading me to the sofa, we sit down, my back sinking into the plush pillows.

"If I swear one more time, she might jump out of her skin. I can't tell who is more nervous, her or me."

"From the sound of the plates clattering in the other room, I'd say her."

I laugh, if anything, to relieve some tension. "Yeah, I think you're right. God, I feel so stupid. I don't even know what to say."

"Hey," Georgia's fingers trace the side of my mouth before she leans forward, brushing a brief kiss across my lips, "there is no formula for this. Shit like this doesn't happen every day, you're not supposed to follow some script. Just be yourself, be honest, and she will love you, if she doesn't already."

"I don't know why I'm acting like a fumbling idiot," I admit. "I feel like a scared little boy."

Before Georgia can reply, Marie is back, the tray she is carrying, filled with baked goods and a pitcher of iced tea, shakes with her every step. I'm quick to jump up, taking it from her before placing it down on the ottoman. She gives me a grateful smile before filling three glasses and handing one to each of us.

Her small frame sits down on the floral armchair across from us, her hands wringing in knots as she watches us.

"This is delicious," Georgia replies after taking a huge sip.

"Thank you," Marie replies before her eyes quickly dart to me then back to Georgia. At this point, these two have said more to one another than I have to her. I need to pull it together and take Georgia's advice.

"It's really good," is all I come up with. Again, I'm greeted with a smile.

There is a slight silence lingering in the air as the three of us sit in this well-loved living room. Poor Marie looks as if she's about to split open with nerves.

"So, uh, I'm sure you're wondering why I'm here," I begin, deciding to jump off the cliff before I second-guess myself.

Her head bobs up and down.

"Obviously, I got your information seven years ago when I turned eighteen. I'm sorry I didn't contact you earlier, *hell*, I didn't even know if you would want to know me."

"I did," she says so quickly I nearly miss it. My body relaxes at her words, giving me the confidence I need to keep going.

"I'm glad," I say genuinely. "I wanted to know you. I just wasn't ready then. But I am now and it's important for me that you know I hold no ill will toward you. I don't know much about your life, Marie; in fact, I know nothing, but the life I was lucky enough to be given, the parents I have, it's all thanks to you. So I just wanted to say thank you. And if you're willing, get to know you."

"You're thanking me?" She repeats my words, an air of astonishment laced through each one.

"Yes. I don't know why you had to give me up, but even from being in your presence for ten minutes, I can tell you didn't make that choice lightly. So yes, thank you for giving me the best shot at life I could have had."

A lone tear tracks down her makeup free face. She is quick to wipe it away.

"All these years, I worried you would hate me for what I did. After you turned eighteen, I waited for you to contact me. To demand the truth about why I left you. But after the first year went by, I gave up hope that you'd come. I just assumed it was my penance for giving you up, that I'd never get to meet you, or know who you became."

I squeeze my free hand together in a weak attempt to get my emotions in check. The thought of her thinking I hated her for twenty-five years gnaws at my insides like a cancer.

"I never once hated you."

"That means the world to me to hear, you have no idea." She pauses, finally taking a sip of her drink. "I'd love to know about your life, what you have been up to."

I waste no time filling her in on my childhood, my lifelong love of hockey, all leading up to my time with Georgia. The more I speak, the more she relaxes, both of us letting go of any preconceived notions we had about one another. By the time I'm finished, we're laughing like old friends. Instead of her feeling like a parental figure, it's more a comfortable friendship, something I think we both need.

"Well, it seems like I left you in great hands, Chase. I'm not sure you could have had a better life."

"I got very lucky," I reply. "If you don't mind me asking, what about you, Marie? Have you had a good life?"

"I have in a way. I lead a very solitary life, but it's the way I like it. I was sixteen when I got pregnant with you. I was raised by a single mom and we didn't have a lot. It just made sense to us that you should be given the best shot out there and when I was honest with myself, I knew I couldn't give you that. It wasn't even about money; I was so young and I wasn't ready. Even if you had hated me, I would still never regret giving you up. I know that might sound harsh, but in my heart of hearts, I knew I made the right choice. Now, seeing you, hearing you, I know it more than ever."

I expected her words to hurt me, but they give me peace more than anything. "Can I ask, and tell me if I'm overstepping, but what about my birth father?"

Guilt flashes across her face, her eyes breaking contact with my own. "I wish I could tell you more about him. He was someone I met at a party one night; he was older, probably in his twenties. Had no desire for a kid, laughed at me when I told him I was pregnant. I'm sorry, I know that's probably not the response you were hoping to hear. If you want to find him, I'm sure I can get his information from someone, I know his name."

"No," I cut in, "he had his chance, as far as I'm concerned, he's a sperm donor and nothing more. I'm just glad I found you."

She nods, clearly grateful she doesn't have to dig up that part of her past.

"So, you paint?" I ask, gesturing to the easel.

Her face lights up. "It's just a hobby, but it keeps me busy. I teach art at the local middle school, so I'm always trying to find new things to bring to my classroom. And when I'm not with the kids, I volunteer at the local community center. I've got a class with them this afternoon."

"You're really talented, Marie," Georgia says from next to me. She's been so silent this whole time, one might forget she's there, but not me. Her hand on my leg has kept me anchored.

For the next hour, our conversation drifts from personal to casual. I learn that her mother passed away ten years back and left her this house. I tell her all about my parents and how one day, they'd love to meet her. She seems nervous but excited at the same time.

She tells me more about her life over the past few years. She shines when speaking of the children she teaches, describing her life as 'simple, but content.' It's the opposite of the loud and rushed life Georgia and I live, yet we still manage to find we have many things in common.

Despite her not knowing hockey, she promises to start watching the games I coach, potentially even coming to one in the future. We're taking small steps for now, not wanting to overwhelm one another.

Our conversation may not be monumental in content, but it means the world to me.

Georgia

We close the door of the car, Marie waving us off as we go. Chase is far more relaxed than his jittery form when we arrived. It's clear their conversation not only gave them each some peace of mind, but also hope for the future.

Despite my initial comments that he would be okay no matter today's outcome, I am thankful as hell that things turned out the way they did. I would have been gutted for him if this went poorly.

I turn on the engine, slowly pulling the car away from her home, knowing we will see her sooner rather than later. Marie has a sweet disposition, her warmth and charm clear from the moment she welcomed us into her home. Her life is the opposite of what Chase and I lead, quiet and solitary, but it's clear she likes it that way. Perhaps we'd all benefit from taking a dip in one another's lives.

"So, are you happy?" I ask as we pull onto the open desert road ten minutes later.

"I am, I really am. I had no idea what to expect. I thought I'd feel hurt and abandoned when I finally met her, but all I could feel was understanding. She was just a kid when she had me, I mean shit, I wouldn't have known what to do with a baby at twenty-five, let alone sixteen. And her actions led me to my parents, so I can't feel anything but grateful for how it all turned out."

"She seems like a really special person, Chase. I'm glad I got to meet her."

"It won't be the last time; I know we will see her again. Plus, I know Mom and Dad will want to meet her. But I don't want to overwhelm her all at once with it. I think baby steps."

Already I can feel his protective instincts coming out for Marie. His words radiating the emotional maturity he's grown into these past few years. We continue to drive, recounting our time with Marie, the glow around Chase undeniable.

We eventually pull back onto the Strip. Despite it only being midafternoon, it's bursting with movement. It's a Saturday in Las Vegas, what the hell do I expect?

"So, I have a little surprise for you," I say, parking the rental in the valet area of the hotel.

His eyebrows squint together. "You do?"

I nod. "You up for it?"

"With you? Always."

I wink at him before exiting the car, handing the keys to the attendant. I give her a tip and a quick thanks, before rounding the car, slipping my hand into Chase's.

"Do I get a clue?

"It may or may not involve some of our nearest and dearest."

His head snaps to the side. "You're not trying to lock me down at a little white chapel, are you, Georgia Monroe?" Despite his joke, I can't deny the fire that burns in my stomach at his question.

"Slow your roll, Cowboy. I have more slot machines and too much tequila in our future."

"Sounds just as good." He winks.

"Hey Mathews!" a familiar voice calls out from above us. Looking up to the hotel balcony, the familiar faces of Logan, Taylor, and Weston stare down at us. Grins adorn their faces as they watch us.

"We're coming to you!" Taylor yells down to us.

Chase turns to me, eyes wide. "You did this?"

"Yeah," I reply on a whisper.

"I know you, Chase. Most people in this situation would want to be alone, but you, you'd want your friends, no matter the outcome."

Clearly lost for words, he just stares at me. "What the hell did I do right in this world to deserve you?"

I don't have a chance to reply before his lips come down on mine. Not usually one for public displays of affection, I shock even myself when I lean into him, wrapping my hands around his neck.

"Get a room," someone mumbles as they walk past us.

Chase pulls away only to reply, "Don't you worry, we have one."

"I still can't believe you guys are here," Chase says, taking a sip of his beer. We're all gathered at the hotel bar, the whole lot of us. Me, Chase, Taylor, Weston, Ash, and Logan. Henry is staying with Logan's parents for the weekend. It's their first time apart from him, but from the looks of it, they are managing.

"When our girl G told us to be here, we couldn't exactly say no," Taylor replies.

"Your girl G?" Chase says, lips curled at the side.

"What can I say, she's a catch!"

I nudge his side. "It's important to me that I know your friends."

I spot Ash grinning at us from across the table. "I still can't believe it. I just never thought I'd see the day where the two of you, not only get along, but are also a couple. It's like a Christmas miracle."

I can't help but laugh. It seems that every time we are together now, Ash comments on this so-called Christmas miracle.

"You best believe it." Chase grins, pulling me into his side.

The night continues on, everyone laughing and reminiscing about the past and what our futures will bring. I didn't mention Maire to anyone, just that it would be nice for Chase if we all spent the weekend together.

But a few hours into the night, he opened up, sharing his glee over finally meeting her, of having me with him. The momentous meaning of me going with him to meet his birth mother isn't lost on anyone. Ash's mouth practically touches the floor as a tear escapes the side of her eye. I never thought I would see the day, but it appears motherhood has turned her soft. Not that anyone is complaining.

After we stop ordering drinks and the waiter hands us our check for the second time, we finally take the hint to fuck off.

"None of you assholes are going back to your rooms," Ash says as we enter the casino. Her usually pale cheeks are tinged a light pink as she leans against Logan. Even five drinks in, this girl can still go all night.

"No one is going back to their rooms," I reply.

"Okay, I have an idea," Ash says, her hand slipping into Logan's.

"What if we get married!"

"Uh, who wants to tell her she's already got a husband," Chase says from next to me.

I level her with a stare. "You do know you've got a husband next to you, Ash."

"No shit. But imagine how fun it will be. And you have to be my maid of honor! I won't take no for an answer."

Despite already being her maid of honor at her last wedding, I lift a shoulder in surrender. "Like I'd say no to you.

"I want a tacky white dress!" she calls out, pulling away from her already-husband.

"Deal," I say, moving toward her.

"What if the paparazzi find you? It's a shock Logan has gone incognito this long," Chase asks.

Logan lifts a shoulder. "Don't really care, man. I'm just re-marrying Ash, I doubt that's big news."

"Fine with me. Can Elvis do it?" Chase asks.

"Duh," Ash replies, clearly wanting to go all out.

Logan turns toward the rest of us. "Looks like we're getting married…again."

Chase

As I watch my best friend re-marry the woman he is already married to, I can't help but acknowledge how different this is from the first time. No longer am I prickled with annoyance toward the maid of honor who I had to walk down the aisle with. No longer do I cringe at the thought of spending forever with someone. All of it has changed. All because of Georgia Monroe.

Georgia Monroe.

Standing across the aisle from me, next to Ash, who looks like a poor man's Madonna, in her dress-up box wedding dress and Logan who is sporting a glitter tux. Georgia managed to escape the costume parade, instead rocking a mini gold dress, with sky high heels and golden locks streaming down her back.

Catching me staring, she winks before turning back to our friends. My chest does that achy thing that happens every time I'm around her. I finally understand what it means when people say love hurts. But man, it's such a good fucking hurt. I'd hurt like this every day for the rest of my life instead of going through the motions like I've been for far too long.

Because after years of nothingness, I finally understand what it means to love and be loved. And god, does it hurt so good.

Georgia

I wake up naked, tangled up in Chase and a thin sheet. My head rests on his bare chest and I try to nuzzle closer, soaking up every bit of him that I can take.

The vibration on the nightstand alerts me to my phone. With a grunt, I lean over, hopeful not to wake Chase as I move. My dad's name flashes on the screen, but I let it go to voicemail. I will call him back before breakfast.

"What time is it?" Chase asks from next to me, clearly awakened by my not-so-subtle movements.

I look at my phone. "It's nine."

I pull open my phone, surprised by what Ash has sent me. "Looks like you were right. Some paps got pics of the wedding, apparently I've also been identified as your new leading lady."

Chase lifts his head from his pillow fortress. "You okay with that?"

I wink at him. "Never better. But I'm also starving, wanna get breakfast?"

He mumbles something I don't understand, but I take it as a yes when he hauls himself out of bed. I don't hesitate to admire the view; it is all mine anyway.

"I thought you wanted breakfast," he teases as he slips into the bathroom.

I toss a pillow at the door before pulling myself up and out of bed. "I'm coming!"

An hour later, we're sitting in a diner across from our hotel. They apparently have the best pancakes around, and Chase is desperate to try them. I, on the other hand, don't exactly have an appetite after the call I just had with my dad.

"So, I was talking to my dad about his new job," I begin, my shoulders set in a straight line. Chase watches me from across the booth, clearly already on high alert because I sat across from him, not next to.

"And as he was telling me about it, I couldn't help but think how familiar the company name sounded." I pause. "It wasn't until I really thought about it, did I remember you mentioning the name of *your* dad's company once. MatTec Industries."

"Georgia," Chase begins, but I silence him with a look.

"Chase, I'll ask you this once then I won't ask again." I pause, swallowing before continuing, "did you get your dad to give my father a job?"

His eyes briefly flutter away from my own. "No," he replies, voice rushed.

"Don't lie to me." My words come out as a hushed whisper, desperate and pleading.

He lets out a gust of breath, leaning back into the worn diner booth. His head rests on it, looking up at the ceiling as if it will give him answers.

"I didn't get him to give your dad a job, Georgia. I'm not lying about that."

"But you're omitting the truth?" I ask, already knowing the answer.

"Yes," he whispers.

"Then tell me."

Seemingly foregoing staring up, he gives me back his attention, focusing solely on me. "When you were telling me about how scared you were for your dad, I heard you, but I didn't fully feel it. Then when I met him, it all became so real, you know? This man had raised you and because of one mistake, he lost everything. You were right when you said the world would be harsh toward him. So, after a few weeks, I mentioned the situation to my father in passing. I'm sorry I overstepped." He pauses, holding my gaze.

"I didn't talk to him under the assumption that he would give your dad a job. I was initially just telling him because he's my dad and the more time you and I have spent together, I've grown to care for you deeply. Everything my dad did after that was his own choice. My dad's a businessman, above all, and he would never hire your father if he didn't think he could do the job at hand."

I raise my left hand, my head coming to lean forward on it. "I don't know what to say, Chase."

"I know it probably feels like I went behind your back, but that was never my intention. And I know you don't want to feel like a charity case, but I swear to god, Georgia, it isn't like that. I'm sorry."

"Chase." I blink back the tears forming in my eyes, hoping if I continue to swallow, it'll take down the lump that's taken residence in my throat. Feeling slightly more composed, I slide out of the booth, his eyes widening slightly, like perhaps I am leaving. But instead of walking out the door, I take my place next to him, linking his hands with my own.

"I'm not mad," I whisper. "I mean, at first I did feel a little betrayed, unsure why you kept this from me. But after I talked with my dad, he helped me realize you did this because you care about me. And to be honest, well, that means everything."

His shoulders drop, relief written on his face.

"I've never really had someone by my side who cared like that for me. I've been dating for over ten years. So, you can imagine why I'd doubt someone who, at the time, I wasn't even dating, doing such a massive gesture. But I see now, there was no ulterior motive, no pity behind it. It was done out of-"

"Love," he says, cutting me off.

I can't help the tear that falls at his words. "Yeah," I reply, voice croaky. "It was done out of love."

"Is this your way of telling me you love me, Georgia Monroe?"

I lift a shoulder. "I mean, you're okay."

He grins, pulling me into him. "I love you, Georgia Monroe. You think you could be okay with that?"

"I think so."

"Do you love me?"

"I really do, Chase Mathews. I love you."

His eyes brighten at my words. "I always thought something would bring me to my knees, I just never thought it would be you, Georgia. But man, am I sure glad it was."

I lean forward, kissing him with everything I have in me.

"I love you, Prick."

"Love you, Brat."

I guess Logan was right all those months ago, misery really does love company.

Chase

I look at Georgia tracing the lines of her face with my eyes, attempting to lock it into my memory as I know in a few short hours, we will, yet again, be separated. She turns to me as if sensing my gaze. I take her fingers, linking them with my own. The pesky airplane seat armrest obstructing both of us from getting closer.

"What's on your mind?" I ask her. "You can tell me."

She nods clearly understanding where my thoughts are taking me.

"I can't keep doing the long-distance thing," she says speaking first. "And to be honest, Chase, I don't think you can either." I exhale a breath, thankful she knows my thoughts before I say them.

"I can admit that I can't do it for long-term anyway. This weekend has changed everything for me."

"For me too," she whispers back, her voice drowned out by the light thrum of the airplane.

"So, what are we going to do?"

"I wish it was that easy to just say I'll quit my job and come to you or you'll come to me, but the reality is, neither of us wants to give up our dreams and we shouldn't have to, but at the same time, we shouldn't have to give up each other either, so where does that leave us?" she says as a laugh trails on her last words even though there isn't much humor in her voice, just a tinge of sadness from our impending separation.

"I wish I had an answer," I reply. "I wish it was like in the movies where you can just snap your fingers and everything turns out okay."

She smiles, her lips tilting up at the side. "I think if we've learned anything, our stories are not like the movies, it's much more complicated and drawn out. Plus, if we were a movie, I think people would've gotten sick of us years into our bickering. I'm surprised either one of us made it this far."

I laugh. "I think all along, the universe was just waiting for us to find the right moment. All the back-and-forth, the bickering, the arguing just led us to right here, right now. I wouldn't change it for anything. Well, maybe our friends would change it, I think they were starting to get sick of us," I say. She squeezes my hand.

"I wouldn't change it. Chase, I think that you're right, it all happened to lead us to this moment. For each of us, I think every little step in our story needed to happen, to not only ensure growth as individuals, but strength as a unit. We're both so strong and self-assured, big personalities in this world, and look how quickly we were knocked off our pedestals. As fate would have it, it was at the same time and the only people who we were willing to open up to was one another."

"I know this probably sounds batshit crazy, Georgia. But I never once thought tearing my ACL would bring any good in my life. I was so certain it was just all over. But I'd go through it all again, just to find you."

Her eyelids blink rapidly, attempting to dispel her tears. "I'd never want you to go through that again, Chase. But I understand the sentiment behind it. There isn't a lot I wouldn't do to get to this moment either."

I don't hesitate to cross the distance, ignoring the armrest digging into my chest. She meets me halfway, connecting our lips. And despite our fears I know, we're going to be okay.

Seattle – 1 year later

December 2020

Chase

"Did you really need all these shoes? I mean, aren't these two identical?" Ash asks Georgia, lifting up two identical pairs of black heels. I stay silent, knowing I don't want to die today. Packing boxes are scattered around our condo, as Ash digs through Georgia's box of shoes. Well, actually there are three boxes.

"Those are two completely different shoes," Georgia says, grabbing the shoes from Ash and placing them in our closet.

Yep, I said *our* closet.

After living in two different states for the past year and a half of our relationship, we're both finally back in Seattle. Despite our desires to be together a year ago, we knew it wasn't realistic for either of us to give up our jobs for the other. We loved what we did and, in a way, I think we both needed that time in our own space to really value what we had when we came together.

But after the year was up, it was clear that things had to change. As luck would have it, I was offered a coaching position here in Seattle. And although Georgia loved New York, she felt certain her time there had come to a close. She missed her family, Ash and Logan, but mostly Elaine. You never know how much time someone has left on this earth and I know it killed Georgia to be so far away from her.

Plus, it was hard to deny that I felt the same way. I missed my family, and it wasn't exactly easy travelling to Vegas to see Marie when I was in Boston. At least being in Seattle, it will be easier for her to visit or vice versa. Despite us meeting over a year ago, we've been taking things slowly, learning who the other one is, and it's been great. I think anything too fast would have been too much for both of us, but I'm happy to say she's become a permanent fixture in my life.

Georgia got lucky when her boss Monica told her she wanted to expand their agency to Seattle. So although it took a few months to iron out all the kinks, we've made it back here.

"I think we're going to need a bigger closet." Georgia looks up at me from her spot on the floor, messy hair piled on her head.

"Let's cross that bridge when we get to it," I reply, knowing full well I'll be contacting my contractor next week.

"I know we want to get this finished, but if we don't get ready, we're going to be late."

Georgia reaches for her phone. "Shit! We need to be there in an hour! I gotta do my hair." She pops off the ground, pressing a quick kiss to my lips before dashing off to the bathroom.

I wait for the shower to turn on before nodding to the other room. Ash follows me out of the room, shutting the bedroom door behind her.

"Do you think she has any clue?" I ask, voice low.

My friend shakes her head, biting down on her lower lip. "None. And trust me, if she had any idea, she would be hounding me. I have to say, I'm surprised. Georgia is like a dog with a bone, and the fact you've managed to hide this from her is very impressive."

I run my hands up and down my jeans. "Okay. That's good."

"You don't have to be nervous, Chase, she's obviously going to say yes."

"God, I hope so."

"Chase, Georgia loves you more than life itself. Look at all the moments you two have shared over the past year and a half, everything you've been through. You've got nothing to worry about."

"You're right," I reply, shaking my head. "I'm just psyching myself out. I've had this ring in my fucking drawer for six months, I think it's just the nerves."

"You used to play in front of thousands of fans and never got nervous, but proposing to Georgia is what gets you?"

"Sounds about right," I confirm, before I hear the shower turn off in the other room.

"You still planning on doing it tomorrow?"

I nod.

"It's gonna be okay, I promise," Ash whispers. "Now I'm going home to my handsome husband and adorable son, and I will see you two tomorrow. Hopefully both sporting shit-eating grins. Tell Georgia I will text her later. Have fun tonight."

She reaches for her black bag, throwing it over her shoulder before giving me a quick hug.

"Thanks," I tell her, knowing I'd never have been able to find the perfect ring for Georgia without her.

"That's what friends are for."

She leaves and I rush back to the bedroom to get ready, knowing full well we can't be late for Elaine tonight. It's her big day.

"I can't believe she's actually gone through with it," Georgia whispers to me as the entire room breaks out in applause. Elaine and Herb are marrying under an altar made out of fake flowers, surrounded by half of their retirement home. Georgia and I are front and center, the two of us cheering louder than anyone in this place.

Elaine turns to us, sending a wink our way before turning back to her husband. The two of them walk down the makeshift aisle, the rest of their guests following suit.

"Me neither, I thought she'd for sure kill him before they made it to today."

After a year of back and forth, Herb decided he wanted to spend the rest of his days with Elaine, and much to our surprise, she said yes. I guess she's more romantic than we thought. So here we are, in the Whispering Palms Retirement Village lounge turned wedding reception.

"She looks happy."

I nod. "She really does." I take her hand in my own, linking our fingers.

"Do you think this wedding has any alcohol?"

"Let's find out," I reply, taking us around the other residents. If we wait behind them, we might be stuck here forever.

An hour later, the Bee Gee's are blasting, Georgia and Herb taking a spin on the dance floor together.

"If it were anyone but my Georgia, I might be jealous," Elaine says from next to me.

I smile at her, taking her hand. "May I have this dance?"

"Ah that pretty boy charm, it never does get old." She places her small hand in mine, and I lead us to the dance floor as the song changes. "Witchcraft" by Frank Sinatra plays and I'm thankful for a slow song.

"So, are we going to be having another one of this type of events soon?"

"You trying to ask me something, Elaine?"

Her lined mouth creases more at her smile. "You tell me."

"Hopefully, if all goes according to plan."

"You better not be trying to steal my shine," Elaine whispers to me, but humor rings out in her voice.

My chest shakes. "Never. But I would like your blessing. You're like family to Georgia and me."

Elaine blinks rapidly a few times, her hand coming away from mine to wipe away her tears. "Well now look what you've done, made an old woman cry." Taking a breath, she rights herself and returns her hand to my own. "It would be my greatest honor in this life seeing you marry Georgia. Knowing the two of you will be together for life."

"That means the world to me, Elaine. Without you, who knows if Georgia and I would have been together. The day she took me to see you, everything started to change for us."

She pats my chest. "You would have found your way, I know it."

We dance until the end of the song, then Georgia cuts in. "Can I have this dance, handsome?"

"Well, how can I say no to a pretty girl."

Herb takes Elaine's hand, spinning her into him as they dance away, the two of them having more stamina than anyone else in this room.

"Miss me?" Georgia asks, placing a kiss on my lips. I lean into her, deepening what she probably assumes to be a peck. Her cheeks are slightly flushed as I pull away. A retirement home perhaps isn't the best place for intense PDA.

"You have no idea," I confirm.

As Georgia and I dance the night away, I can't help but appreciate how my life has turned out. If you had asked me three years ago where I'd be now, I'd have said the NHL. No thought of a partner, only myself and the game. And man, I'm thankful I changed. Because what is the point of having everything if you're alone?

But now that I've found Georgia, neither of us will ever face a single day alone. And hopefully, tomorrow will only reconfirm that.

1 year later

Georgia

"Holy fucking shit, Ash. I'm so nervous. Were you this nervous when you married Logan?" I look to my best friend, taking deep breaths to stop from having a panic attack. I can't sit down as it will crease my satin wedding dress, so I choose to pace back and forth.

"It's okay, drink this." She shoves a shot of something my way, I down it.

"Fuck, what is that?" I ask, my face twisting up.

"Whiskey."

"Really, Ash. Whiskey?"

"It's all I could find in this house!"

I laugh it off before the nerves rear their ugly head again. "Oh god, this feeling inside me is so overwhelming." I fan my face with my hands.

"The nerves?"

"No, not even that, just everything. I'm overwhelmed with how I feel. It's strange really, I've said I love you to people before, but I don't think I really meant it. I think I just thought that's what you were supposed to say to someone after being together for a period of time, but after being with Chase," I pause, shaking my head. "I don't know, it's crazy. I feel like I want to explode all the time, like at any point my chest could burst open from how much I love being with him, being around him. In the past, I was so scared of being hurt by him, I don't think I actually gave him that much of a chance. I just wrote him off, and to think that I could have potentially never experienced this with him because I am so stubborn, now that is a scary thought."

Ash smiles at me, her rosy cheeks high with glee. "I can't tell you how happy that makes me to hear, Georgia. I always thought there was something between you two, but not in a million years did I expect it to be love. "

"Join the club." I laugh. "I bet you never thought you'd see the day we'd get married either."

"Definitely not, but I'm happy it's here."

"Me too," I reply, exhaling a breath. "Okay, I think I'm ready."

My best friend takes my hand, leading me out into the hallway. We're getting married at Chase's parents' house in their back yard. Well, they're really fucking wealthy, so it seems more like a park.

I peek my head out the window, hoping no one will see me. Chase's back is to me, so I don't get a great view, but I spot Logan next to him. We both opted out of having big bridal parties, both of us choosing just Ash and Logan to stand by our side.

Besides them, 100 of our nearest and dearest line the lawn, including my mom and dad, Elaine and Herb, Marie, and Chase's parents and old teammates.

I spot friends I made when I used to visit Ash in Massachusetts, Nick and Winona, Eleanor and Jess, Vivian and Will. It's been years since we've all been in the same place, but somehow, it feels like no time has passed at all.

"It's time, G. You ready?"

I nod. "I'm ready."

The doors to the garden open as the music begins to play. Ash walks out ahead of me, leaving me all alone for the first time today.

The skin on my arms begins to prickle, and I know in a matter of seconds, life is going to change for the better. Chase and I may not know what the future holds for us, but we do know that we'll have each other. And if life has shown us anything, it's that we're stronger together than apart.

The music changes, and it's my time. Suddenly, all eyes are on me. But there is only one pair I care about.

Our eyes lock from the distance.

He smiles at me.

I step forward.

The End

Thank you for taking the time to read Misery Loves Company!

Thank you for taking the time to read Misery Loves Company. In no particular order, I want to thank my incredible team at The Next Step PR. I am so lucky to be surrounded by such amazing women. A special thank you to Jill and Aurora. To Becky, your notes and advice were invaluable. To Amanda, thank you for your time and patience in creating these covers. I adore them. To Kiki, you are not only an amazing businesswoman but a lifelong friend, and I am so lucky to know you. To Emily, as usual, you give me the best notes and feedback. Thank you to all the ARC readers and bloggers who take the time to read and support me. As always, my beautiful readers, you make this all possible. To my sisters for helping me brainstorm the title, and Duck for thinking of the winner! Finally, I want to thank my 0friends and family, and I love you

Scarlett Hopper was born in Sydney, Australia and moved to Los Angeles when she was 10 years old. She currently lives back in Sydney with her family and their two pugs. When she isn't writing or reading, she spends her time traveling and searching for the best record stores while eating at 24-hour diners. Eventually, Scarlett hopes to begin a new adventure in Edinburgh, and then Seattle.

Website: www.scarletthopper.com.au
Newsletter: bit.ly/ScarHopNewsletter
Facebook: www.bit.ly/FBAuthorSH
Twitter: www.twitter.com/AuthorScarHopp
IG: www.bit.ly/SHopperInsta
Goodreads: www.bit.ly/authorshgoodreads
Bookbub: www.bit.ly/SHBookBub
Personal Facebook Group: www.bit.ly/authorshgroup
Website: www.scarletthopper.com

Saint Street

Never Now

Late Love

The Encounters Series:

Brief Encounters

Chance Encounters

Missed Encounters